PALOMA BLUE

Empress in Exile

First edition

ISBN: 979-8-9917349-3-6

Cover art by Luca Mercogliano
Advisor: Greg Fisher
Editing by Flannery Wise

This book was professionally typeset on Reedsy.
Find out more at reedsy.com

For those who seek to soar

Preface

This book takes place during the height of the Roman Empire. The Romans conducted much of their lives in a manner many would consider cruel today. Their treatment of women in particular was not for the faint of heart. This story involves difficult situations involving marriage, childbirth and death. Please be forewarned.

Prologue

The horizon extends before me, a flat mirror of the blazing sun. I detect no birds in the sky as I huddle at the bottom of my small boat.

Only now, fleetingly, different memories surface as I drift.

I remember the blue bird that appeared mysteriously in the garden of our old villa in Antium. How it sat, fat and unafraid, as the dogs sniffed at it and my nurse picked it up with her hands. It never flew, hopping around the garden; until one day, it was gone. Shortly afterward, the emperor called my father to Rome.

My heart pangs as I recall the swan, its giant white wings flapping against the black sky. Moving east, a harbinger of death. The night Geta was lost to me.

Now my tiny craft floats aimlessly on the current, at the mercy of the gods. My fate remains unknown.

Part One

CAELIAN HILL

I.

"You stupid girl!" I threw the broken hairpin as hard as I could at the *serva* bowing her head in contrition. The most important day of my life, and this clumsy cow had dropped my favorite piece of jewelry onto the tiles, shattering it to pieces. How was I to be presented to anyone, let alone the young Augustus, with slaves like these?

I snatched a second hairpin from the table and was about to throw it at the other slaves when Mother's voice echoed from the doorway, firm. "Plautilla, stop this outburst at once. Your father is expecting you."

I reluctantly lowered my hand, defeated. No matter the circumstance, we were all slaves to Father's ambition. "Yes, Mother," I grumbled.

I threw myself upon my couch and flung the pillows fruitlessly against the wall. Mother sighed in disapproval at yet another example of my fiery temperament. I knew I needed to gather my composure before being presented to the emperor's eldest son today, but I didn't have to act like a perfect young lady yet. Glaring at the girls hovering in the corner, I signaled for them to begin.

As the servants attended to my hair, I remembered what I had been taught about Marcus Aurelius Antoninus. He had been made *Augustus*, or senior emperor, under his father, Septimius Severus, at the age of ten. By his early manhood, Antoninus had already commanded legions in battle and enjoyed racing against his brother in the Circus Maximus. He was virile, strong, and the undisputed heir. At least, that was the story Father told us. Other voices, spoken barely over a whisper, told another. *Vain. Cruel. Vicious.* And most damning of all, they spoke of an intense rivalry with his younger brother, Publius Septimius Geta, who remained merely a *Caesar*, or deputy Augustus.

Coins featuring the brothers' faces jingled in the pockets of every Roman merchant, portraying them both as heirs to the throne. This had apparently sent Antoninus into such a rage he had thrown a tantrum that had been talked about for weeks. As far as I was concerned, that was the most interesting thing about him. That a man who appeared to be so strong, ascendant to the highest power in the empire, considered his younger brother his most dangerous enemy. I would have to keep my wits about me with Antoninus, regardless of the truth of this rumor. Assuming he would even consider me a worthy match.

Sighing, I grimaced as the slave girl wove the tendrils of hair around my ears tightly into a braid. I had already seen the drab fabric Mother had chosen for my stola, dyed a hideous olive green. I hated the color, which resembled that of a common girl's garment too closely. Of course, Mother would never select a color such as saffron or indigo, ones that would signify my status as the daughter of the sole *Praetorian prefect*, Commander of the Praetorian Guard. No, Mother turned up her nose at what she considered garish displays of wealth. "It is not the clothes that make you seem provincial. Adornments do not make the maiden, grace and charm do," she would often say. Of course, the other *dominae* mocked our simple garments behind her back. But Mother would hear none of it.

Father, of course, knew that to win the endless game of political intrigue on Palatine Hill, you had to look as if you already belonged. Even though our respective families, the Fulvi and the Hortensii, were among the wealthiest in Rome, there were always a few who turned up their noses to us because Father was from Leptis Magna and spoke with an accent. Of course, so did the emperor and empress, so the last laugh was on them. But in Rome, one never knew which direction the political winds would shift. On this I agreed with Father.

The sharp end of a pin jolted me out of my reverie. "Ow! Clumsy cow!" I turned and slapped the slave's hand. It was the same girl. Her cheeks flushed as her fingers trembled, pinning my stola in place with a shoulder pin.

"I am sorry, Domina Plautilla," she mumbled.

"Be careful," I chastised. "Or I will have my family cast you into the street."

The slave's cheeks reddened further, but that was of no concern to me. Scowling, I gestured to another slave to bring me the box containing my jewelry. I carefully fingered the gold trinkets, finally selecting several bracelets that made a pleasing sound when I moved my wrist and a ring with a green stone that might hopefully offset the color of my stola. Closing my eyes, I let the girls paint my face. As they worked, a fragment of a half-remembered dream entered my mind. I had been staring at clouds, and their shapes in the sky held meaning. I rarely remembered my dreams, but lately they had become more vivid. Perhaps it was the excitement of potentially marrying into the royal family that caused such odd thoughts. Shaking my head, I blinked my eyes open and gazed at my dim reflection. My appearance seemed to have improved, but was it enough to catch the eye of Caesar? I would soon find out.

We had been invited to a banquet celebrating Antoninus' latest achievement. Was it a match in the arena? A race in the Circus? No matter. He would be puffed up and proud, strutting about like a peacock. Ready for his next conquest. It was on this occasion that my father planned to introduce me to the emperor and his son, in the hopes that his alliance with them could be strengthened. Even though Father was one of Emperor Severus' most trusted advisors and a cousin on his mother's side, it was not enough. And Julia Domna, Empress of Rome, had doubts about our family. I had to win her over just as much as Antoninus.

The slave girl held up a second mirror, and I inspected their handiwork. It was adequate, nothing more, but it was getting late and there wasn't time to force them to do it again. Dismissing the slaves with my hand, I left the cubicula to join Mother and my brother Gaius in the *triclinium*, the dining area located just off the center atrium of our house. We resided in a large *domus* in Caelian Hill, closest to Palatine Hill. I sometimes wondered if Father had chosen it so he could spy on the emperor's family even when they were asleep.

Mother was pouring the wine as I entered and reclined next to my brother, who was shoveling dates into his mouth as fast as he could grab them. "Gaius," Mother began, but did not finish her sentence. She never chastised him; he was her favorite. Gaius used this fact to his advantage, always causing havoc around the house and never receiving punishment. As soon as Mother learned of his mischief, he widened his large eyes and begged for forgiveness, and she instantly softened. It was impressive, I had to admit. At least some of Father's wile was in him, though whether he would have any sense once he came of age remained to be seen.

The servants brought in platters of meat, and Gaius tore a pigeon almost in half. I flared my nose in disgust, delicately picking at a bird with my fingers. "Gaius, we have a banquet to go to in a few hours," I said.

"Mmmnot going," he managed, sounding like his mouth was full of pebbles. "Just you."

I turned to Mother, surprised. "You aren't joining me?" The thought of meeting the royal family without Mother by my side made me uneasy. "Is it only Father?"

Mother sipped her wine carefully, but her brow was furrowed. "We were only provided two invitations. There will be many distinguished guests, and Julia Domna needed to reserve space for them." The pain of the snub was clear in her carefully curated words.

A tendril of dislike for the empress unfurled in my stomach. I was not close to Mother, but this was a slight against our family. I coiled my anger into a tight, shiny pebble, ready to drop when the opportunity arose.

"Don't worry, Mother. I will make you and Father proud. I will do my best to win Antoninus' favor." I smoothed my drab stola, wishing again it was any other color.

Mother eyed me warily. "I would hope so." Suddenly she leaned forward and took my hand, startling me. "But be careful, Plautilla. This is not a game, and you will need to keep your wits about you. Remember your upbringing." Her expression was somber, and I sensed that there was more she wished to say but for some reason could not.

Just then, Gaius burped loudly. We laughed, breaking the tension.

* * *

It was dusk when the slaves carried me on my *lectica* through the crowded streets. Our *domus* wasn't far from the Imperial Palace, but the streets were full of shoppers, and the lectica lurched back and forth as the men wove their way through the crowd. Mother always insisted I keep the curtains drawn, but the motion and lack of fresh air was affecting my digestion. I pulled one to the side and the smell of the city hit me in the face: savory food, sour wine, human sweat, and animal excrement. A smell like no other, one of thousands of souls cooking together in this marble pot. The city intrigued me, but Father would never let me investigate it on my own, even though other noble daughters who had come of age would often venture out to shop or dine with supervision.

Father had always been protective of me, keeping me close by when he was home and protected by only eunuchs once I entered marrying age so that my honor was never in danger. When I was young, I had adored him. He would always bring me a gift when he returned from his long trips, either a jewel or beautiful piece of clothing, and sweep me into his arms upon his return. He often showed more affection to me than Mother, and I sensed that Mother resented it, but her aristocratic upbringing armed her with a cool reserve in response to any indignation Father presented.

To the rest of the world, we were perfect, two established family lines coming together to form the model of a noble *familia.* We opened our house to distinguished guests, traveled to our villas in the south and on the sea, and benefited from powerful political ties. Yet we were four strangers living together, each of us keeping our dreams and desires separate from the others.

Father's utmost quality was ambition. Ever since he had cast his political fortunes with Septimius Severus, our lives had been determined by the emperor's desires. Father had spent many years rising through the ranks of Severus' service, starting when they had been in the army in the provinces. Father's dedication had rewarded him well. His loyalty had brought him to the pinnacle of power short only of being a member of the Senate; he was now the highest-ranking officer of the Praetorian Guard, the emperor's personal military force.

Normally, there were two co-prefects, but the other one, Quintus Aemilius Saturninus, had been arrested and killed recently, most likely upon the emperor's orders. While unsettling, it had given Father more opportunities to demonstrate his loyalty to Severus. I had no doubt that he was already hatching plans for a Senate position next. While becoming emperor was out of reach, I knew a marriage with Antoninus would cement our family's legacy permanently among Rome's elite. This motivated Father above all else, even over love and family duty. While this reality pained Gaius and Mother, I understood it. Only with power could you bend others to your will. A powerless life in Rome was a miserable life indeed.

Mother was motivated by loyalty, duty, and tradition. She relished the role of *domina,* leader of the household, and the state of our house reflected this, as shiny as the tiles in our atrium that she ordered the slaves to scrub every day. While we shunned many of the trappings of wealth, Mother's familial line commanded respect, and there were still those who appreciated her fealty to the old values of humility, honor, and duty. Not so for Gaius, who loved spectacle and all things accessible to a young man of wealth. He could not wait to become lord of his own house, and I suspected that if he could, he would have spent his time exclusively competing in the many sporting contests occurring throughout the city.

And as for me?

What desires was I allowed? Of course, like any noble girl, I wanted to be admired and adored. How I wished I could parade about in the latest fashions and hairstyles. If a jewel glittered, I wanted it on my hand or around my neck. If a flower smelled sweet, I wanted to drown myself in its fragrance. If I became empress, I could wear whatever I fancied. This motivated me above all else in my willingness to marry Antoninus, if he chose to have me.

Perhaps I was cynical, but I never felt as if my fevered prayers to Venus were answered. My face was never enough to draw the eyes of anyone. I supposed that was why I wished for silver and gold, so that I would be truly seen and adored. And yet, sometimes, I felt another desire stirring, something I could not yet name. A longing for something—an understanding. Of what, I did not yet know. But it was there, a small flutter of need that grew inside me. I knew better than to discuss it with anyone, but it felt like a secret I needed to share. I felt it most strongly in the mornings, when I woke from my vivid dreams. Lately, I had felt it at dusk, staring at the colors in the sky as they faded into black. Glancing upward now, the sky was hidden by the throngs of people, but I felt it pressing down upon the city. I closed the curtain again and uttered a small prayer to Venus to favor me in Antoninus' presence. We were almost at the palace.

The lectica stopped moving, and the curtains were parted by imperial slaves. I had arrived. I allowed one of the guards to assist me to my feet, and soon, I was escorted up the imposing stairs that led to the heart of the Imperial Palace. Hundreds of years ago, Rome's leaders had lived in more humble abodes, but that custom had been supplanted by a series of emperors who had built and then expanded the palace up the hill until it engulfed almost an entire city block. Tonight, fires illuminated the many guards lining the entrance, where the scent of incense and sound of music wafted into the night air.

There was a gathering of people entering ahead, and I waited patiently until the palace servants acknowledged me. Confidently, I stepped forward, doing my part to project my family's power and wealth. "Fulvia, daughter of Gaius Fulvius Plautianus and Hortensia," I said clearly. Only my immediate family called me Plautilla.

The servant nodded to another slave, and beckoned me in. "Wait here," he commanded. I nodded demurely and stepped to the side. As I waited for Father, I fussed with my bracelets and stola and bit my lips to bring a blush to them. I wished I had ordered the slaves to redo my hair, but it was too late now. I nodded as familiar faces passed by and smiled as a few bowed their heads, acknowledging my status. Finally, I saw Father hurrying toward me.

He was dressed in his armor, polished to a high sheen to signify his status as prefect. Striding up toward me, he looked me up and down, as if inspecting a new recruit.

"Good," was all he said before grabbing my hand. "Come with me."

His pace was quick, and I struggled to keep up with his long strides as he led me through the crowd. The great hall was full of people eating, drinking, and laughing, all dressed in their finery. I gaped at the elaborate hairstyles of the women, done up in the latest fashion. Clearly, I would not impress anyone with the traditional styling of my own braids. The men were equally groomed and wore elaborate jewelry, and some had more paint on their faces than I did. All were drinking from golden goblets as servants presented platters laden with exotic delicacies. It was the grandest banquet I had ever seen, and my cheeks flushed in shame at the comparatively simple offerings Mother had presented when we had hosted our own. Nothing I had ever experienced matched the grandeur of this evening.

I realized Father was speaking. "I will present you to the emperor and empress first, then their sons. Do not speak. Bow to each in turn, and if they speak to you, nod and smile and let me answer. Antoninus is wearing a white toga with a red stripe, his brother's is purple. Don't forget that. Always refer to Antoninus as Augustus and always refer to him first. Don't forget that, either. Don't fidget. Don't eat anything that has a strong odor, and only sip if you are offered wine. Smile."

"Yes, Father," I answered breathlessly, for his pace was unrelenting. At this moment, I was merely another soldier of his to command. We had crossed over almost the entire palace and were heading to the *Aula Regia*, or audience hall, where the emperor formally received guests. Ornate frescoes covered the walls, and the marbled columns shone in the firelight. Father stopped suddenly, and I nearly bumped into him. He pulled me forward and put a heavy hand on my shoulder.

Just then, the ornate doors to our left were flung open and the imperial family entered the hall. A hush fell over the crowd as we lined up to receive them.

Septimius Severus strode in first. The emperor had dark skin and full head of gray hair. He walked purposefully, barely waiting for the crowd to part before barreling through. His demeanor was stern; he nodded at the onlookers but did not smile. His white toga was adorned with gold thread, and the gold laurels in his hair gleamed. Julia Domna was next. The empress was tall with olive skin, and her dark hair was braided in an unusual arrangement, framing her angular face. Her eyes were as black as a cobra's, and I shrank a bit closer to Father at the sight of her. I knew she was a formidable presence in the court. Then I remembered her dismissive words to Mother and stood up a little straighter. If there was anything I had mastered since coming of age, it was dismissive words, and I would wield them on behalf of my family if pressed. The empress may have been a force, but so was I.

Behind them entered the two brothers. Antoninus was first. He had his mother's coloring and his father's curly locks, and he was on his way to growing a full beard. I noted the broad shoulders peeking out of his toga and the gold laurels in his curls, slightly less gilded than his father's but no less impressive. He wore a scowl on his face. It reminded me of a boy mimicking a man, displaying emotions without truly understanding what they meant.

I was so focused on the young Augustus that I barely noticed Geta until he was almost in front of me. Like Antoninus, his eyes were brown, but his were honey-colored and had what looked like amber flames in them. *Tiger eyes*, I thought. His cheekbones were more delicate than his brother's, his hands more slender. The laurels in his hair were silver instead of gold. He was clearly younger than Antoninus but bore an expression of disdain, as if he were already indifferent to our company.

At that moment, my skin prickled with gooseflesh so suddenly that I took a startled step forward, almost blocking Geta's path. Father's hand clamped me back in line, but Geta turned his head toward me, and we locked eyes. Geta nodded at me, and I bowed my head. He continued toward the raised dais as the guests dispersed to their respective dining formations.

Father spun me around and hissed harshly into my ear. "What was that display? You shame me before we've even started!"

"I'm sorry, Father, I was distracted—" I began.

"Foolish girl! We don't have time for your nonsense! Thank the gods Antoninus was no longer present. Now gather yourself and do exactly as I say!" Father yanked me forward again.

"Yes, Father." I sighed. I glanced down at my arms, but the gooseflesh had receded. What had just happened?

* * *

After many speeches lauding Antoninus and toasts to his health, the feast began. Musicians played as we reclined on couches and were served one delicacy after another: boar, pheasant breast stuffed with squib, oysters, octopus oozing garlic and olive oil, and dozens of fruits including plums, apricots, dates, apples, and oranges. Of course, each dish was accompanied by the finest wine. I was too nervous to eat much, but Father ate for both of us, sucking his fingers with gusto and draining each draught poured for him. Over my own cup, I watched the royal family as they reclined on a dais in an alcove above the great room, where they could observe their guests. Both Antoninus and Geta ignored each other, making small talk with either their mother or father. Very little conversation occurred between the emperor and empress. *They're like us*, I realized. *They play the role of a doting family but barely tolerate each other.*

Antoninus was receiving a significant amount of attention from the ladies in the room. He made eye contact with many of them, smiling and then grinning when they tittered. I felt myself growing impatient with Father. Another woman would be betrothed to him before we even rose from our couch, at this rate. I saw my chance at catching Caesar's fancy grow fainter by the minute.

"Father," I whispered. "When is it going to happen?"

"Soon," replied Father. "When the emperor beckons us." He continued eating, seemingly unperturbed.

Finally, after the last sweets were displayed and many of the guests were quite drunk, Emperor Severus glanced our way and nodded at Father. It was time. I rose to sitting and tried once more to arrange my stola, but Father was already lifting me by the elbow.

Carefully, we picked our way across the room through the maze of cushions, couches, and reclining guests. I felt all the eyes in the room on us, and my cheeks grew hot. I only hoped the paint on my face was still presentable. When we reached the dais, Father bowed his head, and I followed suit.

"Plautianus, dear friend, speak," declared Severus. "Who is this captivating young lady?"

"My Imperator, may I humbly present my daughter, Fulvia Plautilla," answered Father. "She is our eldest, and well-bred." He pushed me forward, and I bowed my head again.

Gazing upward through my lashes, I saw Antoninus and Geta observing me. Remembering Father's instructions, I remained silent.

"Does she speak?" asked Antoninus.

"Only when spoken to," said Father. "She is well-behaved."

I realized then that Father was drunk. He had waited too long to act, and his wits were dim. I would have to take matters into my own hands. "I speak my mind often, Caesar, when there is someone interesting to hear it," I said coyly. "Do you think you qualify to hear my thoughts?"

At this, Geta snorted. Father stiffened next to me, but Julia Domna leaned forward. "Clever," she said, though there was no warmth in her tone. "Tell us, girl, what do you think of tonight's festivities?"

"I think they are a fitting celebration of a truly accomplished individual," I responded smoothly. "Rome benefits from your grace and his honor."

Antoninus glanced over at his mother with a furrowed brow, then turned back to me. "Thank you for the compliment," was all he said, before reclining backward and pouring himself another glass of wine.

This seemed to end our interaction, and Father and I slowly returned to our table. Mercifully, many of the guests were no longer interested in us, as dancers had entered the hall and were performing lewd pantomimes. I dared a glance back over my shoulder. Only Geta was still watching us.

Shortly after, the royal family departed the great hall. The guests, many of them too drunk to stand, were escorted out of the palace. Father and I were among the last to leave. We walked slowly under the large columns of the atrium, followed by a cohort of Praetorian guards, ensuring that no visitors decided to sneak back into the palace uninvited.

"What happens now?" I asked. I felt both exhausted and exhilarated by our efforts. I only hoped it was enough for Antoninus to consider me.

"We wait," replied Father. "I will continue to advocate on behalf of the union. The emperor well understands the advantages of uniting our families, but the empress and Antoninus must also agree to the match. In this regard, the emperor is unusual. He will summon you again if he cares to."

But it was Julia Domna who sent for me.

The invitation arrived the next day, calling me to a private audience with the empress. This new development sent our house into a flurry of activity. Father was pleased, which allowed me to press for more suitable garments. Mother reluctantly agreed. Soon, I was happily choosing from among the finest fabrics in Rome for new stolas and veils. I needed to present the picture of a modest, cultured girl from the noblest of houses (with the latest in cosmetics and hairstyles, of course). Sparing no expense, Father arranged for both *cosmetae* and *ornatrices*, slaves that attended to the faces and hair of the most fashionable women, to prepare me. As they fussed and fidgeted, I finally felt worthy of admiration. If I was empress, I would have slaves like this at my beck and call whenever I wished. I was giddy with excitement, but I was also nervous.

Shortly thereafter, the day of my audience with the empress arrived. I woke earlier than usual. The house was quiet. I padded toward the atrium looking for the slaves, but they were busy in the kitchen preparing for *ientaculum*, the day's first meal. I passed the *laraium* and thought of making an offering to Venus, but for some reason, I wandered out to the garden instead. The air was still fresh, free of the smells of the city. A light breeze blew, causing my nightshift to wrap around my legs. The chickens were pecking for scraps. I shooed them away with my feet as a few leaves skittered across the tile. I bent down to pick one up. My fingers traced the veins along the ridge. It had been a long time since I had looked at a plant— or anything in nature, for that matter. Suddenly, I recalled a dream from the night before, once again about clouds. I looked up at the sky, framed perfectly by the rectangular perimeter of our garden. The morning was clear, with no clouds in sight. Yet I felt a charge in the air dancing along my skin, as if the sky were about to crackle with lightning.

An enormous hawk landed on the roof of the house, its appearance so sudden that I gasped. The chickens scattered, clucking and flapping their wings. The majestic bird glanced down at the sound, and its eerie yellow eyes studied me. For a moment, we stared at each other, and then it took flight and flew straight overhead, heading for Palatine Hill. As it did, the hair on my arms rose. I felt the charge even more strongly. I stood quickly, watching as the hawk fluttered farther into the city. The edges of its wings and tail were dark, as if it were a smudge against the sky. Turning, I looked for others, but there were none. I realized that my heart was pounding and my fists were clenched. Slowly, I opened my hand to find the leaf was crushed within my palm.

I had just seen an *auspice*, but I did not understand what it meant.

Auspices, or bird behaviors, were interpreted as signs of Jupiter's favor by a class of priests known as *augurs*. Public officials consulted augurs on every major decision, from generals in the army seeking the most auspicious day to begin a military campaign to determining whether a public meeting should be held. To become an augur was very prestigious, even more so than becoming a Vestal Virgin. Augurs held both the ear of the emperor and sway over official magistrates who consulted them before taking public action regarding elections or events. Even my father had consulted them when faced with major decisions involving military tactics.

Many patrician families used augurs for private decision-making as well, and of course, every Roman could determine omens by observing the eating behavior of their own chickens. Hungry chickens meant good luck—every child knew that. But to my knowledge, no girl or woman had interpreted a formal *auspicia ex avibus*. It was ridiculous to consider it. I was just startled. It was just a bird, out for the hunt early in the morning. Nothing more.

Yet every fiber in my being knew that to be false. I had *felt* the bird's presence before I had seen it. Had it been hunting me? What did it signify? Hawks were predators. Was someone being hunted? Who was the prey? Was it I?

"Plautilla?" Mother's voice startled me, and I turned swiftly to see her standing in the doorway of the house. "What are you doing out here? You need to prepare for your visit."

I nodded dumbly, unable to find my voice. A servant appeared behind Mother, and both women stared at me. "Plautilla? What is the meaning of this?" Mother asked again, less patient this time.

"Coming," I whispered. Slowly, I followed them into the house, suddenly afraid of what was to come.

II.

Unfortunately, my composure did not return before I was presented to Julia Domna several hours later. My nerves were still frayed, and everything I encountered upon my return to the palace seemed laden with dark meaning. The rooms were cold and quiet, and it felt as if I were in a mausoleum when I passed through the grand atrium. The smoke from the *turibulum* on the altar was too thick, and it seemed as if the empress was seated behind a gray veil when I was presented to her in the tablinum. Behind her were imposing busts of ancestors from both her family and Emperor Severus'. Their marble faces were a silent tribunal, judging my worthiness.

"Domina Augusta," I began. "I am honored to be your guest today. Thank you for the invitation." I bowed my head deeply. The deep blue silk of my stola fluttered with my movement, reminding me of waves in the sea. *I must keep my wits about me,* I thought. But it was difficult, as the empress was an imposing figure. Her sharp mind and even sharper tongue were well-known in noble circles. No one dared speak ill of her, for their family's good fortunes could be sunk on her slightest whim. Today she wore a stola of blood-red, the deep stain of the color contrasting against her olive skin. Gold laurels gleamed in her raven-black hair, matching her ornate earrings and necklace. Her dark eyes measured my appearance as I rose, and I received a short nod of approval. Thank Venus Father had granted my wish for new garments and allowed me to be presentable. Otherwise, the audience would have been over before it had started.

"Come," Julia Domna commanded, gesturing to a low couch. "Sit." The empress reclined upon her lectus.

Carefully, I took my seat and accepted a cup of wine from one of the slaves. I took a delicate sip, the picture of a proper young lady. Julia followed suit, gazing at me all the while. I felt as if I were a fresh goose presented at the butcher. I recalled the hawk's yellow eyes upon me and shivered.

"Tell me, Plautilla, what interests you most about our family?" asked Julia.

I thought carefully before I responded. "That you are provincial yet have ascended to the pinnacle of Rome's power."

"Similar to your own family," responded Julia.

"Only through the blessing and patronage of our wise emperor. Father is deeply humbled and grateful for the opportunities presented to us by his friend and cousin."

"Oh, she's very good, Mother." Geta's voice carried into the room. "She's almost as formidable as you."

Though I was startled when Geta appeared, I did my best to hide it. Julia's lips pursed, and I could tell she was irked at Geta's intrusion. "I did not recall asking you or your brother to join us," she said curtly. "Though I suppose it would be more appropriate for him to do so, given the circumstances."

Geta casually stepped forward from behind the curtain that led to the atrium. He was dressed relatively simply in a white toga, and his head was free from adornment. "Antoninus has other engagements," he said softly. "But fear not, Mother. I will report back to him on the suitability of this match."

"I did not know you were on speaking terms with him today," Julia said dryly. She gestured for the slaves to bring Geta a cup of wine. He accepted it and drank deeply, then wiped his mouth with the back of his hand. His every movement mesmerized me. For a moment, I forgot a potential match with Antoninus was the reason I had been invited. *Careful, Plautilla. This is another test.*

I cast my eyes down toward my feet and away from Geta's, willing myself to remain placid. My heart was beating as quickly as it had that morning. Geta continued to pace along the periphery of the room, and I could feel the currents in the air shift with his passing. Julia Domna asked another question, and I answered, but my mind was preoccupied. What was Geta playing at? Was this some boyish foolishness, like something Gaius would do? Or a way to make his brother jealous? I tried not to let my cheeks grow warm as Geta stepped deliberately behind me. I willed myself to remain calm as the gooseflesh returned upon my arms.

Thankfully Julia Domna signaled for Geta to leave us before inviting me to the palace's verandas, overlooking the gardens. We strolled past many statutes of previous Augusti. I made knowledgeable and praiseworthy comments about each one, silently thanking Father for drilling this knowledge into me. Eventually, the empress was convinced I'd had a proper upbringing. "You reflect very well on your family," she commented, gazing out across the city. "If you were to be matched with Antoninus, you would be under much scrutiny. To be an Augusta is to never know privacy. What do you think of such a life?"

I thought of the endless banquets I would host, the servants that would cater to my every whim. I thought of the jealous looks of the other noble women and the admiring looks of their husbands. The thought of all this made me smile. "I would enjoy it, Domina Augusta. And I would enjoy learning from you on how to navigate this life with poise." I smiled and bowed my head once again. Julia Domna snorted, sounding very much like Geta.

"We'll see," was all she said.

* * *

Having passed the first test, there was soon another. Our family was invited to a private audience with the imperial family. This time, we were to dine with them at *cena*, the main midday meal. Father spared no expense this time. Both Mother and I wore new gold jewelry, and costly togas were fashioned for both him and Gaius. I shook my head from side to side, reveling in the swaying motion of the earrings Father had selected for me. The *ornatrices* had arranged my hair in a flattering style that revealed them and my neck. Father was taking no chances.

If only Antoninus would demonstrate the slightest bit of interest. As we made small talk and ate each delicacy presented, he acted as if he would rather be anywhere else. My attempts at engaging him in conversation were unsuccessful.

"Which charioteer are you sponsoring in this week's race at the Circus Maximus?"

"The usual one."

"What sort of horse do you enjoy riding?"

"One that gets me where I want to go."

"Do you enjoy banquets?"

"No."

It was harder than pulling teeth from a snail. I looked at Father, but he simply nodded his head encouragingly. *Keep trying.* I glanced briefly at Geta, who was reclining on the couch opposite Antoninus. He held an amused look on his face, as though he was very much enjoying my fruitless efforts. A flash of anger passed through me, and I decided to serve both brothers a taste of their own medicine.

Turning toward Geta, I leaned forward and asked coyly: "Tell me, Geta, is it difficult to be a spectator to Antoninus' many accomplishments? I would have a terrible time not comparing myself to them." Geta's smirk quickly vanished. Antoninus laughed for the first time, regarding me with newfound interest.

"Anwer her, brother," he said. "Surely it is your turn to respond to one of Plautilla's endless questions."

Geta sat up ever so slowly, and a faint scowl appeared between his brows. Underneath, his eyes were piercing. "Does an eagle compare itself to a wolf?"

How interesting. "So, you fancy yourself an eagle and your brother a wolf? Which is the true embodiment of Rome?"

"What a silly question. The Aquila is carried on every standard by our legions. It symbolizes our superiority, our intellect, and our culture. Rome is the light, and those who huddle in its distant provinces tremble at the thought of it."

Spoken like one who does not remember where he comes from, I thought. I turned to Antoninus. "Do you agree?"

"No," he said quietly. "Rome was founded on the strength of the wolf. The brothers Romulus and Remus were nourished by the mother wolf's strength and depended on the loyalty of her pack to stay alive. The wolf runs deep in our blood."

"And yet, it was vultures that determined their fate," I responded. I chanted the children's rhyme that all of us knew:
"Six for the brother first on the hill
Twelve for the brother who stabs 'til he's still
Who was the best and who was the least
Only the birds knew, ready for the feast."
Julia Domna cleared her throat, and I realized that the others had been listening to this exchange. The emperor looked displeased. I knew I was playing with fire, but I didn't care. My temper flared. I was tired of being a pawn in an endless competition between two spoiled brats. I swung my legs to standing and stretched my arms overhead, as if I had just awoken. "The air grows stale in here," I declared. "I recall your verandas have fresh breezes. I am in need of one. Who will accompany me?" I set off in the direction of the gardens without a look back.

When I reached the open air, I felt dizzy, for the rush of anger had dissipated, leaving only remorse. What had I done? Surely I had disgraced our family with my actions. I had thrown away all of Father's efforts and Mother's guidance for a momentary sense of power. How could I have been so thoughtless?

"I believe your little outburst has made your mother quite faint," a voice said behind me. "Our slaves attend to her."

"And yours? Has she disavowed me?" I turned to find Antoninus slouching against a pillar, his arms crossed. He had a quizzical look on his face.

"Time will tell," he answered. "But I would not make a habit of it."

"So I should be a dutiful, silent wife? Is that what you seek?" I was tired of flattery and polite decorum to be sure, but part of me was genuinely curious to hear his answer. And my outburst had drawn him out, which was more than polite conversation had accomplished.

Antoninus crossed to the balcony and looked out over the city. I studied his strong profile as he considered my question. His curls reflected red and gold strands in the light. "I do not want a wife at all," he said quietly. "But I will do my duty to Rome."

"At least you are honest," I said. I gazed out at the buildings, thinking of the thousands of people who lived in them. I wondered if any of them were truly happy with their circumstances.

"Honesty is important to me, Plautilla. I will give you what you seek, which is significance. You will be an Augusta, a glittering jewel by my side when I am in Rome. I can see that you are born to it."

"And when you are not in Rome?"

Antoninus turned toward me, and his dark eyes were piercing. "You will reflect on the glory of my name. I ask nothing more, but I will not accept anything less."

I considered his words. I knew that he proposed a fair arrangement, and my circumstances could have been far worse. For all his temper, he held unlimited wealth, and my daily circumstances would be comfortable. I held no illusions that he could kill me on a whim, for what woman in Rome did not live in fear of her husband? Men could philander all they liked, but women were put to death if there was even suspicion that they had wandered. Some lost their lives over trivial matters. As Augusta, I would be under constant scrutiny. Could I survive a loveless marriage? *Mother did,* I thought. At least I wouldn't be a spinster in that cramped house. I'd have space to call my own, and more importantly, all the riches I could ask for. The leering of men held no interest for me, and I doubted I would miss Antoninus when he was absent. Perhaps I would take up a new pastime, such as learning the lyre. One made of gold.

"I accept your bargain, Marcus Aurelius Antoninus, if you accept mine. I will bear your sons. I will reflect on your glory. All that I have will become yours, except my thoughts. I will not bring dishonor to your name, but I will not be silent. I speak my mind, for good or ill." I held my head up and met his gaze.

Antoninus' face was unreadable. Finally, he took my hand. His fingers were rough and callused from familiarity with both the sword and bridle. The sinews in his shoulders rippled with the movement.

"It's a match," he said. "Let's tell the others."

* * *

That night, I dreamt of walking barefoot in the palace in the moonlight. Standing on the veranda, the full moon rose over red smoke that hovered above the city. Overhead, an eagle wrestled with a snake, its talons wrapped around the coils as it streaked toward the ground. I leaned over to catch it before it fell, but only the tips of the feathers brushed my fingers.

III.

The process of negotiating the marriage contract was not a simple one. Father spent weeks arranging the details of my dowry. He kept much of the arrangements a secret, only to say cryptically that it would be "memorable." Obviously, we were not as wealthy as the imperial family, but apparently Severus was as keen to unite our families as Father was. Despite this, (or perhaps because of it) Julia Domna took over the planning of the ceremony, determining which priests would officiate and who merited an invitation. For all their previous scorn of us, it seemed all of Rome's wealthiest families were competing to be considered.

Mother oversaw the details of my preparation. I began (with much help) to weave my *tunica recta*, the white wool sheath I would wear underneath my *flammeum*, the orange veil that would symbolize my transition from girl to domina. A month after the announcement, Antoninus presented me with a gold ring during a public ceremony called the *sponsalia*, or betrothal. It was fashioned with an etching of two clasped hands. As he placed it upon my finger, Father and the Emperor Severus signed the final contract, which included the promise of a *consular insignia* for Father. He would obtain his coveted Senate seat at last.

For such an important event, it was essential that the date be fortuitous. For this, naturally, the augurs were consulted. I had never given much thought regarding the declaration of *auspicia* before. But this time, I was fascinated by the process. This was *my* wedding, and the selection of a favorable date would have a tremendous impact on my life. I asked Mother and Father endless questions over the course of these weeks, desperate to learn more.

"How do they interpret the signs?"

"Do they ever disagree with each other?"

"How are they selected to become augurs?"

"Are we allowed to watch them divinate?"

"Have they ever been wrong?"

Finally, Mother had enough. "If you're so insistent, go visit them yourself," she said, exasperated at the subject and my slow progress with the spindle. At this rate, I would have white hair before my white tunic was completed. "Father will take you to see them if you fulfill your duties."

It was the inspiration I needed to finish my task. As I gritted my teeth and forced my clumsy fingers to weave the wool fibers into something presentable, my mind wandered. I thought about Antoninus. What preparations was he making for our union? Was he nervous? As I slowly stitched the garment, I realized that I was laying a path from girlhood to womanhood, on which I would pass from my father's protection to my husband's. I remembered Antoninus' large tan hands, and how my fingers had disappeared inside his palm when he had grasped them. I then thought of Geta's pale hands. How could two brothers from the same mother be so different? Why did they dislike each other? I wondered if my arrival into their family would upset this delicate balance.

* * *

Once my tunica was finished, Mother allowed me to accompany Father to the *auguraculum* so that I could observe the taking of the auspices for that day. It was on a hill located between the Temple of Concordia and the Tarpeian Rock. At the crest was a rough area surrounded by stones, where the sixteen members of the College would gather to study the skies.

Unfortunately, auspices were taken at dawn, so that the day's business would not be delayed if the signs proved favorable. I trudged alongside Father toward the hill, bleary from lack of sleep.

"Will they be taking the auspice for our ceremony?" I asked. There had been no word from the palace on whether Julia Domna had consulted the augurs yet. The emperor was known to be more interested in astrology and had even erected a façade to the palace called the *Septizodium*. It bore statues of the seven planets surrounding Severus; he represented the sun.

"Unlikely, but I will see," Father said. "It has been many weeks, and I wonder what the delay is. The emperor is preoccupied with developments in the north. He may need to visit the front and take Antoninus with him. This may be why there is no consult yet."

As Father and I approached the auguraculum, we could see several augur priests standing in a line, each holding a *lituus*, a large staff featuring a curve at the end. All of them were much older, with stern expressions on their faces, and I tried not to giggle as they muttered and argued with one another as various birds flew this way and that. From our vantage point, it seemed almost silly. Father explained each quadrant of the sky held significance, as did the direction from which the bird flew. Birds traveling from left to right signaled Jupiter's favor. Those traveling from right to left, his disfavor. The type of bird was also important, as vultures, eagles, and owls held more significance than ravens and crows, who in turn were more significant than woodpeckers. I nodded along while Father droned on but began getting confused and eventually bored. What were they casting for? What could be more important than the nuptial wedding date of the soon-to-be-emperor? I felt annoyed that the entire process was anticlimactic. So much of our daily lives were governed by what these men interpreted. Was this all?

None of what I observed resembled what I had experienced in the garden. It seemed like a pantomime in which, at any moment, the stern frowns would morph into wild smiles, and the play would turn from tragedy to comedy. I stifled yet another giggle as the augurs gathered to scowl at one of the holy hens which had wandered from the flock. I snuck a glance at Father, but he appeared confident in their abilities. I knew these augurs held tremendous sway in religious rites and with our leaders. A small thought half-fluttered to the forefront of my mind: *they do not truly see the birds, only pretend that they do.* I quickly cleared my head. To even think such a thing was sacrilege.

Father recognized a senator, and ever eager to make a good impression, strode off to greet him. Sighing, I followed half-heartedly. "Cassius Dio, my good man!" Father raised his hand in greeting. "What a pleasant occurrence to find you here. What brings you to the auguraculum this morning?"

Cassius Dio smiled politely at Father, though the sentiment

did not reach his eyes. I recognized the telltale attitude of Roman snobbery, as if Father was not wealthier than most members of the Senate. "Mere curiosity," the senator responded. "It is always of interest what imperial business the augurs are called upon to decide so early in the morning, when most citizens are still asleep." Dio then noticed me, before glancing back at Father. "Are you seeking a wedding auspice?"

"Yes, we are hoping for a determination of a date," Father said, pretending to be bashful. "Obviously, such an extravagant celebration will require much planning, and my dear Plautilla is anxious to begin." Father placed his arm around me dotingly. Playing the part, I smiled at Dio. The senator gazed at me, and I felt the odd sensation of being assessed.

"I look forward to celebrating with you when a date is chosen," Dio said politely. He then abruptly turned and headed up the hill, dismissing us.

Father gave me a little push. "Give me a moment," he said, before following the senator.

Annoyed, I set off toward a bench under a nearby walnut tree, wishing I could return to my bed. From my bench, I watched two augurs crouch down to observe the runaway hen as she lifted her tail and scattered droppings at their feet. I resisted the urge to laugh out loud.

The sun had risen, and the heat of the day was beginning to build. I leaned my head back against the tree, enjoying the cool shade. The leaves shifted in a slight breeze, and a piece of walnut shell fell near my feet. Then another. And another. Looking up, I spotted a raven trying to break apart a walnut with its beak. Fascinated, I watched as the bird twisted the nut this way and that, lifting it up off the branch and then thrusting it down, until eventually the remains of shell fell off and the bird enjoyed the prize.

Clearly, augury was not as interesting to me as simply watching birds. I could have done that from my garden. Still, it was nice to be out of the house and away from Mother's constant fretting. I had been relatively calm about the match, but Father's comments about the auspice's delay worried me. Had Antoninus changed his mind? Did Julia Domna find me wanting? Had Father displeased the emperor in some fashion? After a few minutes, I saw Father beckoning me. I stood and gazed up at the raven, who was now pulling at another walnut from the branch. "Careful, greedy one. The augurs will say you are bad luck," I teased. The bird turned its head and looked at me and once again. I felt the hair on my arms rise. It was as if it had *heard* me. "Do you come here to mock them," I whispered. Spying a nut on the ground, I reached down and held it out in my palm. "Here."

The raven squawked. I shook my head. "That won't do. Come here." I crushed the nut with my fingers and lifted the pieces higher in my palm. The bird cocked its head, then hopped closer. I stood still and held my breath. Finally, the bird descended in a graceful swoop and landed on the bench. I shook my head. "Closer." The bird flapped its wings, as if uncertain. "Do you want it or not?" I glanced toward Father, who was now speaking with one of the priests. He would be angry if I did not come to him soon. "Raven, let us show these augurs a thing or two. Come now!" I stamped my foot impatiently.

With that, the bird hopped up and into my hand. Its taloned feet were sharp against my skin, and it was lighter than I had imagined. Slowly, it bent its head down and took the walnut in its beak, looking up as I laughed. Now that I held it in my palm, I didn't want to let it go, but I needed one more piece of crucial information. "Tell me, my friend, if Aprilis is the correct month to marry my intended." I raised my hand and launched the bird to see which way it would go. Instantly, it streaked to the right, flying so quickly it was as if it were a smudge of kohl against the sky. My heart raced. The bird had just told me that a date in Aprilis was not favored, I was sure of it. I needed to tell Father. I ran up the hill as fast as I could.

I was panting by the time I reached him. "Father," I gasped. "I need to tell you—"

"The augurs have decided the date of your union!" Father declared. "The signs have indicated that the date shall fall between the date of novem and quindecim in Aprilis!"

"But Father—"

"It took much scrutiny, but the entire college is certain. You will be blessed with a spring union!"

"Yes but—"

"Come, we must tell your mother. This is a day of celebration!" Father grabbed my hand and pulled me behind him once again. I knew it was no use. No matter what I said, my word would never mean more than the words of the acclaimed members of the College. I tried not to think of the implications of a girl knowing more about the will of Jupiter than the most lauded priesthood in the city. *It can't mean anything,* I thought. *How could this be? What is happening to me? Could I call the bird again?* Turning back, I searched for the raven, but it had vanished.

IV.

As the date of our nuptials grew closer, Antoninus showed little interest in me. I barely saw him save for the few banquets that were held in our honor. During one particularly interminable meal, he only talked of the military campaigns he was planning with Severus in Tripolitania. "Father and I must travel to the provinces in Africa, for there is unrest there," he said, reaching across the table for another cup of wine. "I will depart as soon as we are married, for time is of the essence."

"Not too soon, I hope," I jested, daring to touch him lightly on the arm. I had hoped Antoninus would admire my stola, woven from the palest yellow thread, which favored the gold jewels in my hair. But he had barely noticed. Annoyed, I glanced over at Geta, who was feeding grapes to a young girl named Livia from the Claudii family. Every time he fed her another, she giggled in a high-pitched squeak, and I found the tone of her voice unbearable. How I wished I could dump a carafe of wine onto her head. Gritting my teeth, I turned once again toward my future husband, painting the picture of a future empress, cool and above the fray.

"It is a lovely evening," I said. "Perhaps a walk in the gardens will help with digestion."

Antoninus grunted. "My digestion is fine."

I glared at him, willing him to rise and take my arm. I wanted to parade through the crowd and have the guests admire us. Regardless of his surly disposition, my soon-to-be husband looked handsome, wearing a burgundy toga that brought out the deep brown of his eyes. Together, we resembled the royal colors of Rome; a matched pair, set to rule. But Antoninus would not play the part.

"If my stubborn brother refuses to accompany you, I volunteer as your servant." I turned to see Geta smirking at us. Behind him, Livia pouted. I knew Geta only offered to walk with me to taunt his brother, but my heart quickened nonetheless. I was beginning to realize that Geta had a strange hold over my emotions. I found myself observing him frequently when he was near. His eyes were fascinating, appearing tawny in sunlight and obsidian in shadow. Geta did not speak as often as Antoninus, but when he did, he captivated everyone in the room. I sensed that Geta was as ambitious as his brother, and I felt an odd sense of kinship at this. Both of us were forced to navigate our desires in the shadow of Augustus. I wondered what Geta thought about me. Did he see me as another ornament of Augustus, or as a kindred spirit? It was another mystery, like my strange dreams and interactions with birds, and it added to my unsettled feelings as the wedding drew near.

As always, Antoninus could not resist Geta's challenge. "No need," he responded, rising quickly and reaching for my hand. The crowd quieted as we carefully stepped down from the dais and headed out into the evening air. I kept my eyes down, the picture of a modest girl, but I walked with my head held high. Behind us, Geta followed, accompanied by Livia. A few other young couples joined us, but mercifully, the rest of our families did not.

As promised, the sunset was spectacular, the scent of blossoming lemon trees wafting in the breeze. A few butterflies fluttered around the potted plants. As Antoninus guided us toward the fountains, I exhaled, realizing that I had been holding my breath. The *aula regia* had been stifling.

A knot of us gathered to look over the city. I turned to Anontinus. "Do you ever feel afraid?" I asked softly. Something in the air made me feel melancholy.

"Not in Rome," he answered. "Not by my father's side."

"What do you fear?" I asked, genuinely curious. It was rare that Antoninus spoke frankly about himself.

His brow furrowed, creasing the lines in his forehead as he thought. Finally, he answered. "Not fulfilling my destiny."

I nodded, considering his words. I too held a destiny, one that was tied up in his. It was to bear him an heir and little more. Unexpectedly, bitterness rose in the back of my throat. I had never held the desire to lift a sword in battle, but at that moment, I wanted a fight. *By Jupiter, I want more*, I thought, but I didn't know what *more* meant. I just knew I wanted it.

It was Livia, of all people, who broke my reverie. "Look!" She pointed toward the Colosseum. We all turned to see a flock of starlings alight from the upper rim of the enormous structure and gyrate in the fading light. For a moment we stood as one, watching in delight as they danced in and out of circles, creating patterns in the sky.

Of course, the accolades to Augustus could not be withheld for long. "They honor you, Antoninus. It is an auspice from Jupiter in celebration of your accomplishments!" Antoninus laughed, and the others cheered. Only Geta and I were silent.

I realized at that moment that he was standing next to me at the balcony ledge, his pale fingers curved over the stone. I turned to gaze at him and found his eyes already watching me.

"All hail Marcus Aurelius Antoninus," he said softly, and his voice dripped with sarcasm.

"That is not what the birds tell us," I whispered. "That is not the auspice at all."

Geta raised his eyebrows and cocked his head to the side. "What do they say, little one?" He was mocking me, but I didn't care. Turning to look at the flock again, I watched as the gyrations moved farther out to the river. I closed my eyes and tried to remember how the sky looked in that moment; the birds forming a V, diving and swirling, coiling tighter and tighter. The hair stood on the back of my neck. I opened my eyes. "We bind ourselves tightly to our fate, for good or for ill," I whispered.

Geta sucked in his breath, laughing softly. With an odd look on his face, he twisted the rings on his fingers. "You'll fit right in with this family," he finally said.

It was only later, when I was alone in my cubicula, ruminating on his words, that I realized what he had meant: I was entering a gilded cage.

V.

On the thirteenth day of Aprilis, I woke filled with dread. My cubicula was still dark. I strained my eyes to take in the walls and ceiling, knowing it would be the last time I woke in this bed. Perhaps it was the last time I would wake alone. Starting tonight, my bed would be in the palace. I wondered if Antoninus was awake, and thinking similar thoughts. I doubted it.

A series of celebrations had marked the days leading up to this one. Three days ago, the imperial family had held gladiatorial contests in Antoninus' honor. Two days ago, there had been chariot races in the Circus, where his team had prevailed. I tried not to think about the dozens of competitors who had perished in front of my eyes. While Gaius had been an eager spectator of this sort of entertainment during our childhood, Mother had never allowed me to attend with him. After viewing the violence first-hand, I was both grateful and resentful of her decision. Grateful in that I had never seen anyone stabbed or trampled before, and resentful that I'd had to endure it for the first time under scrutiny. Viewing violent displays was not something I enjoyed, and maintaining my composure was difficult. The past two nights, I had dreamt that the sky was filled with thousands of vultures descending to eat the flesh off the bones of the wounded.

Yesterday, I had ritually sacrificed a small bundle of childhood clothes and toys, signifying that I was ready to become a woman. There was little I had cared to lose, but I admit, when I had seen the doll and clothes catch fire, I had felt a lump in my throat.

Now as I lay in the dark, I took a deep breath, for today would be the most important day of my life. I made a silent prayer to Juno: *make me a worthy Domina of Rome*. Kicking off my coverlet, I glanced at the window. It was still dark outside, and there were no sounds of slaves preparing for the day. I had awoken earlier than anyone else. Perhaps I needed to say another prayer. Closing my eyes, I prayed to Venus: *bring me love*.

* * *

Six hours later, I was the picture of purity. My long white tunica recta fell to the floor, held together by a knotted belt clasped by a special knot called a *cingulum*, meant for my future husband's fingers only. My hair was woven into six ceremonial braids, to represent my fellowship with the Vestal Virgins at this threshold of womanhood. Upon the braids, I wore a crown of flowers, placed underneath the ceremonial saffron veil known as a *flammeum*. The orange cloth was made of wool and felt scratchy on the back of my neck.

The entire house had been filled with fragrant blossoms, and their honeyed scent filled my nostrils. As was custom, the imperial family, along with their magistrates, augurs, and members of the Senate, were traveling to our house for the ceremony, which was to be followed by a series of spectacles throughout the week in honor of Severus' *Decennalia*. Mother and Father had been preparing for this day almost as much as I had, ensuring that the floors were spotless and our atrium was cleared to accommodate all the guests attending. After the ceremony, the guests would gorge on an extravagant feast provided by our family. Additional slaves had taken over our kitchen at daybreak, and shouts could be heard as our regular slaves tried to navigate around the newcomers as well as various corralled animals waiting to be slaughtered. I hoped our house was presentable enough, but I was too nervous to care much about Julia Domna's judgments. I had more to worry about.

For some reason, a Roman girl's wedding day was considered the best time to inform her of what to expect on her wedding night. Every woman, from the lowliest chamber slave to my own mother, had been whispering all sorts of unpleasant facts into my ear all day. I learned more than I had ever cared to know about men's rank breath, how sweaty they were, how much hair they had on parts of their bodies one didn't expect, and most distressingly, how painful the act was. Unfortunately, this made me quite cross. I slapped more than one slave trying to braid my hair that morning.

Mother was not pleased with me at all. "Plautilla, you dishonor our family with this behavior!" she scolded. "Compose yourself!"

How could I compose myself when the excited male organ had just been described to me in excruciating detail? By the time guests started to arrive, I wanted to scream. My next best course of action was to get so drunk I wouldn't feel anything, though then I risked being sick in my marital bed. Something told me Antoninus would not take kindly to that.

Soon it was time for Father to lead me to the atrium, where the guests were assembled and waiting for me. The imperial family and their entourage had just arrived. Our ceremony was to be conducted by Claudius Livius Sulla, the preeminent augur of the College. His role was to divinate the omens of our union before we spoke our vows. I clutched Father's arm as he solemnly led me into the center of the crowd, followed by Mother and Gaius. Slowly, I took my place next to Antoninus. Next to him stood Emperor Severus and Julia Domna, and beside her, Geta.

I was grateful that the veil hid my face as a squealing pig was led into the atrium for Sulla to stab with a ceremonial knife. Sulla then methodically cut the liver into sixteen sections and laid them in a circle on a large stone. The augur was muttering to himself, using his knife to arrange the liver pieces this way and that while I tried not to gag. The crowd was hushed, waiting to hear his declaration. Finally, he looked up, smiling. "The omens are positive. Augustus will conquer his enemies in the north, south, and east. You see how the liver indicates this here." Sulla poked a few bloody chunks with his knife. "The pieces naturally gravitate to the east, which indicates victory in battle." I wondered what this had to do with our marriage, but the crowd was murmuring in approval.

Next, Julia Domna stepped forward and arranged Antoninus' hand over mine. Together, he and I spoke our words of consent to one another: *Ubi tu Gaius, ego Gaia.* Mother then stepped forward, offering a spelt cake made with her own hands. Both Antoninus and I took a piece and ate it before the cake was laid on our altar as an offering to Jupiter. Finally, Father and Emperor Severus formally signed the marriage agreement, and Father bowed and handed the emperor a gold coin with our faces etched upon either side. This was mostly symbolic; my dowry was primarily a significant portion of property in Leptis Magna. I suspected that was the primary reason why Antoninus and his father wished to travel there so soon. Finally, the ceremony concluded, and the feast began.

Couches were placed in every conceivable space, and animated chatter soon echoed off our immaculate tile as partygoers dined and drank. The guests were presented with platters laden with the favored delicacies of the day: stuffed dormice, roasted flamingoes and peacocks, jellied eels, snails, and goose liver. After an hour, more slaves entered, bearing golden plates and cutlery, and they presented these new place settings to guests with a flourish before vanishing. A hush fell as people looked about expectantly, awaiting the next course. I spotted Cassius Dio in the corner, inspecting his golden plate with a bemused look upon his face.

With a squealing sound, nearly a dozen boars stampeded into the room, chased by slaves. The looks on the guests' faces quickly turned from anticipation to horror. Several women shrieked and lurched behind their husbands, fearful of getting attacked by one of the agitated beasts. One woman ran screaming from the room, followed quickly by her husband and two of the smaller boars. At this, Severus roared with laughter. "These patricians have grown soft, Plautianus! I see they have forgotten how to catch their dinner!"

Father guffawed and raised his cup in response. "Just like the old days, eh? I knew you would find it amusing!" He continued to chuckle as one of the creatures rushed over and snuffled at my feet. Before I could react, Antoninus reached forward and gored the creature in the neck with one of the golden knives. When the animal collapsed, its blood spurting onto the hem of my tunica, my husband called for more wine.

The next few hours were a blur. It felt as if most of imperial Rome had taken over our house and proceeded to become increasingly drunk. Wine and mead were spilled; entire platters slid upon the floor, cracking Mother's precious tile; someone let the chickens out of their pen, and they ran amok, scattering among the crowd and pecking for scraps of food (a few were eaten by one of the boars). Antoninus was lounging on the couch that was usually occupied by Father, devouring a pheasant. I reclined by his side, unable to eat much. My nerves were fraught with the thought of what was to come next. Mother sat next to me, and for once, did not scold me but simply patted my head. Father was off in the corner boasting to several senators about some political matter. Gaius was flirting with a girl, and with a start, I realized it was Livia. I glanced at Geta to see if he noticed, but he was lounging on a couch in the corner, staring at the ceiling, seemingly bored. For some reason, this angered me. Our entire family had turned their lives upside down, and Publius Septimius Geta couldn't even be bothered to act like a proper guest!

I stood up, taking care not to disturb my garments. "Where are you going?" asked Antoninus.

"Out into the garden for a moment," I responded. "Is that all right?" I had turned automatically to Mother for permission but realized mid-sentence that I belonged to Antoninus now. I smiled my sweetest smile. "Husband?"

"I don't care where you go," he said dismissively. "Just be ready for the procession at sunset." How could I forget. I nodded and then made my escape.

Outside, I gulped fresh air, leaning against the wall. The

noise was lessened out here. Even the slaves were enjoying themselves with jugs of wine behind the house. I had a temporary moment to myself.

"Any auspices?" Geta's soft voice echoed behind me. Irritated, I refused to turn around.

"What does it matter? Even the most auspicious sighting would bore you," I snapped. "I see you feel we are beneath you."

Geta laughed, making me even more aggravated. Why was this man so frustrating? I balled my hands into fists. "I didn't realize what I said was amusing," I said, trying to be as haughty as possible. "You disrespect your *Augusta*."

It was bold of me to assume the title within hours of the vow, before the marriage had even been consummated. But I wanted to land a blow. Geta whistled, and I saw him grimace as he stepped forward out of the shadow. "That was cruel, Domina."

"You deserved it," I countered. "I can suffer one rude brother but not two."

Geta laughed again, but this time it felt as if I was being let in on a secret. "So chastised, my lady." He leaned against the balcony. "I'll be good from now on."

"I doubt it," I countered. Why was it so easy to jest with him? Why couldn't I do this with Antoninus? I was suddenly conscious of his nearness to me. He smelled of drink, but the scent was not unpleasant. Geta leaned forward and inhaled the sharp scent of rosemary growing from a pot. "The air inside is stifling," he said. "I need to sharpen my senses."

"And I need to dull mine," I said. Suddenly, I turned crimson, realizing the meaning behind my words. Geta turned and gazed at me for a long moment.

"It's not that bad," he said softly. "You'll come to enjoy it. You'll see."

"And you know this how? You have much experience?" My cheeks were flaming, but I couldn't stop.

"Yes," he whispered softly. "I have experience." His eyes flickered over me, and I felt as if I were already naked. I desperately needed something to steer the conversation away from this topic. Noticing one of the chickens, I crouched down and held out my hand to it. Geta watched as the chicken waddled toward me. "You do have a way with birds," he said. "Perhaps we can secure a peacock in the palace to entertain us."

"Your brother would eat it," I retorted, and Geta laughed again. Something turned warm in my belly, and I knew I was courting danger. We had been alone for too long. If Antoninus discovered us, my marriage would be over before it even started. "We should return," I said. "Augustus will be missing me."

Geta snorted. "No, he won't." He strode rudely into the house without looking back. I resisted the urge to throw something at him. How someone could aggravate me one moment and make me blush the next was a mystery, and one that I dared not solve. A soft clucking pulled me back into the present, and I looked down at the chicken, who was pecking at the hem of my tunica. "Dear hen," I whispered, "will my marriage bring happiness?" I stretched out my fingers to caress the back of the hen's neck. The bird lifted its head and suddenly pecked at my hand, drawing blood.

* * *

By the time we all gathered for the procession, the sun's dying rays had turned the walls of the city bright orange. As I left my childhood home for the last time, I quickly grabbed a nearby glass of honeyed wine and downed it in one swallow to calm the nerves in my belly. As was custom, I was to lead the way toward my new home.

Slowly, we set off on the road toward the palace, our drunken procession surrounded by Praetorian guards, who kept a careful eye on us. I walked in front, enduring the eyes of the citizens who had gathered to watch us pass. Some of them tossed nuts at me, a sign of fertility. As they crunched under my feet, I thought of my raven and wondered where the bird was now. Emperor Severus and Julia Domna were behind me, followed by Antoninus and Geta, my family, and our guests. At the rear of the procession were the slaves, who were carrying enormous pots filled with gold coins. There were fifty of them, and my mouth dropped at the thought of how much wealth was being displayed for all to see. I was glad for the protection of the guards as a few people rushed at us to scrounge for dropped coins. My feet hurt and the hem of my white tunica frayed as we trudged through the streets. As we approached the palace, the butterflies in my stomach began to flutter anew.

At the palace stairs, Antoninus was handed a large torch, which he held aloft. The wedding party proceeded single file up the steps into the large atrium, and then down the hallway toward the marriage chamber. At the doorway, I was given a bucket containing suet and oil, and a ball of sheep's wool. I rubbed the ointment along the archway of the door, fulfilling another ancient custom, though I could not remember what it was for. Antoninus handed the torch to Emperor Severus and then turned to me. In the flickering light, everyone's faces resembled satyrs, even those of my parents. I closed my eyes as Antoninus lifted me up and swung me over his shoulder, carrying me over the threshold. His arms were so strong I sensed that he could have tossed me across the room like a doll.

Two more servants greeted us, each holding a ceramic bowl. One held glowing embers, the other water. I pressed my fingers into the embers and then quickly dunked them in the water, another symbolic gesture to ward off ill omens from our wedding night. My fingers throbbed from the heat, and, unthinkingly, I put them in my mouth.

"Plautilla," I heard my mother murmur. I quickly removed them.

And now the moment was here. Antoninus and I had arrived at our marriage bed, surrounded by our families, servants, and half of patrician Rome. I stood awkwardly, wondering what to do with my hands. Finally, I let them drop to my sides. I gazed directly at Antoninus, and he beckoned me. "Come," was all he said.

Slowly, I walked toward him until our noses almost touched. I felt, rather than saw, my husband reach for the knot that secured the belt around my waist.

As if on cue, the crowd began to file out. I kept my gaze on Antoninus as the room emptied. Finally, the servants shut the door, and we were alone at last. I concentrated on breathing as the belt fell to the floor, followed by my veil and tunica. Soon I was naked, my only adornment the flower crown in my hair. Antoninus shrugged his toga off his shoulders and let the cloth fall to the floor. We stood for a few moments, eyeing each other's bodies. Antoninus was breathing heavily, and I hoped his breath wasn't rank. *Venus, help me.*

Antoninus gestured to the bed, which was covered in flowers. "Get on your knees," he commanded. Slowly, I crawled onto the bed and felt Antoninus behind me, his hands encircling my waist. I closed my eyes and felt him arrange himself before he pushed into me.

For the next few minutes, I did my duty. It was not as bad as I had feared, but not as good as I had hoped. Afterward, we lay together until Antoninus dozed off and began snoring softly. I watched the flickering candlelight on the tiles above and thought once more of my raven. *In the morning, I shall try to tame another one.* It was the last thought I had before falling into a dreamless sleep.

Part Two

PALATINE HILL

VI.

A year later, the bars of my cage shone brightly indeed.

I had yet to bear an heir. Of course, it would help if Antoninus tried to bear one with me, but after the first month, he had lost interest in our marriage bed. Father had arranged for our eunuch servants to follow me to the palace, so there was no other man to impregnate me even if I wanted them to. The entire act of coupling was not interesting to me regardless. The furtive grabbing of flesh, the panting, the pain between my legs—and for what? I understood that men gained pleasure from it, but I did not. If only a child could arrive another way. I fantasized about finding an infant left on my doorstep that I could sweep into my arms and call my own.

Soon after Antoninus left my bed, he departed for Africa with the emperor, leaving me to attend to his duties in Rome as *Augusta*. During this time, I hosted many banquets in his honor, dressed in the imperial finery I had long coveted. I joined Julia Domna to make public offerings at temples and to speak to wealthy senators asking for support of the emperor's proclamations. During this time, it was Father who truly guided the daily administration of the empire. Yet Julia Domna held sway of her own. With Severus gone, the administrative *consuls* and judicial *praetors* did not make

51

any decisions without her tacit approval. No one, not even my father, had as much knowledge about the actions of the magistrates, priests, and senators as she did.

Ever ambitious, Father rapidly gained power in the Senate. I sensed rising tension between him and Julia Domna as he did so. Father had always been relentless about furthering his own interests, but now, his interest was butting up against the empire's imperial coffers. One night I overheard Julia Domna complain to her chief magistrate that Father was a "profligate spender of the emperor's coin." I only hoped it wouldn't affect my purse, for I enjoyed the gold and silver trinkets I bought for myself. I would often visit the finest merchants and spend hours selecting the best silks or jewels to add to my collection before returning to the silent mausoleum that had become my home.

Besides my servants, I rarely spoke to anyone when I was inside the palace. I did not even dine with the royal family but took my meals in my chamber alone. With so much time on my hands, I found myself becoming more interested in the natural world. I had taken to walking in the palace gardens at sunrise, as the early morning birdsong was one of the few things I enjoyed. Similarly, I was learning to map the stars, and I began to mark their march across the sky as the seasons passed. Unfortunately, I did not encounter any ravens during this time, much to my disappointment. I needed a companion and had no one to confide in.

My efforts to establish friendships with other young ladies of the court fell flat, for they were not interested in my company, only Geta's. Though not an Augustus, he was still a Caesar, a coveted prize for any woman seeking his affection. I frequently heard female laughter late into the evening as I lay in my bed or sat tucked away in a forgotten alcove gazing at the night sky. I could have tried to join in on the festivities, but it would not have been appropriate as the bride of Augustus. Why would I care to watch yet another empty-headed girl simpering away at his jokes? I had better things to do with my time than watch Geta seek attention from what seemed like every woman in Rome.

Geta kept his distance from me over these months, and we only saw each other at official functions. Both of us were ornaments, trotted out as pretty things to distract the populace from yet another tax increase. Geta was a champion of many gladiators and charioteers, and thousands joined my brother Gaius in support of the games every week. He also spent considerable time in the Senate and had developed a cordial relationship with Father. I was pleased to hear this, for Father's unfettered access to the palace had been severely curtailed once Emperor Severus was no longer present. As the weeks and then months marched on, I longed for Antoninus to return. I needed to fulfill my duties as wife and mother to a future heir, and the longer my husband was absent, the more foreign I felt in my surroundings.

* * *

On the first anniversary of my wedding, my parents received a rare invitation to dine at the palace. I greeted them politely under the empress' watchful eye, but I really wanted to be embraced in one of Father's bear hugs. Instead, I gracefully reclined on the couch between him and Mother, with Julia Domna across from us and Geta beside her.

We ate in silence for several minutes. Platters of suckling pig, dried fruit, and fragrant bread were brought forth. Mother and Father exclaimed loudly how excellent the food was, but I felt shame because I knew better—this was a simple meal at the palace. It was insulting that Julia Domna did not consider my family worthy of a proper feast. My cheeks burned, but I kept my composure, grateful to be near familiar faces.

Finally, Mother cleared her throat. "Have you had word from the emperor? Has the campaign in Africa gone well? We have received little news."

Julia nodded slightly with a slight smile. "But of course. The campaign is successful, as the auspices predicted. But surely Plautilla informed you of this?" The empress turned her dark eyes toward me with a slightly disapproving look.

I smiled, but inside I seethed. I had received no correspondence from Antoninus in nearly a year, and Julia knew it. This was a subtle way to suggest that I was unworthy of Antoninus' attention. But I was no longer a naive girl cowed by brittle speech.

"Unfortunately, it seems Antoninus' many letters expressing his devotion to me have been waylaid," I began. "But I anticipate when he returns, I shall receive a suitable expression of his love. Perhaps a giraffe or rhinoceros, to accompany me in the gardens for my morning walks." Geta almost choked on his grapes at my retort but masked his amusement by grabbing his wine.

Father laughed as well, but I caught Julia's stern expression at my seemingly lighthearted jest. I knew I could pay a high price for displeasing her, but I could not reveal how much Antoninus' silence pained me. While we did not have much in common, he was still my husband. I was surprised when Geta spoke next. "Senator Plautianus, you have known my father from a young age. What was he like as a boy?"

Father preened at this unexpected opportunity to reinforce his significance. "He was much like you, Caesar. A clever orator and a natural leader. He quickly won the trust of those who served in the legions with him."

Julia smiled indulgently at Father's words, and the hair rose on my arm. "I have always understood that Severus had little time to fritter away with idle chatter. It was his mastery in military tactics that ensured his rise to power. I am gratified to hear that at least Antoninus demonstrates this essential skill."

Once again, the empress' words cut to the bone. Only this time, it was Geta who absorbed the blow. He didn't show it outwardly, but I saw it in the stiffening of his shoulders, and how his eyes hardened even though he still smiled. In that moment, I realized how lucky I had been, coming of age in a home where I wasn't belittled in front of others. My temper flared again, but this time on Geta's behalf.

"There is more to leadership than military tactics," I said sweetly. "Mastery of diplomacy, oratory, and learned study of history do more to further an empire's ambitions than any battle."

I received a brief flicker of gratitude from Geta's eyes before he poured himself another cup of wine. Father patted my hand. "Of course, my dear, but you need both to truly succeed. Thank the gods we have such a gifted leader as Severus to ensure our peace and prosperity for thousands of years. To the emperor!" Father raised his glass for a toast, and we followed suit.

"To Antoninus," I chimed in, playing the part to the hilt. "I look forward to my loving husband's return, as I am sure you do as well, Augusta." I bowed my head in a show of solidarity. Geta gave me a sly look that said *well-played*.

Julia's lips were pressed together in a firm line. I knew she was displeased, but she arranged her face into a smile. "Your comments are fortuitus, Plautilla. I have received word that Antoninus will return to Rome within a month. Let us drink to his health and a safe return." The smile froze on my face as I absorbed this news. Antoninus was finally coming home.

After dinner, I bade Mother and Father farewell and decided to stroll in the garden before returning to my chamber. The night jasmine was blooming, and the sweet scent helped to clear my head. The news that Antoninus was returning filled me with relief but also an odd fear. *I have nothing to fear*, I thought. *I have obeyed his wishes.* Why was I feeling this way? As had become my habit, I scanned the night sky for clues, but there were no birds. I had not thought of auspices in a long while, and for a moment, I wondered if I would ever sense another one. It felt as if a part of me had been slumbering ever since becoming Augusta. Would it wake again?

* * *

The next morning, I woke later than usual. After a light breakfast, I sat in the center of the room as the slaves combed and braided my hair. The endless hours of the day stretched before me, as they had so many times before. I decided that I would try to learn more about Antoninus' preferences so that I could be fully prepared for his return. Perhaps some of the palace slaves could share his favorite pastimes, or I could order them to make food that he liked to eat. I even considered traveling to the Colosseum so that I could speak

56

knowledgeably about the games.

A commotion at the door drew me from my thoughts. Suddenly, Geta burst into the room, holding something wrapped in his hands. "What are you doing?" I gasped, shocked to see him in my personal chambers. Geta knelt and placed the object onto my lap. It was a fledgling crow swaddled in cloth. It was so young its feathers looked wet, and its beak opened and closed weakly as it made little squeaking noises.

"I think it fell from the roof," Geta said. "I was heading to the Circus when I saw it on the ground. I knew you could help." He said this matter-of-factly, like it was obvious. "I trust you will take care of it."

I looked at him as if he had sprung two heads. "I'm an Augusta, I can't take care of an animal!"

Geta shrugged. "You'll find a way," he said, rising and walking out. Once again, I felt an overwhelming urge to throw something at his back. The man was impossible.

The little crow squeaked again, and my hands instinctively cupped the cloth holding it. It opened and closed its little beak, barely able to lift its head. No matter the proper protocol for an empress, this little creature needed me. Geta thought so, at least. "We shall see what we can do, little one," I whispered.

A short while later I was in the kitchen, feeding it cut up pieces of wild strawberry and currant, followed by small bits of bread mashed with goat milk from a spoon. The tiny black bird swallowed everything I gave it, apparently ravenous. I re-swaddled it in a clean cloth and clutched it to my chest as I set out looking for its nest. Several of the young slaves from the palace followed me. Soon there was much shouting as the children ran about, coming up to me to breathlessly report that there was no sign on any of the eaves of the palace. Eventually, I ordered them to collect insects, and they scampered about, grabbing grasshoppers and beetles to place into pots. The bird ate everything they caught and more.

For days, caring for the little crow consumed me, and I forgot completely about Antoninus' return. Because the creature needed to be fed constantly, I let my hair run loose down my back and only donned simple tunics as I had not time for anything else. Luckily, Julia Domna had traveled to Ostia, so there were no disapproving eyes to prevent me from dressing (or not) as I saw fit. My fancy stolas and pallas were temporarily ignored.

A few nights later, I was in the kitchen, nibbling on strawberries as the slaves cut up more fresh fruit. After days of my constant care, the bird had started to open its eyes and even hop a little. I smiled as it leaned over the edge of the small basket I was carrying and inspected the mound of fruit. I picked up a currant and placed it in its little beak.

"See? I knew you could do it," Geta's voice echoed off the kitchen tiles. "Though I didn't think you would bring the entire palace to a screeching halt in the process."

I didn't look up as he approached the table. His long fingers snatched a strawberry from the pile, and he popped it into his mouth. I continued to feed the bird while Geta watched. His fingers reached for more fruit, and I slapped his hand away. Geta chuckled and waved away the slaves who were preparing the evening meal. Soon we were left alone in the corner of the kitchen.

"Does it have a name?" Geta asked. I blinked, realizing the idea of naming the bird had not occurred to me.

"No, not yet," I said. "What do you think its name should

be?"

Geta thought for a moment. "Corvus."

I snorted. "Typical."

"Oh? You would do better?" Geta asked. Once again, the banter between us was light. He was dressed simply, in a white tunic. If not for the surroundings, we could have been any two Roman citizens in a kitchen.

"Naturally," I said. "Since he fell from the sky, I think we should name it Caelum."

"Falling from the sky is not a good quality in a bird," jested Geta. I threw a strawberry at him and he laughed. "Temper, temper, Augusta. I see you are very protective of your baby."

I winced at his words and heard his sharp intake of breath. The silence between us grew heavy once again. I continued to feed the crow, who was now bobbing his head in anticipation of more fruit.

"Forgive me, Plautilla," Geta said quietly. "I did not mean to offend."

I shrugged, no longer caring what he thought. "Caelum is too long. I think we should call him Cael." I gathered up the basket and the bowl of fruit. "Good night, Geta." I marched out of the kitchen, leaving Geta to contemplate my back for once.

* * *

Cael continued to improve, and soon he was hopping onto my shoulder or arm when I whistled to him. The slaves found an ornate birdcage, which I placed in my chamber with the basket on the bottom. The crow had other ideas. He was determined to spend as much time with me as possible, pecking and squawking at the bars, and so I left the door of the cage open. I would take Cael out into the garden and the fledgling would flutter and hop, seeking insects and sometimes worms from the garden beds. Soon he would be able to fully feed himself. It remained to see if he would stay at the palace or fly off into the wild, but I was grateful to have him by my side in the interim.

That night, we received word that Severus and Antoninus would return in two days. The palace slaves were put to a frenzy, polishing and shining every surface, and I began the many rituals Roman women performed to enhance their beauty. I visited the baths and pumiced my skin until it shone. My hair was oiled and braided, and I ordered new cosmetic paints and a had the finest cloth I could find dyed deep red to offset my gold jewelry. When we received word that the legions had marched through the city gates, we traveled to the Temple of Mars and stood atop its steps, holding laurels to welcome our brave emperors home. A crowd had formed, cheering as the legions marched past. Soon the chariots holding Severus and Antoninus could be seen approaching. My heart fluttered in anticipation.

Emperor Severus' chariot arrived first. The emperor waved to the crowd before climbing the steps and kissing Julia Domna's hand. He was handed a ceremonial sword, and the crowd roared as he lifted it above his head. It was a show of vigor and strength, and it seemed that the provinces in Africa had agreed with him.

Finally, Antoninus' chariot pulled to the bottom of the steps and he leapt out. My husband's bronze skin and golden armor shone in the sunlight, and the muscles in his arms rippled. His beard was fuller than it had been a year ago, and his was hair darker and longer. Clearly, Africa had favored him as well. He pumped his fist into the air, and the crowd cheered wildly.

"I have missed his engaging wit," Geta murmured drily. I was so shocked I almost laughed. It was bold of Geta to say this at the moment of his brother's triumphant return.

"Geta," I chided. "Stop."

"Yes, *Augusta*," he whispered as my husband approached.

Antoninus greeted his mother first, bowing and kissing her hand as Severus had done. He then nodded at Geta, and finally, he was standing in front of me. I felt tiny in his presence. I bowed and held out the laurels I had been holding for this purpose.

"Welcome home, Augustus, husband. Rome hails your great victories and honors you with these laurels!" I placed the laurel wreath in his curls. His hair was coarse and felt rough against my fingers. I smiled and leaned forward. "Welcome home," I whispered. "I have missed you."

Antoninus nodded. "You look well," was all he said before he headed into the temple. Geta raised an eyebrow at me before following. I walked behind, wondering what would lie in store for me that evening.

After enduring a long ceremony in which a sacrificial offering was made to Mars, followed by much feasting, I retired to my chambers to prepare for Antoninus' arrival. I had the servants rub scented oils on my skin and pinch my cheeks to bring out their blush. However, it was not until the stars had traveled halfway across the sky that Antoninus lurched into my chamber, smelling heavily of wine. He fumbled with my tunic, and soon, he was performing in a perfunctory manner. His body was heavy on top of me, and his sweat smelled different than I remembered.

"I have missed you, husband," I whispered into his ear, clutching his shoulders with my hands. Antoninus grunted in response. The bed began to thump against the wall, disturbing Cael, who had been asleep. With a squawk he awoke and began to hop agitatedly in his cage. Before I knew what was happening, a dark blur swooped toward us, and Cael landed on the table next to the bed. Antoninus turned his head and stared at the little crow just as Cael leaned forward and pecked at his hand.

"What is the meaning of this?!" Antoninus shouted as he swatted at Cael and the bird hopped away, swooping to dip again.

"Cael, no!" I tried to sit up, but Antoninus pushed me back down.

"I'm not finished yet," he grunted and thrust into me several more times before collapsing on top of me with a sigh. I closed my eyes and prayed to Vesta that it was enough to conceive. After a few moments, Antoninus rolled over and sat up. I opened my eyes and reached out to the bird with my fingers, stroking his soft head. Antoninus stared at Cael, who was hopping up and down on the table. He then turned his dark eyes to me. "Plautilla, I have seen many exotic animals on my travels, but none have entered a bedchamber. Explain the meaning of this."

"He fell from the eaves, and I nursed him back to life," I answered. "He was a fledgling."

Bird and man assessed each other. Cael fluffed his feathers, as if to look bigger. After a minute, Antoninus shrugged, swung his legs over the side of the bed, and reached for his robe.

"Do you not wish to stay?" I asked in a small voice.

"No," Antoninus said gruffly. "I have been away for many months and would like to feel the comfort of my own mattress. Remove the bird, I don't want to see it again." And with that, my husband departed.

The room grew quiet. I slowly sat up and held out my hand. Cael hopped into it. I slid my own legs onto the floor, then padded to the cage and placed him tenderly in the basket. The little crow tilted its head and looked at me, its black feathers gleaming in the moonlight.

"There, there, little one," I whispered as I gently stroked top of his head. "It will be all right." It wasn't until Cael responded with soft squeak that I burst into tears.

VII.

Though my heart was heavy, I obeyed Antoninus' wishes and moved Cael's cage to my servant's quarters. Cael hopped up and down in the now locked cage, pecking at my fingers through the bars. "It's only for a little while," I whispered, though I feared my words were untrue. "Just for a few days."

Yet despite my sacrifice, Antoninus did not continue his visits for long. After two more nights of hurried coupling, he retreated to his own chambers. While my ears did not hear of any dalliances with courtesans or slaves, it still anguished me greatly. I continued to present myself as a proper and desirable Augusta, painting my skin near alabaster and ensuring that my lips were as red as my stola. My hair was braided in ever more elaborate styles; my jewelry glowed in the candlelight. I made polite and astute conversation and even played a few notes of the lyre for distinguished guests one evening. Yet Antoninus preferred to confer with the officers from the *legio* unit he had served with in Africa, drinking with them until late. During the days, he did not dine with me in my chambers or walk with me in the gardens. Even though my husband had returned, I was still alone, with only a crow for company.

One morning, I woke early and dressed in a simple stola before fetching Cael for our walk. The sky was cloudy, and tendrils of mist hovered around the vines, as if the sky itself lurked in the shadows. I walked with my shawl drawn about my shoulders, enjoying the cool air. I could feel the season beginning to shift to autumnus, when rains would soak the city and engorge the river. I wondered if I would still be able to walk outside during the rainstorms. I was finding more solace in nature as my loneliness grew. If I were to remain inside the chilly marbled walls of the palace for weeks, I feared I would lose my mind. There was only so much mending, dining, and lyre-playing I could stomach. Once again, I envied how men could follow their interests in sport, politics, or languages wherever they fancied. Only women had to remain in their *domus* unless they were allowed to shop or accompany their husbands. No wonder so many women embraced the role of *domina* with a vengeance; it was the only power they wielded. Yet I could not even do this in my home—Julia was clearly the *domina,* not only of the palace but the empire itself.

As I ruminated, my steps took me downward toward the *schola praeconum,* a series of rooms constructed just above the entrance to the Circus. As I approached, I saw Antoninus, Geta, and several of their personal attendants entering the building below. Carefully, I stepped into shadow and approached out of sight, for I was curious what they were doing. It was unlike the brothers to attend anything together without Julia forcing them to, and the presence of guards was unusual. I reached a corner wall and pressed against it. The conversation inside echoed off the tiles, and I closed my eyes as I concentrated on listening.

Antoninus was speaking. "These schemes must stop. Word of your plotting reached me in Leptis Magna. More importantly, it reached Father." I could tell he was angry by his clipped tone.

Geta's voice spoke next, softer. "Your imagination runs wild yet again, Lucius. There is no such plot." Geta's use of Antoninus' boyhood name was a slight.

"Do not try me, Geta. Remember, I am Augustus, and Father's designated heir. I will crush any rebellion that surfaces, and trust me, brother, there will be no survivors. Not even you." There was the sharp sound of steel, and I wondered if a blade had been drawn. I wanted to see what was happening, but I dared not risk peering in farther.

Geta's laugh echoed off the tiles. "You think everything is a battle. There is nothing to conquer here. Why don't you spend some time conquering your wife. You are ignoring your duty, brother. If you do not administer to her, it's only a matter of time before someone else will."

I gasped at this and quickly clamped my hand over my mouth. Cael dug his talons into my shoulder, startling me further. I had forgotten he was there. It grew quiet, and I wondered what was happening. When Antoninus spoke again, his voice was lower and more menacing.

"Careful, Geta. I have spies everywhere. Plautilla may merely be a pawn in her father's desperate quest for power, but she's not stupid enough to risk her life with a dalliance behind my back. She belongs to me. But hear me: if I catch word you are caught up in one of Plautianus' plots, I will kill you myself. That man is a menace to our family. I cannot prove it yet, but when I do, I will dispose of that viper, and his little snake too. Stay far away from them both if you know what's good for you."

My stomach lurched, and I clutched the side of the building with my nails. What had happened for my husband to speak of me this way? What did he mean by a plot? Father had no plans to usurp Severus! What was this madness? The sound of footsteps jolted me into action. I quickly slunk backward into a small crevice between the buildings, praying that the shadows would hide me. Cael flew from my shoulder and landed on the eave above. I made myself as small as possible as several Praetorian guards exited the building, followed by Antoninus. I watched as they marched back up to the palace. When they were out of sight, I crept forward from my hiding place. More voices echoed off the tile.

"Master Geta, we should report these threats to the emperor."

"No. We have no proof, and it would weaken my standing. I will speak with some sympathetic members of the Senate, but I must bide my time. We must be patient."

My stomach lurched again. These words, too, seemed as if they had come from a stranger. Who was this cool and calculating Caesar? It was not the carefree and humorous Geta that I thought I had come to know. I glanced up at Cael, who hopped up and down on the eave and flapped his wings. I shook my head. *No, little one.*

Cael cocked his head to the side, and then suddenly swooped down from the eave and landed in the window farthest from me. I froze in terror. What was he doing? As if he could read my thoughts, the crow squawked and flapped his wings. The voices grew silent, then I heard heavy footsteps and a guard appeared in the window. "Shoo," he said, poking at Cael with a blade. Cael fluttered away but swooped down and pecked at the man's helmet.

"Stupid bird!" The guard swatted at Cael but couldn't reach him. Then I heard Geta's voice again.

"It is a sign we must confer with the augurs. Send word to the magistrate that I will visit the College. Go now, for it is better for us to leave separately."

A few moments later, two more guards departed and headed for the palace. Cael landed back on the window and squawked again. I remained frozen as Geta poked his head out of the window and searched the grounds until he caught sight of me. I felt pinned in place by his eyes. Eventually, he lowered his gaze. "Your husband is not the only one who has spies, I see," he said.

Slowly, I walked to the window, and Cael hopped onto my shoulder. I then entered the room, which was rectangular and featured mosaics of soldiers on the walls and floor tile. Geta was leaning against the wall, his arms folded. I took one step more and stopped. The silence between us was heavy once again.

"I don't have to ask you how long you were there. Your face says it all," he said. "I'm sorry you had to hear that, Plautilla."

"What…what was he talking about, Geta?" I asked. "I know of no plot from Father. There is nothing to fear from him."

Geta shook his head as if I were a child. "Your first statement does not necessarily have anything to do with the second."

I was suddenly conscious of my simple stola and shawl, and my unbraided hair, which must have looked wild around my face. Yet I was not ashamed. Rather, I felt anger. My husband had called me a snake, and now his brother was hinting that Father was committing treason. I balled my hands into fists, and for the first time in my life, I considered striking a man with them.

"These are lies, Geta. You call me a viper, but your family is full of them. The only lies that are spoken spill from your forked tongues."

Geta smiled then. It was sad and sardonic at the same time. "I will not argue with you there." He continued to slouch, as if we were having one of our typical jesting conversations. My cheeks suddenly burned hot at the memory of his words.

"How dare you speak about me to my husband. How *dare* you. Our marriage bed is none of your concern." I wanted to grab his dagger and stab him. Why was I suddenly so enraged? I was terrified for Father, for I knew that rumors like this could put his life in danger, yet I could not stop. I stalked toward him as my fingernails dug into my palms. Cael's talons dug into my shoulder. At that moment, I felt as powerful and reckless as Nemesis, the goddess of vengeance. I came so close to Geta I could feel his breath on my cheek.

"You arrogant peacock," I practically spat. "I trusted you."

"I know you did," Geta whispered. His eyes searched my face, and I was once again struck by how expressive they were. They reminded me of a turbulent sky before a storm. "You may not believe me, but I trust you too, Plautilla."

"Trust me to do what?" I asked, suddenly confused.

"Keep a secret," he whispered.

Then he reached for me.

Three things happened at once. Geta's fingers encircled my arms and drew me against his chest. Cael catapulted from my shoulder and began to flap wildly above us. And Geta's lips pressed against my mouth. I was so shocked I barely had time to react. As I opened my mouth to protest, the tip of Geta's tongue caressed mine. At that moment, all my thoughts vanished. I felt electricity charge my skin as it had on the day of that very first banquet. The sky went dark, and fire burned in my belly. Before I knew what I was doing, my arms were encircling his shoulders. We proceeded to devour each other.

In all the months we had been together, Antoninus had never kissed me this way. I didn't understand what strange alchemy was at work, but everything that had seemed wrong with my husband seemed right with Geta. The smell of his sweat tinged my nostrils, and he tasted like the sweetest wine. His skin felt soft, and his sinewy muscles were firm underneath my fingertips. His curly hair was softer than Antoninus', and the sounds he was making in his throat filled me with desire. I was ravenous for him. I wanted *more*.

Suddenly, I remembered the words Antoninus had spoken minutes before: *she's not stupid enough to risk her life with a dalliance behind my back.* What was I doing? I pulled myself away and took a step back, trembling. Geta laughed then, and I noticed he was panting. I suspected that he was slightly mad. Why had I never seen it before? And yet I burned for him. I had burned for him all along. The realization filled me with shock.

"Geta," I began, but then fear took hold of me and I fled. I ran as fast as I could up the hill to the palace and raced through the halls, clutching my shawl. I sensed more than saw Cael flying behind me. Slaves and guards turned in astonishment as I raced past them. Finally, I reached my chambers and flung myself on the bed. My servants gathered around me as I screamed into a bolster. Finally, I lifted my head and glared at the nearest attendant. "I need to bathe at once," I demanded.

"Of course, Domina. What happened?"

I thought for a moment. I needed to come up with a story no one would question. Yet I couldn't think of anything. If I claimed to have seen someone or something upsetting, they would send guards to investigate, and they might see Geta. I needed a story that no one would try to verify. A dozen slaves were now staring at me, resembling a row of pigeons on a branch. Suddenly, I knew what I could say.

"I saw an auspice," I said faintly. "My husband is in danger."

* * *

As I underwent my bathing ritual, the news of my vision traveled quickly throughout the palace. By the time I was presentable, I received word that the emperor himself required my presence. I swallowed hard when I learned of this, but I nodded and accompanied the guard down to the library, where Emperor Severus was waiting.

In my year on Palatine Hill, the emperor's personal library was one of the few rooms I had not visited. As I was ushered in by the guards, I gazed at the walls, which featured a few tapestries surrounded by shelves with papyrus scrolls. There were no windows; the only light came from the fire and several sconces that were placed along the walls. Along the ceiling was a detailed fresco of the planets, a large sun located at the center. Emperor Severus was seated behind a sizable desk, reviewing scrolls. He did not acknowledge me for a long while as I stood before him, continuing to write on a parchment. Eventually, he signaled to a nearby scribe, who stepped up to the desk and rolled, tied, and sealed the parchment. Severus then looked up at me.

I bowed my head. "Imperator, I am honored you have called upon me."

"It is not an honor," he replied tersely. "You speak of an auspice that threatens my son. I was not aware you were able to interpret the auspices, seeing as you are simply a girl." He gestured to the scribe to hand him another parchment. I felt the slight keenly, but this worked to my advantage.

"Honorable Imperator, you are correct. I have no formal training in interpretation. Yet sometimes…the birds reveal things to me."

The emperor raised his head at this. "What sort of things?"

I kept my face neutral. It was unnerving to speak directly to Emperor Severus, for I saw traces of both Antoninus and Geta in his face. "Whether it is advantageous for certain banquets to take place, or if a journey should be undertaken on a certain day."

Severus snorted. "And this leads you to interpret danger to Antoninus."

I paused, because I needed to weave this very carefully. "This sign was…different, My Imperator. This morning on my walk I saw Antoninus and Geta enter the schola. I thought nothing of it, but I then observed two vultures flying from the east land upon the roof. I thought it was fortuitous, but a few minutes later, when Antoninus returned to the palace, one vulture took flight and flew to the west, even though Antoninus was not heading in that direction." I took a deep breath. "I was afraid, for I understand vultures to have much influence from Jupiter. I fear that if Antoninus were to set off on a journey or undertake a contest today, he may come to harm. I was overwhelmed at the thought of losing my husband, and I became upset and ran back to the palace." I hung my head, as if in sorrow, but mostly to hide my emotions. It had taken enormous strength to spin this falsehood.

The emperor sat back, contemplating me. I glanced at the scribe, but his expression was unreadable. "Forgive me, Imperator, but where is Antoninus?" I asked timidly.

"He is with his *legio*, inspecting horses," the emperor replied. The disdain in his tone reflected what he thought of my auspice tale. "We shall speak more of this when we dine at *vespurna*." With that, he waved his hand, dismissing me.

I spent the next few hours in my chamber feeding Cael and stroking his feathers. I had dismissed all the servants. I needed to gather myself in solitude, as tonight would require even more artifice. I would need to mask my emotions and play the part of the dutiful wife as if my life depended on it, for it did. Yet a part of me hoped Geta would see through the charade. I tried not to think about the feeling of his soft lips against my jaw, or the surprising strength of his arms. I wondered what coupling with him would be like. If the women who often dined at the palace were any indication, he probably had far more skill in this than Antoninus. The thought of Geta touching me this way gave me goosebumps. *If I only I had been married to Geta.* The gods laughed at us all, it seemed.

When the sun was low in the sky, I entered the triclinium and bowed to Emperor Severus and Julia Domna before taking my place on the middle couch. Antoninus then entered, wearing a long cloak over his armor. He took his usual position next to me and proceeded to pour himself a cup of wine before downing it in nearly one swallow. He still smelled faintly of the stables, and I resisted wrinkling my nose. Instead, I moved closer to him and kissed him on the cheek, which startled him. "I am grateful to see you, husband," I said. It was true. Having him near me would make playing the part easier, for I simply needed to attend to him and not think of myself. "I am relieved to see you hearty and hale as ever, and with an appetite to match." I poured him another draught of wine. Antoninus looked at me as if I had two heads. I dared not look at Julia, for I knew she possessed the skill to see through my artifice.

At that moment, Geta entered the triclinium. At the sight of him, I clutched the pitcher of wine so tightly my fingers ached. He had bathed, and the oil on his skin matched with the gold in his laurels made him resemble Apollo. He draped himself over the couch in a careless fashion, but I could sense his tension in the way he held his jaw. He nodded to Antoninus before flicking a glance at me. His eyes were cold, and I felt an odd pain that quickly turned to anger. Why should Geta act as the wounded party? He was the one who had kissed *me*. I felt my temper rising and willed myself to control my emotions.

We ate in silence, and I held my breath, for I knew the true inquisition was coming. Eventually, Julia reclined with her cup of wine and studied me before raising her glass in a toast. "To Antoninus, who is favored by the gods, despite their unfavorable auspices." She tipped her head back and drank. Antoninus looked up, confused. Geta kept his gaze on the floor, his face a mask.

"What is the meaning of this?" asked Antoninus, who turned and looked at me. I smiled weakly and raised my own glass.

"I observed two vultures land on the roof of the schola when you and Geta met this morning. One flew to the west when you departed, and I was concerned it was a bad omen."

"You saw us?" Antoninus' brow furrowed. "What were you doing there?"

"I was walking with Cael, as I always do," I said, desperate to change the subject. "We were heading to the gardens, but I wanted to walk through the mist."

Antoninus scrutinized my face but then grunted, apparently satisfied. I exhaled and took another sip of wine.

"If there was a mist, how could you see which direction the birds flew from?" asked Julia. My stomach dropped. Antoninus, Severus, and Geta turned back to look at me. I felt my face grow hot. *Think, Plautilla.*

"A sunbeam pierced the cloud, which is what drew my attention. It was then that I saw the birds. That made me believe it was a sign from Jupiter."

"Luckily it was an empty-headed fantasy. Antoninus is as strong as ever, as we can all see for ourselves. Stick to your lyre instead of this bird foolishness." Severus grunted, sounding exactly like Antoninus. I smiled, but inside, I seethed. *I am not the empty-headed one, old man. You are blind to the mutual hatred of your two sons even though it is right in front of you.* I despised being thought of as simple, but it was the price I had to pay to remove suspicion surrounding what I had seen and done that morning. The five of us fell back into silence as we continued to eat.

Then Geta spoke. "How odd that this particular auspice was not accurate, as I have heard tell that Plautilla is quite skilled at reading the birds. I would still sleep with one eye open, brother. The day is not over yet." He delicately popped a morsel of eel into his mouth.

My blood turned to stone. What game was Geta playing?

"Is that so?" asked Julia, her sharp eyes upon me once again. "Do tell us more."

"Plautilla has correctly read the auspices for many events. She has a natural gift. Why do you think that crow follows her? He brings tidings of Jupiter to her ears."

They were all staring at me. Severus looked confused, Antoninus angry. Julia's expression was calculating, and Geta's was smug. I wanted to cry. How could Geta do this to me? Had my refusal angered him this much? Did he not understand that my life was at stake? I realized that I hated them all and I hated this place. I wanted to go home, one way or another. It was this knowledge that calmed me as I sipped my wine before responding.

"Geta is too complimentary of my skills. I merely find birds interesting when I walk outside. I did not realize that my every endeavor was of such interest, and that he was observing my every movement, seeing as he is not my husband."

The blow landed, and I saw Geta blanch. Antoninus leaned forward. "Yes, it is quite curious that my brother has such intimate knowledge of your activities." I winced at the word *intimate*. "From now on, you shall remain in your quarters unless accompanied. You draw too much attention to yourself otherwise."

"What?" I gasped. This was a prison sentence. "No, husband, that is not necessary."

"It's for your own protection," Antoninus declared. "And there will be no birds to distract you."

It was all too much. My eyes welled up, and tears ran down my face. Without a word, I silently stood and went back to my chamber, leaving them to each other.

* * *

I knew better than to expect any member of the imperial family to comfort me. But I was surprised when Julia Domna visited me the next morning. I was staring at the fresco of a garden painted on the wall as Cael hopped on my fingers. I was contemplating how cruel it was to paint the walls of a prison with images of nature when she suddenly marched into the chamber. I was so shocked I forgot to feel shame at my unkempt appearance, for I was still in my night tunic. I had dismissed my slaves yet again and refused to get dressed. I hastily rose and bowed my head as Julia approached. She stood for moment, gazing at Cael as he turned at cocked his head at her. After a moment, she nodded. "The bird is quite tame, that much is true."

"Yes, Domina," I did not know what else to say. Why was she here?

Julia turned and observed my unmade bed and the jewelry and paints scattered upon my side table. She then stepped forward and picked up the lyre from the floor where I had left it. Finally, she ran her long fingers along the bars of Cael's birdcage. I had demanded that my slaves bring it to me the night before, for if I was to be a prisoner, I would not be without my only trustworthy companion.

"You know, I believe you may be skilled in augury after all, Plautilla. While many scoff at the idea of a girl interpreting the auspices, I don't see why it is not worth investigating further. I have arranged for you to visit Claudius Livius Sulla himself. He will be able to discern the meaning of your auspice and if you indeed have the gift."

I did not know whether to celebrate or fear this development, but I nodded. "Yes, Domina."

Julia stepped up to me and lifted my chin with her long fingers. It was unnerving to be so close to her, far more than it had been with Severus yesterday. I could fool the men with my tale, but I knew she was too clever. I stared at her as she gazed sternly back. "You have been a dutiful wife to Antoninus, Plautilla, but that is not enough. You have not borne him an heir, and you act foolishly. Such foolishness distracts my sons from their destinies. If you have the skill, we shall use it to ensure Antoninus survives the many forces that gather against him. If you do not, well…" She left the latter part unsaid, but I knew what she was thinking. If I did not bear a child to Antoninus soon, I would be useless to them. As terrified as I was of facing a true augur, I knew it was my only chance to prove my continued worth.

"I understand, Domina," I whispered.

"Good. Now get dressed." With that, she swept out of the room.

VIII.

I was not taken to the auguraculum this time, but rather to the Temple of Jupiter Capitolinus, the most significant temple in Rome. Also known as the Temple of Jupiter Optimus Maximus, it had been erected in honor of Jupiter, Juno, and Minerva upon the grounds of an ancient shrine to the god Terminis. It was located at the southern peak of Capitoline Hill above a vast plaza. Nearly all political rituals and swearing-in ceremonies were performed there. The temple had survived two fires more than a hundred years ago and had eventually been rebuilt even more lavishly, with gold and bronze interwoven on the tiles of its roof. The political power of the College of Augurs was evident in their ability to conduct rites and business on Capitoline Hill.

I swallowed hard as I ascended the steps and walked under the vast atrium, surrounded by Praetorian guards. People stared at us as we passed, wondering what merited such a presence in this sacred place. I felt as if I were being served up to the gods. Jupiter was seated on a shrine in the middle of the temple behind a massive golden door, flanked by smaller doors that led to the shrines of Juno and Minerva. Their stern stone countenances bore witness to the offerings made at the grand altars at their feet. In front of Jupiter's door stood Claudius

Livius Sulla, who was obviously waiting for us. The Praetorian captain marched up and spoke to him, then gestured toward me. I gathered my palla around my arms and stood as straight as I could.

Sulla had the air of someone who knew they were important. He had rings on every finger, each trinket larger than the last. When he had officiated our wedding, my flammeum had obstructed my view of him, but now I saw a round face that bore paint, a portly figure, and oily hair. Nothing about this man indicated sensitivity. I wondered how one so wrapped up in oneself could interpret the auspices. Sulla beckoned me closer, and I approached warily.

"Fulvia Plautilla Augusta, it is an honor." Sulla bowed low before me, making a grand show of propriety. I gaped at him for a moment before I remembered my manners.

"The honor is mine, Claudius Livius Sulla. I am gratified you have taken time from your weighty responsibilities to speak with me." We smiled at each other, the picture of courtesy.

"But of course! When the empress requests our time, the College is eager to be of service. I hear you have seen auspices of your own. Very interesting, very interesting. Come." He gestured for me to follow him down toward another smaller temple at the end of the plaza. Glancing at the guards, I carefully fell into step beside him. The guards followed behind us like overgrown ducklings.

"So, tell me about this auspice that you saw yesterday. Very troubling, very troubling." Sulla waddled so quickly I had a hard time keeping pace. Breathlessly, I repeated my story of seeing the two vultures appear in the sunbeam, and one flying to the west when Antoninus departed the schola. Sulla nodded along as I spoke, but I sensed he already knew the story, he just wanted to hear me retell it. Eventually, we reached the doorway the smaller temple that housed the augurs and the cages of the sacred chickens. Sulla turned to me and smiled yet again.

"My dear, I shall give your omen much thought. For indeed, even if Antoninus is free from harm at this moment, I agree such an auspice is worth investigating, for perhaps he may come to some other harm. We shall take another auspice at sunrise and ask the gods directly to declare Antoninus' fate. Of course you will join us." He beamed at me, delighted to have an audience.

"Sunrise?" I repeated faintly.

"Or just before. At the auguraculum. I trust you won't be late!" And with that, Sulla entered the College to attend to the sacred chickens. I glanced backward at the guards, but it was of no use. If I was to dig my way out of this falsehood, I would need to join the augurs at daybreak.

* * *

I awoke before the slaves and stared at the ceiling. Cael was sleeping on one of the light sconces, his sleek head tucked into his wing. I briefly considered taking him with me. He had become so tame he would perch on my shoulder for hours while I played the lyre or went on my walks. The slaves fed him morsels of food or insects when they saw him. Even the guards smiled and playfully lifted their swords for him to swoop onto them. It seemed everyone in the palace liked the little bird, except for the imperial family. Sadly, I knew he would be a distraction. I gently stroked his feathers, and he woke instantly, hopping into my palm. "I will see you soon, little one," I whispered as I gently led him to the cage.

The servants stirred when I carried Cael into the atrium, and they hurriedly helped me dress before accompanying me down to the kitchens, where the guards were waiting. I was already annoyed with constant company when I moved through the palace, though it made it easier to avoid Geta. I did not fully understand how we could continue to remain cordial, but I knew we must. *I will solve that problem after I solve this one*, I thought.

The journey to the auguraculum was brief. The sky was beginning to turn pink in the east when I climbed to the top of the hill. I found the augurs standing in a line facing south, with Sulla in the center, holding an imposing lituus that was nearly taller than he was.

"Ah, Augusta! You grace us with your presence," he greeted me unctuously, as if he had not invited me at such an early hour himself. "We are excited to have you join us as we cast the first auspice. Come, come." He led me quickly to the line with the others and arranged my shoulders until I too was facing south.

I gathered my palla against the morning chill, feeling foolish. What was I supposed to look for? I tried to remember Father's words from the last time we visited this place—was the northeast quadrant an auspicious flight path, or was it the northwest? If two birds flew in opposite directions did one cancel out the other? Did the determinations of imperial chickens hold more sway?

Stop fretting, Plautilla, I told myself. *Just watch the sky.*

The breeze died down, and it grew quiet. The augurs appeared as sentinels overlooking the city. The orange glow of the sun tinted the roofs to our left as the sun began to rise. I realized I didn't hear any birdsong. Perhaps the birds knew we were watching. I knew how they felt. How could any creature sing if they were constantly under scrutiny? My thoughts turned unexpectedly to Geta. I wondered if he was still asleep, and if there was someone lying next to him. I knew I needed to concentrate on Antoninus, but I couldn't help myself. *Which brother will prevail?* I asked Jupiter. *Which brother deserves my heart?*

At that moment, a black cloud began to take form next to the river. My breath caught in my throat as thousands of birds rose as one, swirling and swooping into various shapes across the sky. Even Sulla gasped out loud. We stood in wonder as they danced against the clouds, silent as snow. The shape split into two halves and twisted around itself, birds flying in perfect formation as the sun glinted off their gray feathers. I gave up trying to figure out which quadrant or direction they flew and just opened myself up to the majesty of them. I knew that only the smallest and dullest water birds flocked together this way. *Together, they make beauty,* I thought. A small sound escaped me as I realized I had answered my own question.

I was deep in thought as the augurs convened to interpret the morning's auspices. The gyre had provided a heightened sense of significance to the day's questions. The augurs discussed the various events that awaited their determination. Sulla turned to me. "Young Augusta, what did you make of the sky this morning? Do you still interpret Augustus Antoninus is in danger?" The circle of augurs turned to face me. Sulla's expression was smug, and I felt small. Closing my eyes, I imagined soaring among the birds, the freedom of spreading my wings and taking a leap of faith.

Drawing a deep breath, I answered. "Those who follow

their leaders without faith will eventually come to despair. Those who follow their leader with trust reflect the gods' will. Antoninus shall remain safe as long as those who surround him have trust in his leadership." I opened my eyes to find twelve mouths gaping open. Even Sulla looked taken aback. Eventually, he composed himself.

"Those are wise words, Augusta. Wise beyond your years." Sulla bowed his head toward me and the others followed suit. "While you may not be formally trained, your interpretations of the birds are not without merit." Relief flooded through me. I had passed whatever test Julia had set. Little did she know I would soon fail a bigger one.

* * *

I returned to Palatine Hill, and nothing more was said about my auspice. Antoninus did not appear to change any of his activities. Rather, he seemed to court danger, as if in defiance of any unlucky omens. He visited the Colosseum daily and met with the gladiators, sometimes even challenging them to combat. One day, he came home bloody and exuberant because he had fought a boar in the arena and won. Julia Domna chastised him for it, but Severus roared his approval at the sight of his bloody armor.

There were a series of banquets at which patricians, generals, magistrates, and senators dined with the imperial family, discussing policy and military campaigns. Notably, Father was not among them. I smiled my way through these dinners and played my lyre, but my insides were in knots. I had not spoken to my family since Antoninus' return. I needed to visit them. Unfortunately, such a journey now required the approval of my husband. I chafed at these new restrictions on my movement and wished for Antoninus to leave on yet another campaign. I was tired of being confined to my chambers, tired of monotony and the endless talk of war. Geta, when he chose to dine with us, ignored me completely. He had taken to spending much of his time in the Senate and with the magistrates, learning about the administration of the empire.

The next night, I took the bold step of visiting Antoninus' chamber to win his favor. He was surprised but acquiesced as I led him to his bed. Afterward, I smoothed the fabric of my stola across my lap as Antoninus rose and poured himself a draught of wine. He was still naked, and his muscular frame glistened with his sweat in the firelight. Once again, I wondered how two brothers could be so different.

"Husband," I started, keeping my voice even, "I have not seen my family since your return. It has been many weeks, and I miss them. With your favor, I would like to visit with my mother and brother. I do not seek to have them here, only to spend the day there while you are at the Colosseum." I smiled at him, as a dutiful wife should.

Antoninus grunted and poured another cup of wine. "Very well. Take that damn bird with you."

"Thank you," I said, grateful for this small courtesy. Antoninus seemed calmer than he had earlier, and I took the risk of asking what had been on my mind since that morning in the schola. "Father has also not dined with us recently. Do you know why?" I kept my eyes deliberately on my lap, for I feared my face would reveal my concern.

"Plautianus remains busy as a bee. Your father is fine," he said shortly.

I turned to look at Antoninus as he donned his tunic and

lay down onto the bed. His hair was still ruffled, and his freshly shaven face made him look younger. "Husband, would you…like me to stay with you?"

Antoninus studied me for a long moment. I bit my lip and smiled again. Eventually, he shook his head. "Good night, Plautilla," he said. He then turned onto his shoulder and faced the wall. My face turned hot, and I nodded though no one could see me, then turned toward the door where my escort awaited.

Walking down the darkened hall, I hurried ahead of the guard, trying to hide the sorrow on my face. My husband did not love me. But worse, he did not trust me. For some reason, he believed I was part of a plot to usurp the emperor that I had no knowledge of. Nothing I could do or say would make a difference. How was a supposed to conceive an heir if he wouldn't look at me? The tears in my eyes prevented me from seeing Geta until he crossed my path. I stopped short as he nodded curtly before continuing toward his own chambers. Suddenly, my sorrow turned to rage.

"It is customary to wish your Augusta a good evening," I huffed. "Your manners leave much to be desired, Publius Septimius Geta." I straightened my stola as best as I could and marched forward.

"It seems you have already had a good evening, though I don't know if it contained any desire," Geta retorted. I stopped again, shocked at his words. I looked to the guard, who had his hand on his sword, when another two guards stepped forth from the shadows. It seemed that every member of this family required armed guards in their own home. I signaled to my guard to stand down, then turned and gave Geta my most imperious stare.

"How hollow your life must be, if you feel the constant urge to be cruel, Geta." My chest was tight, but at least I wasn't crying anymore. We stared at each other, and I knew I looked unkempt from my coupling with Antoninus. But I would not stand to be spoken to with such derision, even if it was from a Caesar.

Geta took an unsteady step toward me, and I realized that he had been drinking. He bumped into one of the columns. "Plautilla," he began.

"You will address me as Augusta," I said icily. I eyed him warily as he wobbled closer. We were face to face for the first time since that moment in the schola. Geta's eyes burned into me, and I glared back, though my heart was beating nearly through my chest. Slowly, he leaned forward, and I tensed as his lips brushed my ear.

"I can't stop thinking about you," he whispered.

At that, I turned and fled.

* * *

The next morning, I sent word to my mother that I would be visiting the following day. I dismissed my slaves yet again and lay in bed, terrified of leaving my chamber. But whether I was more afraid of what Geta would do or my own desires, I did not know. I felt as if I were in the center of a knot of ropes and the cords were pulling tighter. Antoninus wanted nothing to do with me, Julia was ready to dispose of me, Father's life was in danger and he did not know it, and Geta was fixated on me. If I warned Father, it would further confirm Antoninus' suspicion that I was part of the plot. If I did not bear an heir soon, Julia would find a way to have me removed from the family in disgrace. If I coupled with Geta, Antoninus would have me killed. I pulled the bolster over my head and screamed in silence.

I composed myself eventually and dined alone in my room that evening with only Cael for company. The next morning, I woke early and dressed in a plain stola, grateful for the opportunity to escape my prison for a day. I called Cael to me from across the room and fed him a strawberry. "I need you stay with me," I told him. As I was escorted to my lectica, the little bird flew alongside, swooping from one statue head to another. I called him to my shoulder and held him tightly to my chest during our journey.

When I saw my old villa, my heart turned. Never had I thought I would miss this simple domus, with its modest portico and slightly faded paint. I felt like a stranger as one of the Praetorians knocked loudly upon the door. When Mother opened it, she paled, then color returned to her cheeks when she saw me. She was beginning to bow her head when I ran to her and threw my arms around her for an embrace. Cael fluttered above our heads as she returned the hug tightly. "How I have missed you, Plautilla," she said, kissing me on the head. Cael croaked and landed on my head as Mother looked up. "Is this a pet?"

"I have much to tell you," I laughed, my heart suddenly light. "Let us eat."

Soon we were seated in our cozy triclinium, dining on my favorite childhood dishes: poached eggs with savory fish sauce, cheeses, honey cake, and fresh oranges from the grove above the city. I gasped when Gaius entered the room—he had grown nearly a foot and was sporting a scraggly beard under his chin. "It is good to see you, brother," I said, hugging him tightly. He awkwardly hugged me back and settled down to shove an entire egg in his mouth. Some things hadn't changed.

Mother smiled at me and sipped her wine, but she looked wan. I wondered again where Father was. It saddened me that I could not speak as freely as I wanted. Still, this was my family. After feeding Cael a slice of orange, I sat up and addressed Mother.

"We have hosted a series of banquets with members of the Senate, consuls, and ex-consuls as guests. Yet Father has not participated. I am keen to see him. Do you know why he has not been to the palace?" I sipped my wine casually, but the momentary look on Mother's face filled me with dismay. Ever the patrician, she quickly rearranged her features into a placid expression before answering.

"Your Father has been tasked with overseeing the *Legio II Parthica*. They will now come under his authority with the Praetorian guard. The emperor will need additional protection if he chooses to travel to the provinces."

"Which provinces?" I tried to recall details of the endless discussions I had endured, but the names all blended together.

Mother smiled ruefully. "That much I do not know." We sipped our wine in silence, as Gaius ripped open oranges with gusto. Mother eyed me shrewdly. "There is something you are not sharing with me, Plautilla." I sighed. I should have known I could never hide my emotions from Mother.

"I fear Father has fallen out of favor with Severus. He has not attended these banquets, and it is unusual. I worry that if he falls out of favor, or if I...do not continue to stay in their favor, it will reflect badly on our family."

Mother glanced at Gaius and then leaned forward to speak in a low voice. "It is not the emperor who finds your father out of favor, but rather the empress. Father has advanced many capable men from the legions he controls, but at the expense of two of her family members, Avitus Alexianus and son-in-law Varius Marcellus. She has clashed with the emperor regarding this matter, but Severus sided with your father. The empress… has held a grudge. Unfortunately, she has turned to other means to discredit him." Mother's face was grim. "Indeed, we hear rumors that there is talk your father has become too powerful, that he holds too mighty a sway over the emperor. You have now confirmed this, Plautilla."

"It's more than that," I said. "Antoninus believes Father and Geta plot against him and Emperor Severus to overthrow them so Father can rule. This belief has…affected Antoninus' affection toward me." I hung my head in shame. Cael fluttered over and squeaked softly, and I stroked his feathers. Gaius gasped in surprise and leaned forward, trying to follow suit, but Cael skittered away. I was distracted by this when Mother reached over and took my hand.

"I am sorry to hear this, Plautilla, for I know you have done all that you could to please him. You must stay the course. Do not worry about Father; he commands the prefects of the Legio II Parthica, and has nurtured relationships with others in the Senate who still hold some power. Fear not, for these rumors will be quashed. Now, tell us about this little fellow here. How did you tame him so well?"

While I did not share Mother's confidence, I was grateful for the change of subject. "He fell from the eaves and was brought to me to nurse as a fledgling. Would you like to see him do tricks?"

The rest of the afternoon passed in an enjoyable fashion, as Gaius played with Cael in the garden and Mother and I sat in the sun and traded news of friends and family. It was the happiest I had been in months. I nearly cried when I was summoned by the Praetorian guards at sunset and clung tightly to Mother before I departed. "Do not fear, Plautilla," Mother whispered. "The Praetorians are with Father, and they will ensure no harm comes to you." I nodded, sorrowful that she felt the need to reassure me this way. For all of Mother's knowledge and upbringing, she did not truly understand the darkness at the heart of the imperial family as I did. It burdened my heart that I had to shelter her from it. I smiled bravely, kissed her on both cheeks, and began the journey back toward my prison, Cael at my side.

IX.

Soon after I returned, it was decided we would travel to one of the imperial villas in the countryside to enjoy the cool weather. Julia Domna declared that it would be better to have fresh breezes and sunshine away from the cramped streets of Palatine Hill. The slaves spent a day making all the necessary arrangements before we traveled in our caravan to Villa di Sette Bassi, located in the hills southwest of the city. Indeed, the rolling landscape and poplar trees did much to soothe my nerves as Cael rolled along in the lectica with me, this time in his cage.

The villa was colossal, featuring two stories and extended rooms that had been built out on the top of the hillside by three successive owners. Even better, behind the villa lay an enormous garden with ornate fountains, exotic plants, and cypress trees that lined the paths leading to the thicker woods above. When I saw it, I felt like I could breathe for the first time since leaving my family a few days before. I couldn't wait to get lost in its winding paths. Cael fluttered at the bars of his cage, seemingly eager to fly amongst the trees. "Soon, little one," I murmured to him. "We'll find freedom together soon."

I was given a first-floor cubicula behind the kitchen, tucked away from the others who were residing upstairs in the grander chambers. Even though I could not help but recognize the slight that was made with this decision, I did not mind at all; I was ready to take my leave of the entire family. Antoninus seemed to forget I was even there, giving me freedom to roam while they entertained various scholars and musicians in the great atrium. The first banquet Julia was planning for that evening was one of the grandest yet, inviting dignitaries of the Senate and various generals, though there was still no word of Father. Restless, I coaxed Cael from his cage and set out to explore the grounds.

The scene in the villa's kitchen was chaotic, as household servants, imperial slaves, and local farmers were busy preparing various delicacies or carrying supplies for the occasion. I wandered outside to see a few casks of wine being carted to the edge of the garden. Several women and girls followed, holding baskets of fruit. Curious, I followed them, for this was unusual. Cael hopped from my shoulder and fluttered about the lower branches of the trees, drawing the attention of several children. A young girl smiled and offered him a small slice of orange, and he flew down and snatched it before heading to a nearby rock to greedily wolf it down. I nodded my head in thanks and gestured to girl's basket. "What is this for? Will the banquet be outside?" I asked.

"No, Domina, it is for the festival of Faunalia," she answered shyly. "We will celebrate it tonight." She gestured to a makeshift altar that was being prepared at the edge of the woods beyond the garden.

I smiled kindly. "What is this festival? I do not think I have ever heard of it." The girl giggled at my question before scampering behind the skirts of an older woman who was carrying a basket of fruit. One of the oranges slipped out of her basket and rolled toward me. I bent to pick it up before handing it to the woman. "Is this a harvest festival?" I asked her.

"Yes, Domina. We will make an offering to Faunus, so that he will continue to bless our fields and ask him to guard our flocks for the winter." I nodded, for I had heard of various festivals of the countryfolk that we did not celebrate.

"I hope Faunus grants all that you seek," I said politely before heading toward a garden path.

* * *

Later that evening, the sounds of drumming and music wafted through the windows of the grand triclinium, a distraction from the conversation around me. The vibration from the music was making me restless, and I found myself drumming my fingers along the edge of my couch, wishing for the banquet to end. At least the food had been unexpectedly good. It was considered more rustic fare, but I enjoyed the fresh fruit and vegetables prepared simply with warm breads and cheeses. If I could go the rest of my life without having to look at stuffed dormice again, it would be fine with me.

I glanced at Antoninus, who was enjoying the spicy wine that had been specially prepared for the festival. Remembering Mother's words, I tried to look engaged in what he was saying. He was jesting with a general from one of the legions he commanded. I kept a smile pasted on my face as they proceeded to discuss the best way to disembowel an enemy with a knife. After a particularly colorful exchange, I felt faint and turned away, only to find Geta eyeing me with a sardonic smile. Once again, I felt trapped between the two brothers, a pawn in a game I didn't fully understand.

"Plautilla, what is the matter? You look ill." Julia Domna's words cut across the conversation and the room grew silent. All eyes turned to me, and I felt my cheeks grow hot.

"Forgive me, Domina," I said meekly. "This strong wine does not agree with me." I gestured to my cup, though I had barely had a drop.

"I do not remember you having such a delicate disposition before," Julia said with a tone of concern, though I knew better. This honey contained venom. "Perhaps you should get some rest. We would not want an upset stomach to ruin your visit."

It was a clear dismissal, and my cheeks burned even more with humiliation. I bowed my head in acceptance. I was to be banished to my cubicula yet again with only Cael for company. As I slowly sat up, a rush of anger jolted through me. Before I knew what I was doing, I placed a hand across my belly.

"Thank you, Domina, for your consideration. My indigestion has indeed been worse recently." I added a second hand to my belly for emphasis.

All eyes turned to my midsection. Antoninus' mouth dropped open. Julia's expression grew sharp. Two patrician noblewomen whispered to each other. I smiled sweetly at them and ducked my head modestly, as if I was embarrassed about my newly disclosed condition. I dared not look at Geta, for he would certainly see through the charade. Carefully, I took my leave, enjoying the temporary power of all eyes upon me as I brushed past them. Once out of sight, I ran straight to my room. The halls were deserted, as the slaves had been given the opportunity to enjoy the festival. I quickly removed my jewelry and snatched one of my plainer pallas, wrapping it around my head as a disguise. Cael fluttered at the bars of his cage, but I shushed him. "I cannot take you, little one, or they will know where I have gone." Before anyone could stop me, I fled into the gardens.

I ran. I ran from my anger and fear. I ran from the falsehood I had told. I ran from disapproving stares and whispers behind my back. I ran from neglect and obsession. I ran as hard as I could, wishing Cael could streak through the dark sky above me.

The night air felt cool against my skin as I raised the hem of my stola above my knees, my palla now flapping behind me. I raced up the path toward the woods, where the sounds of music echoed off the stones. As I rounded the bend, I saw that the countryfolk were still celebrating alongside several bonfires. Many were dancing to music. A goat kid had been presented on the altar to Faunus, and its singed flesh wafted pungent smoke into the trees. A man was pouring wine from a cask for several women. Panting, I stopped and observed, entranced, from my position on the hill. I was captivated by their freedom. I had never envied countryfolk before, but now I wanted nothing more than to dance barefoot under the full moon with them. I was tired of being judged for everything I said or did. I just wanted to be a simple girl for one night.

Throwing my palla once again around my face, I approached the man with the wine casket. I snatched a cup from a nearby rock and held it out with the others. If countryfolk recognized me as an interloper from the villa, they said nothing. The man poured the wine, and I tipped my head back and drank it in one large swallow. I wiped my mouth with the back of my hand and gestured for another. After downing the second cup, I shed my palla upon the ground and joined several women in a frenzied dance around one of the bonfires. I shook my braids free and tossed off my shoes, reveling in the feeling of dewy grass underneath my feet. I stretched my arms wide and spun in circles, the wine warming my belly. I closed my eyes, giving into the sensation. I twirled faster and faster, until I bumped into a man who grabbed me by the hand and yanked me roughly toward him. I opened my eyes to see that Geta had prevented me from nearly twirling into the open flames.

Of course he had followed me here. I stamped my bare foot upon his, but he simply laughed. "Careful, Augusta. This rich wine has gone to your head." Geta clutched at my fingers and pulled me into another dance, this one with both men and women. "I would think you would be resting, given that you are expecting the heir to the empire."

"I do what I please," I snapped. Geta raised an eyebrow at this.

"So it pleases you to make a fool of yourself?" he asked softly.

"Quiet! Can't you give me peace?" I retorted, but I did not let go of his hand. We wove through the dancing couples, following the ancient steps.

"I haven't known peace since you married Antoninus," Geta shot back, though his arm encircled my waist.

I felt another retort on the tip of my tongue, but the music sped up once again, and we were caught up in a swirling parade of dancers. Geta danced with fervor, lifting me up and swinging me above before twirling around me. I forgot my anger and simply tried to match his energy, and soon we were at the center of the clapping crowd. The musicians stepped into the circle with us, and we spun together, faster and faster, giggling and clasping fingers tightly, until the music rose to a crescendo and we ended the dance crashing into an embrace.

Geta's face was flushed, and his curly hair was free of laurels. His lips were parted and flames from the bonfire reflected in his eyes. Before I knew what I was doing, I stood on my tiptoes and kissed him fiercely.

The dancers cheered for us until Geta pulled away, clasping my wrists in his. I felt heat rise through my body. I no longer cared what anyone thought. I only knew I didn't want this night to end. I looked Geta directly in the eye. "How do you see me?" I asked.

Geta did not answer but continued to contemplate me. Finally, he said, "You are a phoenix. You rise from the ashes, and you are a mother to Rome."

This took me aback, and I hung my head in shame. "I'm not a mother to anything," I mumbled.

Geta's fingers lifted my chin and he stepped closer, until our noses were touching. "I will make you one," he whispered.

I was his after that.

* * *

Geta led me to a stone gatehouse located on the far edge of the gardens, hidden behind a row of poplar trees. Slowly, with nothing but moonlight streaming in the hole in the roof to guide us, we undressed each other and lay down upon the simple pallet against the wall.

"Geta, I—" The words died in my throat.

"Shhhh," he whispered. "Close your eyes."

I did as he asked and tried to relax. I felt his kisses, featherlight, on my breasts, then stomach, then thighs. I drew my breath in sharply as I felt his tongue explore between my legs. Before long I was clutching at his curls, moving my hips in rhythm with his mouth. The only sounds were that of his mouth upon my skin, and this amplified the intense pleasure I was feeling. The sensations crested and I felt myself falling into ecstasy. Geta continued his ministration until I pulled sharply on his hair to make him stop. Slowly, I blinked my eyes open as he crawled back up to face me, his face flushed and lips swollen. His eyes were wide, and he broke into a sad smile.

"What is it?" I asked, tracing my fingers along the delicate bones in his cheek.

"I need you, Plautilla," was all he said. His words landed like a weight on my heart, and I nodded. Geta then kissed me gently on the forehead and tucked his head between my neck and shoulder as he entered me.

Never had coupling felt this way. The pleasurable sensations returned, not as intense but still encouraging me to move my hips with his. Geta's fingers were exploring my breasts, and he raised himself up onto his hands as he drunk in the sight of our bodies joined together.

Every sense I had was heightened. I did not shy away from staring at his nakedness filling mine; I did not hold back the sounds he brought forth from me. The smell of his sex permeated my nostrils, and I inhaled it deep into my soul. I tasted every inch of him, even between his legs. I had no thought but to pull as much of him into me as I could.

So this was love. This, the movement of our bodies that unlocked the keys to our souls. I felt like crying with joy. Every moment of this was precious, and worth the risk. I was not truly alive until this night. Geta set my skin on fire and kindled something deep within me.

We coupled until the sun rose; our mouths fused together

with kisses. I entreated him to protect me from Antoninus, and he vowed he would give me the heir that I wanted. In his arms, I was both Plautilla and *Augusta*, a girl blossoming into womanhood and a powerful empress to be worshipped. To me, he was both the impish boy who teased me and Cupid, the god of love himself. Finally, we fell into a deep sleep, curled against each other, as the sun's rays warmed our stone sanctuary and birdsong filled the morning breeze.

IX.

It was Cael that warned us. I woke to the sound of croaking and opened my eyes to see a bird poking his head frantically through a hole in the thatched roof. I realized it must have been late morning and gasped, which in turn woke Geta. Sitting up, I reached out my hand and softly called to the bird. Cael disappeared, only to flutter in through the small window shortly after, eventually flying onto my palm. Geta donned his toga and went to the door. Cautiously, he peered outside before quickly shutting it.

"Praetorians are in the gardens," he said quietly. Neither one of us needed to say what would happen if they found us together. With a sickening feeling, I realized they had released Cael in the hopes of finding me. Unwittingly, the little bird had shown them the way.

"Go now," I said to Geta. "I'll stay here. I'll tell them I fell asleep."

Nodding, Geta hurriedly grabbed his sandals and exited. I heard his retreating footsteps head toward the woods. I quickly donned my stola and lay down on the pallet, covering my legs. I pretended to be slowly waking from sleep when the door to the cottage flew open and two guards entered, swords drawn. I yawned and stretched, looking at them with confusion. "What happened?" I asked.

* * *

I was escorted back to the villa by a phalanx of guards. Cael swooped above our heads but did not land, as if he knew to keep his distance. As we approached the entrance to the kitchen, Antoninus strode out to greet us. He nodded to the captain and stepped forward to grab me by the arm. "What is the meaning of this?" he asked through gritted teeth. His fingers pinched too tightly, and I knew bruises would form on the very skin his brother had caressed so gently just hours before. Before I could answer, Antoninus' nostrils flared and he sniffed my palla with distaste. "You smell like a goat," he said. "Clean yourself." With that, he signaled to his attendants and headed to the stables.

I exhaled in relief before nodding imperiously at the guards. "Fetch my slaves," I commanded. "Augustus requires that I bathe."

Later, after I had scrubbed all traces of Geta from my body and adorned myself for the day, I was presented to Severus and Julia for an explanation. Mercifully, neither Antoninus nor Geta were present. The emperor and empress were in the atrium, gathered on the far end of the *impluvium*, or drain pool, in the center. Severus was pacing back and forth, but Julia stood as still as a statue as I carefully walked toward them. Her eyes scanned my stomach, and I knew she was trying to determine whether I was truly with child. I sent a brief prayer to Aphrodite that Geta had indeed made it so.

After a respectful nod, I stood calmly with my hands clasped in front of my stola. I did not look down but gazed directly at them with a pleasant smile on my face. I had risked much last night, but seeing their disapproving frowns, I knew I would do it again if I had the chance. Severus gestured to the servants to close the doors.

Julia did not wait for niceties. "Where were you? Antoninus sent for you, and you were not in your chambers."

That is a lie, he has never sent for me, I thought. But my face remained placid, for I had prepared my answer while soaking in the bath. "I was curious about the music, so before I returned to my chamber, I followed a few of the slaves to the top of the hill. There was dancing and I was…intrigued, so I joined a few of the village girls. Afterward, I was thirsty and was offered some of the strong festival wine. My digestion was not used to it, so I must have fallen asleep in the shack."

This was a simple narrative, but I needed to know how much they already knew. My intuition told me they hadn't bothered to seek out information about what I had done because they simply didn't care. Antoninus was different, but if I satisfied his parents, I suspected he would accept the story and move on, for the same reason. The only one in this wretched household that truly cared about my happiness was Geta; I no longer felt any remorse about lying to the rest of them.

"Odd, that you would consider such reckless behavior in your…condition." Julia clearly had doubts about the veracity of my claim.

"I was overcome with joy and wished to make an offering to Faunus in my own fashion," I replied smoothly. Julia's brows furrowed, and I knew she was trying to find fault with my words, but I had given her none.

Severus grunted and poured himself a draught of wine. "Nonsense. There are more appropriate gods to honor here in the villa. You should have made an offering to Vesta the moment you knew."

"It was at the banquet when I realized. I did not have time to make an offering on my way to my cubicula," I answered, trying to keep a respectful tone in my voice.

"She is full of facile answers, Severus. We won't learn the truth today of where she was." Julia drank from her own cup of wine. I had not been offered one. I perceived yet another slight, but was unperturbed, as I needed to keep my wits about me. My head still throbbed from what I had drunk the night before.

"I do not speak anything but the truth, Domina." I bowed my head again for emphasis. As I looked down, I marked their distorted figures reflecting up at me from the water. Suddenly, a shadow rippled across the pool, turning the water dark. In the reflection, I saw a bird soar across the sky high above, but what type of bird I could not tell. Neither Severus nor Julia noticed, but I knew in my bones that the shadow was an omen. I felt a chill as the meaning of the auspice hit me with a jolt: the fate of this dynasty was far from certain. I felt the color drain from my face and placed a hand on my belly.

"Domina, my digestion troubles me yet again," I gasped. "Please excuse me, for I need to lie down."

Something in my face must have convinced Julia, for she nodded, dismissing me. I turned and hurried back to my cubicula as fast as I could.

* * *

As much as I wanted to hide from prying eyes, I could not stay in my cubicula forever. Reluctantly, I entered the triclinium

104

at sunset for *cena*, the evening meal. Tonight, there would be no invited guests, just the family. Carefully, I sat next to Antoninus, arranging my palla across my arms. Uncharacteristically, he poured a glass of water and handed it over himself. "For your digestion," he said gruffly. I nodded in appreciation, and for a moment, felt a pang of connection. This simple gesture was the kindest thing he had done for me that I could remember.

At that moment, Geta sauntered in and threw himself down on the couch across from us. I dared not look at him as I drank, feeling my cheeks flush. His very presence sent my heart racing, and I felt faint. I smiled weakly at Antoninus as Geta helped himself to several grapes and began eating them with gusto.

"You certainly have a healthy appetite tonight, Geta," Julia said conversationally. "What is it that has made you so famished?"

Geta shrugged as he reached for an apricot. "Must be the country air."

Antoninus rolled his eyes. "Must be the country girls. You didn't return to your rooms last night. Find another gullible wench, brother?"

I froze, the glass of water still in my hand. I could feel my heart beating nearly through my chest. I glanced up at Geta, but he had merely raised one eyebrow at Antoninus. "I had no idea you were so interested in my night-time adventures, brother. If you wanted to better learn how to please Plautilla, you could simply ask her yourself."

My face turned red. I was too shocked to be afraid. What was Geta doing? Antoninus did not move from his reclined position, but I heard the edge creep into his voice. "Once again, you speak of things you should not, brother. You will address my wife as Augusta and only refer to her when invited to do so." His face was placid, but I could sense the anger radiating from him.

I glanced at Severus and Julia, who were calmly eating as if this exchange meant nothing. I wanted to scream at them both—*do you not see what you have created? They will destroy each other*—but instead forced myself to continue sipping water. My appetite had vanished. Geta shrugged and picked up an apple. He turned it around in his long fingers before biting into it. "Very well," he said, his mouth still full. "To answer your question, brother, yes I did find a gullible wench, and she was sweeter than this fruit." He suggestively sucked the juice from his fingers.

"That is *enough*." I was as surprised by my outburst as anyone. I slammed the glass of water down on the table so hard it shattered. I sat up and grasped Antoinus' hand. "You behave like a boor, Geta. What my husband does with me is none of your business. What you do with your whores is distasteful and not appropriate family conversation. Your words are disrespectful to your parents, to Augustus, and to me. Apologize."

Geta stared at me, confusion and anger playing across his face. Antoninus sat up and placed his hand on the knife at his belt. "My Augusta has spoken, brother. It would be best if you heeded her words."

Geta looked at Antoninus, then me, then at Severus and Julia. The emperor sighed, but he did not correct me. Julia remained as still as a statue. I felt truly angry at Geta's reckless behavior and salacious words, and for some reason, jealous of the thought that he had been with anyone else. All these feelings swirled around in my chest. A small, guilty part of me also knew the best way to throw suspicion off myself was to cast it upon another, for this family always needed a scapegoat. I felt low for doing it, and to Geta most of all. Yet I did not take back my words.

Geta's throat flushed red and his full lips pursed into a thin line. He looked down at his hands and fiddled with the ring on his middle finger before mumbling "My apologies, Augusta." I nodded my head in acceptance. Without another word, Geta rose and marched out of the room. My heart felt it was being cleaved in two, but I squeezed Antoninus' hand. "Thank you," I whispered. Antoninus nodded and proceeded to eat a sardine. I caught the eye of Julia, but she seemed deep in thought. I was no longer the subject of scrutiny and had endeared myself temporarily to Antoninus. Relieved, I forced myself to eat.

* * *

Antoninus escorted me to his chamber after our meal, and he initiated coupling with me. I tried not to think of Geta during the act, but I couldn't help it. When I began to kiss Antoninus along his throat the way I had kissed Geta the night before, he looked at me strangely. I resorted to lying back with my arms around his neck as he continued pumping into me. *Vesta, give me a child,* I prayed. *I will make offerings every day, please give me peace from these brothers.* I would have prayed to Jupiter if I thought it would help.

Afterward, Antoninus had me escorted back to my cubicula by his servant. After nearly two years of marriage, my husband still preferred to sleep alone. As we walked through the dark halls, I thought of Geta's arms around me while I had drifted off to sleep only a few hours earlier. It seemed like another lifetime.

When I entered the room, I noticed that it was dark. The slaves had not lit the lamps for me. I turned to call the servant back, but Cael chirped agitatedly behind the bars of his cage, drawing my attention. I stepped forward in the shadows to open the door and let him out. The small bird flew to my shoulder. "I'm sorry I have been ignoring you, little one," I said softly. "You deserve better."

"And what of me? Do I deserve better?" Geta's voice echoed from the darkness. I took a startled step back as Cael fluttered his wings next to my head. As my eyes adjusted further, I saw Geta lounging on my bed, holding a bottle of wine. "Did you think of me when he was inside you?" he asked bitterly, before taking a long swallow directly from the jug.

"What are you doing here?" I hissed, quickly shutting the door. "You'll get us both killed!"

Geta laughed, and I could tell he was extremely drunk. "No one cares enough about either of us to notice. They think I'm sulking in my room, and your husband discarded you once he was done with you. The servants have all gone to sleep." He rose unsteadily and staggered toward me. "It's just you and me."

"You're drunk." I gently put Cael back into his cage but left the door open. "Go to bed, Geta."

"Trying to," he whispered, his arms encircling me from behind. He whirled me around to face him.

"This can't happen again—" The words died in my throat as Geta kissed me. And my body betrayed me in an instant, giving in to desire. I clutched at his toga and pulled him closer to me, desperate for more.

If last night's coupling was gentle discovery, tonight it was combat. Geta punished me for lying with Antoninus, and I punished him for his rude behavior. What did it say about me that I enjoyed it just as much, if not more? We were rough with each other, but our hunger was insatiable. Geta did not object when I bit his throat, and I writhed when he pinned me down with my wrists above my head. "Did he make you feel this way?" he growled as he thrust his hips savagely between my legs. I whined in answer.

Later, when the sweat on our bodies cooled, we lay together in the dark. Once again, Geta's arms engulfed me as he lay against my back, his face tucked into my shoulder. Somehow, not being able to see his face made it easier for me to unveil my deepest fears. "Geta, are you asleep?" I asked as I gently stroked his forearm. I received a soft kiss on the side of my neck in response. "Do you think Antoninus would really kill us?" I whispered.

Geta was quiet, and I could sense that he was thinking. I heard a soft rustle that meant Cael was preening his feathers. I suddenly realized that despite our rough coupling, Cael had not flown to my side. Somehow, the bird had known I was never truly in danger. Geta kissed my shoulder, interrupting my thoughts. "I think he would be angry enough to use it as a pretense to have me assassinated, but I'm not sure he would kill you."

"What about the emperor or empress?" I asked in a small voice. I felt Geta stiffen.

"I don't know," he said quietly.

We lay in silence. Then another dark fear surfaced in me. "What about my father, Geta? Would Antoninus have him killed?"

Geta gently pressed on my shoulder until I turned on my other side to face him. I felt his forehead touch mine. "Why so many troublesome questions? Don't you have faith in me? I will protect you, Plautilla. When I am Augustus, I will make you my bride, I swear on behalf of Apollo. Your family will be safe then." Geta began to kiss my cheeks.

"How—" Geta cut my question short with his kisses, and so I let the dark thoughts go. I knew the only way Geta could accomplish what he pledged was for Antoninus to die. I was never privy to any plot from one brother against the other, but I couldn't have stopped one if I was. I had to trust that Geta had a plan, and that he would prevail. In hindsight, I should have known better. But I was desperate to love and to be loved, and so I buried my head with my heart and wrapped Geta in my arms once more.

X.

I journeyed back to Palatine Hill feeling as if I had finally transformed from a girl into a woman. I held my hand against my belly as Cael and I jostled along the winding paths in my carpentum. I couldn't explain it, but somehow, I knew a shift had occurred. A few weeks later, I discovered that I was indeed with child. I did not know if the father was Antoninus or Geta, and at that point, it did not matter. My growing belly secured my position definitively within the imperial family.

Naturally, once Father heard about my condition, he could not resist capitalizing on the situation. "We shall commission a series of coins to commemorate the occasion!" he boasted to Severus during a raucous Saturnalia banquet. "Augustus and Augusta and the child on either side!" He was preening because it had recently been arranged that Gaius would marry Aurelia, the only daughter of ex-consul Lucius Aurelius Gallus. With his own dynasty in the making, Father felt more self-assured than ever.

"Dearest, we should not anger the gods. Let us wait until the child is born and healthy." Mother, always the reasonable one, placed a mollifying hand on father's knee. "Let us make sure Plautilla survives the birth."

I smiled at her, but inside I felt trepidation. I was not looking forward to the birth. "I shall make an additional offering to Vesta," I volunteered, "to ensure a healthy heir to the empire."

Antoninus was pleased with the situation, but my condition allowed him to give up the pretense of enjoying my company in his bed. Our coupling was no longer a requirement of our marriage; his duty was done. I knew he occasionally took his pleasures elsewhere, but I no longer cared. Geta also reverted to being cool and distant. There were too many prying eyes in the palace for us to be alone together. Often, when I pulled my palla tightly around my shoulders under the chilly marble pillars, I longed for the touch of warm orange blossom scented air on my skin, and his sweet kisses. I wondered if he felt the same, but he had retreated from me.

Winter had come, and with it the rain. I felt as if Cael and I were slowly going mad together. I wandered the labyrinthine halls of the palace, my gait growing more unsteady as the child slowly grew in my belly. Cael fluttered above the maze of hallways connecting the dwellings, his dark wings casting shadows along the brightly painted ceilings. I made daily offerings to Vesta, as promised, asking for a son to continue the Severan dynasty. I became preoccupied with health and would call for doctors and midwives to come to the palace for advice. I arranged for a room to be prepared for the birth, even though it was months away. Mother had kept her birthing chair, and I ordered to have it brought to the palace. I left nothing to chance.

If my place among the family had been secured that winter, the rift between Antoninus and Geta only grew. They quarreled incessantly at meals and refused to spend time with each other unless directly commanded by Julia. They both became more overt in their efforts to curry political favor:

Antoninus had strong support in the military, and Geta was favored in the Senate. While both claimed they did this to shore up support for Severus, everyone knew better. Geta and Antoninus each commanded their own personal Praetorian units, which added to the hostility. I tried my best to avoid them both during this time. Each time I looked at one of them, I remembered coupling with the other.

On the kalends of March, we celebrated the Festival of Matronalia. The imperial family, along with Mother, Father, and Gaius, accompanied me to the Temple of Juno to pray for her to bless me with an easy childbirth. As was the custom, I dressed simply in a tunic and wore my hair unbound as I made an offering of fragrant flowers to the goddess. Even Antoninus made an offering of gold to wish me good health. Later, we watched the Vestal Virgins rekindle the sacred fire of Vesta into a great blaze. I had to take a step back from the heat, lifting my hair to cool the sweat from the nape of my neck. As I did so, I caught Geta looking at me, his eyes brimming with desire. I glanced quickly at Antoninus, but he was staring at one of the Virgins. I let my hair down once again and closed my eyes, praying that no one had marked the look on Geta's face.

After the rains ended, spring finally crept over the hills into the city, and the chariot races began anew in the Circus Maximus. Both brothers became obsessed with beating the other. If Antoninus' favored team won, Geta would see to it that his team would claim victory the next week, whatever the cost. When that no longer sufficed, they began to drive the chariots themselves. During this period, I was forced to spend endless hours in the heat watching, trying not to gag at the unrelenting stench of horses. One particularly horrible day, Antoninus' chariot overturned at the far end of the track, pinning him underneath. I held my breath as he was dragged from the wreckage, my fingers gripping the edge of the balcony. Luckily, he was alive, but his leg was badly injured. After that, both brothers were forbidden from racing, though the damage had been done. Antoninus' leg would heal, but his anger at Geta had hardened into irreversible hatred. When I visited with him to administer tonics or play my lyre, he spoke bitterly of how he would punish Geta, and anyone who threatened him.

One day, as I was trying to help him feel more comfortable, he muttered something about enemies in the Senate. I kept my face placid though my heart lurched. "Surely, you must have allies in the Senate who would inform you of any danger? Father—"

"Do not speak to me of your father again, Plautilla," Antoninus grunted between clenched teeth. "You do not know his mind as well as you think you do. He plots against our family."

I put down the cup of tonic I had been holding. "Husband, our family is his family. Why would he plot against the father of his own grandchild?"

Antoninus shook his head. "Again, you do not understand his mind, Plautilla. Do not question me on this."

"But—"

"Do not!" Antoninus' shout brought the guard who was stationed at the door farther into the room. "Go now. I no longer am in need of your company." Antoninus dismissed me with his hand, his face a mask of pain. I realized then that he would not accept anything from me, whether comfort, solace, or truth. Silently, I nodded and left the chamber. For a moment, I even considered seeking out Geta for any news, but I knew it was the worst thing I could do. I did not want to trouble Mother, and Father would never reveal his mind to me. Suddenly, I thought of Gaius. He had come of age and was soon to marry. Perhaps he had some insight into Father's situation.

I invited Gaius to dine with me at the palace, on the pretense of having him visit with Antoninus. I knew Antoninus would never take an audience with him, so our conversation could be private. As expected, Antoninus claimed to be too ill for company, and so Gaius and I were left to ourselves. After we dined on simple bread and fruit in my chamber, I led Gaius on a walk through the lower gardens, far from prying eyes and ears.

It was a fine summer day, and Cael perched on my shoulder as I tucked my arm into Gaius' for support. Soon I would be too far along to walk on the stairs in the outer gardens of the palace—something I was dreading, for it was only here that I truly felt at peace. Cael fluttered off toward the hillside and landed on the grass, his beak poking into the dirt.

"Will he ever take a mate?" asked Gaius. Cael lifted his head and cocked it to the side, as if he understood the question.

"He is mated to me," I jested. "The bird cares for me like no other."

"More than Augustus?" Gaius asked. I sighed. Though he towered over me, my brother was still so innocent.

"Of course, I meant that Cael would not accept anyone but me." I teased, though in my heart, I felt the familiar pang of loneliness. I had been so long since that tender night with Geta, it was almost as if it had never happened. We walked in silence for a while longer. "How do you find Aurelia?" I asked.

"Pretty and agreeable," answered Gaius matter-of-factly. "A

good match. Father and Mother are pleased."

"Of course Father is pleased, Lucius Aurelius Gallus is another powerful ally to add to his growing stable," I responded. "We all know what motivates Father."

"He has good reason, Plautilla," said Gaius. The hair on the back of my arms stood on end. Gaius did know something.

I put my other hand on my belly and looked down at it to hide the emotions crossing my face. "What do you mean?" I asked.

Gaius sighed, and I suddenly felt like the younger sibling. "Father has earned much wealth from his relationship with the emperor. He courts allies because without them, he would be a target."

"So it is to protect himself and our family?" I asked.

"Of course. What else would it be?" Gaius laughed, sounding like Father. "You have spent too long in the palace listening to idle gossip, Plautilla. Father only gathers allies to protect our family's fortunes and for the good of Rome."

"Gossip is not idle, it is currency, Gaius," I chastised him. "You would do well to heed it, for what is whispered is often true, if the imperial family believes it." I stopped walking and faced him, hoping he would understand.

Gaius shook his head. "The emperor is Father's staunchest ally. He would not have half of his political power if Emperor Severus did not give his blessing."

"I am not only speaking of the emperor, Gaius. Severus does not control everything on Palatine Hill. Father would be wise to remember that."

Gaius was silent then, and his brow furrowed the way it always did when he was lost in thought. I hoped it meant he would share my concerns with Father. Just then, Cael fluttered to the wall next to us, holding a shiny object in his beak. I called him and he flew to my hand, dropping a ring covered with dirt into my palm.

"Perhaps he is your mate after all, Plautilla," quipped Gaius, and we both laughed.

* * *

The last month of my pregnancy was the hardest. The heat returned to Rome with a vengeance, and the imperial family decamped to another villa in Campania near the coast. I, however, was deemed too far along to travel safely and so was left at the palace. In truth, I had no desire to go. While the city heat was unrelenting, I was glad to be free of them. I arranged for Mother to stay with me while we secured the midwives, for I was getting close to the birth. I walked the halls of the palace barefoot, my back aching while my swollen feet were soothed upon the tiles. I avoided the gardens, mostly to avoid the heat, but I was also afraid to see an auspice. I continued making offerings to Vesta at the palace lararium, but I did not travel to any temples in my condition. In the evenings, I submerged my feet in the impluvium pool in the grand atrium. On the night of the Volturnalia festival, when we celebrated *Volturnis*, the god of the river Tiber, even the servants joined in. It was one of the most festive nights of the summer and we laughed and splashed our feet as we drank. Even Mother participated.

My labor began shortly thereafter and lasted for nearly two days. Mother kept trying to make me rest, but I continued to walk in circles around the palace; it was the only way to bear the unrelenting pain in my back. Eventually, I couldn't stand up any longer and was led to the birthing chair. Surrounded by the midwife, attendants, and Mother, I strained for hours, exhausted. Finally, in the middle of the second night, I gave birth to a daughter. She was still as a statue, blue and cold, the cord wrapped tightly around her neck. Her coloring was dark like Antoninus, but her face resembled Geta's. I held her until sunrise, when Mother gently took her from my arms and gave her to the doctors. I was too tired to cry or protest. Her name died on my lips, and I never repeated it to anyone, not even Cael. I took to my bed and did not rise for days.

Word was sent to Campania, but none came back in return. I knew Mother was surprised, but I wasn't. I lay in a trance, neither asleep nor awake, barely eating or drinking. During this time, Cael stayed perched by my side. If anyone attempted to rouse me, he pecked at them until they retreated.

After a week of this, Mother entered my chamber briskly, her lips pursed into a thin line. "Plautilla, this has gone on long enough. You must make an offering to Vesta. I beg you, rise and ask her to bless you with a healthy child. You cannot wait any longer."

I was so horrified by this thought that I began to laugh hysterically. Cael fluttered his wings above me. I must have looked like a madwoman to Mother. How had she ever birthed this monster, with her tangled hair and filthy, bloodstained tunic, and tear tracks on her face. Mother, who was always properly adorned, never a hair out of place. For some reason, this thought only made me laugh more, until I was weeping so hard I thought I would never stop.

"Go," I croaked, dismissing her with my hand. "Go, Mother. I need to be alone."

"Plautilla, the last thing you need—"

"Leave me!" I commanded, summoning every vestige of Augusta I had left. "Please. I promise I will do as you ask, but Father needs you more than I do now." Mother stiffened at my words, but I held out my hand to her and she took it, squeezing my fingers. Then she was gone.

That night, I rose from my bed and walked through the palace in the dark. It was as if I was a ghost of myself as I passed through the silent halls. Eventually, I reached the perimeter gardens, dimly visible under the new moon. Cael flew above me, a silent sentinel. None of the slaves or the guards followed us, for I suspected they understood my grief more than they let on.

I stood on the veranda facing the city, in the spot where Geta and I had seen the flock of birds gyrating together. The night was unusually warm. No breeze wafted up from the Tiber in the darkness. Cael perched on my shoulder as I waited silently for the auspice I knew was to come.

There was no telltale rushing of feathers or slight breeze. It was utterly silent before it appeared. Out of the black, an enormous owl swooped overhead. The creature landed on the eave of the roof above and looked down upon me with glowing red eyes. For a long time, neither of us moved. I knew this bird was considered the evilest auspice of all, yet it held a terrible beauty that entranced me. Suddenly I spoke. "You do not frighten me, for you have done your worst," I declared. "Go now, back to the darkness, and trouble us no more." The owl turned its head to the side and then swiveled again to face us in an unnerving manner. I felt Cael's talons dig into my shoulder. The little bird flapped his wings and squawked, but I shushed him.

The owl contemplated me. I pointed to the north. "Go," I

commanded. "Go, or I will visit you, and take what is precious to you for my own."

I knew I wasn't making any sense, but I didn't care. The owl continued to stare at me, a silent challenge in its eyes, as if to say, *you are still just a silly girl.*

"Cael," I whispered, "fetch me a stone."

Cael shot into the dark. The owl blinked and swiveled its head, following Cael with its eyes. I screamed and it turned back toward me. Trembling, I held out my hand as Cael landed and dropped an object into my palm. It was a black rock, shiny and with sharp corners. I threw it as hard as I could, screaming curses. The owl launched skyward before the object reached it, beating its enormous wings into the dark. Then it was gone.

Guards rushed onto the veranda, swords drawn. "Augusta, are you all right?" asked one.

My heart was beating wildly, my hands clenched into fists. But I was standing. *I am not finished yet*, I thought.

Turning, I gestured to my bloody clothes. "Wake my slaves. I need to bathe."

XI.

The imperial family returned on the first cloudy day of Septem. Once again, I greeted my returning husband atop the marble steps of the palace. This time, there was no acknowledgment. Antoninus marched past me as if I were a mere servant, followed by his retinue of personal Praetorians. My breath caught in my throat as Julia and Severus did the same. Only Geta nodded his head slightly in greeting. His eyes lingered sadly over my face before turning away.

I learned later that Emperor Severus' brother, Publius Septimius Geta (and Geta's namesake), had died during their sojourn. The emperor had traveled to visit him on Creta shortly beforehand. We were now entering an official mourning period for nine days, where we would honor Septimius Geta's memory. Professional mourners soon arrived to loudly wail and lament his passing. There was a grand funeral procession through the streets, even though Septimius Geta's body was not present. I attended these rites, as was my duty, but I was angry that there were no equal rituals for my lost child. As was custom, the death of a newborn did not merit a funeral, but my heart screamed otherwise.

To make matters worse, Father had commissioned a series of *denari* coins that featured Antoninus on one side, and my visage alongside a child on the other. A few additional coins also featured Severus on one side and Father on the other—and these had been discovered on Creta while Severus was there. Apparently the denari had been distributed far and wide throughout the provinces, celebrating a birth that had never come to be. Once again, Father's ambition had stained not only his reputation but mine, and this insult was added to the long litany of grievances Antoninus held against him.

The evening meal held the first night we were all together again was tense. During our strained small talk, there was no mention of the birth. Finally, as the slaves cleared away my uneaten plate of food, I cleared my throat. Four pairs of eyes, so similar and yet so different, stared at me as I tried to smile.

"I am glad you have returned, husband," I began haltingly, "for it has been…it has been a difficult season. I have missed you." I paused, waiting for the polite reply that did not come.

"I trust you have fully recovered?" Julia asked pointedly.

"Yes, Domina, I have recovered," I whispered. "We will try again."

Antoninus did not look at me as he poured himself another draught of wine. "You must make better offerings. Perhaps some coins could be collected on behalf of your Father and brought to the Temple of Vesta."

Julia snickered at this. Severus' face remained stern. Geta intently studied his rings with apparent fascination. I wanted to murder all of them with my bare hands, but I took a deep breath and continued. "Father meant no harm; he was only excited about the possibility of becoming a grandparent." My words sounded hollow to my own ears. We all knew that Father was excited to link himself to the imperial family by blood, even Severus. "But I will take Augustus' advice and redouble my efforts, so that we may be successful."

Julia gazed at me shrewdly over her cup of wine. "We shall see," she said.

I did not expect Antoninus to send for me later that evening, but when he did not, it stung all the same. The heat had returned, and I tossed in my bed, wondering if my husband would ever lie with me again. If I could not bear an heir, where would I go? Would I return to Father's house and live out the rest of my days as a spinster? Would I be allowed to remarry? Would Father scorn me for thwarting his ambitious plans?

The intrusive thoughts would not let me rest, so once again I freed Cael from his cage and tiptoed out of my chamber to walk in the palace. There were more slaves and guards present this time, but they took no notice of us. I retraced my steps down to the outer gardens, seeking solace. Cael remained perched on my shoulder until we reached the night air, when he launched himself into the dark and flew in loopy circles ahead. "Are you showing off?" I asked, but I followed him down the steps toward the schola. The moon was full, and the ivy that grew along its walls looked luminescent in the pale light. It was dark inside, and I saw nothing when I peeked through the window. I was nearly past it when I heard someone softly call my name.

Retracing my steps, I entered the darkened building and paused in the doorway. As my eyes adjusted to the dim light, I saw the outline of Geta sitting in the shadows. I walked over and quietly sat down on the floor next to him. Cael perched in the window, his feathers outlined in silvery moonlight.

"I come here sometimes when I want to think," Geta said softly.

"Do you ever think about that day?" I asked. I didn't need

to ask if he knew which day I meant.

"Always," he answered, and took my hand. I curled into his shoulder and inhaled the smell of him: wine and musk, yet sharp and clean. Geta reached up and stroked my hair.

"I'm sorry," he whispered. "I'm so sorry, Plautilla."

I began to cry quietly, and he held me until my tears subsided. Slowly, I sat up and wiped my cheeks. "I should get back," I murmured. Geta nodded, but he did not rise as I stood and straightened out my stola.

"Was it mine?" he suddenly asked, and I felt a fresh stab of anguish.

"I don't know," I said in a small voice. "Perhaps if she had lived, I would have known."

"Perhaps," he said. "I wish I had been here." The bitterness in his voice cut through me.

"I wish that too," I murmured.

Geta stood then and took my hand. "I will be next time, I swear it," he said, pulling me closer. "I swear upon Jupiter, Plautilla. I will not betray you." I hugged him fiercely, but I didn't believe him. I saw no way out of the gilded prison that trapped both of us. Cael croaked softly and I knew it was a warning. I leaned forward and kissed Geta gently, then turned toward the door to head back.

* * *

Gaius' wedding was bittersweet. Even obscured by her flammeum, we could see Aurelia's face beaming with excitement. There was no hesitation in her part about marrying Gaius. And why not? My brother was a good match. He was strong, handsome, and connected to the imperial family by marriage.

124

What girl wouldn't want to join with him? But I sensed that it was more than duty with Gaius and Aurelia. The way he held her hand tenderly during the banquet, and how he ensured that she was comfortable at every moment, made me wistful. I saw what I had been missing from my own unhappy marriage. I was glad for my brother, but his happiness only added to my sorrow. At least Mother seemed truly pleased with the union; and of course, Father was at his boastful best. Only I felt isolated from the festivities.

It was a measure of Father's political power that the emperor and empress, along with members of the Senate, attended the betrothal of his son to an ex-consul's daughter. It was more surprising to me that Antoninus also joined us on this night. Geta did not, and I tried not to wonder what he was doing as Antoninus and I wandered throughout the atrium of the enormous villa. Perhaps it was due to my melancholy, but it seemed to me as if Father had grown even more arrogant since I had last seen him. The wedding was being celebrated in a villa that had been recently confiscated from one of Father's political enemies. Father had granted the estate to Lucius Aurelius Gallus as a wedding gift for Aurelia. I tried not to think of the family that had occupied the home merely weeks before, leaving traces of their lives for us to gawk at during our celebrations.

"How swiftly the fortunes of the favored fall," I murmured, as we encountered a marble statue of what I presumed to be the villa's previous owner.

Antoninus smiled wryly at my comment. "Your words ring truer than you know, Plautilla," he said cryptically. But he did not elaborate further.

During the banquet, I noticed that the imperial family

seemed colder toward Father. I knew Julia had always disliked him, and the feeling was mutual. They simply both loved power too much and loathed the thought of the other having influence over Severus and the empire. But tonight, as I observed her scrutinizing him, I felt a difference in her manner, almost as if he were beneath her instead of an adversary. Antoninus, too, seemed to be unnaturally focused on Father. Oddly, even Severus did not laugh or drink with him as he often had in the past. I began to feel a sense of unease as the night wore on and the wine flowed. Father tended to partake too much in general, but tonight I feared he was well on his way to being foolishly drunk. I glanced at Mother, but she was sitting next to Gaius and Aurelia, deep in conversation with them both.

Father was boasting of the expanding ranks of Praetorians that now served as Severus' private army within the city. "Never has such power been accumulated," he proclaimed. "And they are only loyal to you and I, Severus, you and I. What adventures we shall have." Father raised his glass and tipped his head back, swallowing the wine with a loud gulp.

"Loyal to both of us?" asked Severus softly. "Both, Plautianus?"

"But of course!" Father exclaimed, unsteady. "I must ensure the loyalty to my command of any officer that swears an oath to serve. We shall never need to fear the machinations of any officer in my guard. They know who ensures they receive payment." Father stuffed an olive into his mouth. "He who controls the purse controls Rome, Severus. I have always said it was so."

"Your attention to administrative matters is quite impressive, Plautianus. I have always wondered how you have managed to keep track of so many expenses and ensure all runs smoothly," said Julia. "Perhaps one day you can share more about these efforts, for they quite interest me." The empress' words were flattering, but I sensed the veiled threat underneath. *Careful, Father,* I thought.

Unfortunately, Father was too far gone to sense the danger. "The administrative needs of the empire are of no interest to a woman, not even one as inquisitive as yourself, Augusta. Stick to what you know best."

"And what is that?" Antoninus asked suddenly.

Father shrugged his shoulders dismissively. "Gossip," he said. I knew then that Gaius had indeed shared my concerns with Father, and that those concerns had not been taken seriously. To speak so ill of the empress in front of Severus indicated that Father held little fear of retribution from the emperor. I could only hope he was not mistaken.

Antoninus' mouth curled into a sneer as his hands balled into fists. "You're drunk, old man." Desperate to calm the situation, I placed my hand on Antoninus' knee.

"Husband," I said quietly, "Do not let Father's words upset you. Indeed, he is too full of drink, yet for good reason, as this is a happy occasion. I apologize for any unsavory behavior on his behalf and will ensure it does not continue." Father looked at me in amazement, and for a moment, I felt a flash of satisfaction. I was no longer the flighty girl who relied on him to navigate imperial protocol, but rather the one who now used her position to advocate on his behalf.

Antoninus continued to glare at Father, ignoring my entreaty. "You walk on a knife's edge, Plautianus," he growled. "And remember, your daughter's fate is bound up in your own."

The hair rose on the back of neck as Father rose to stand,

towering over Antoninus. "What do you mean?" he said. The anger in his tone drew the attention of several senators gathered nearby. Even drunk, he was an imposing figure in his armor, and his hand flew to the knife at his belt. At this, the entire crowd quickly quieted, and the musicians stopped playing. All eyes were on Father and Antoninus, who remained reclined on his couch but was smiling a savage smile.

"Just remember where the power in Rome truly lies," Antoninus said. "There is only one heir to Augustus here tonight."

"Indeed, I thought there were two," Father countered. "Yet he has not joined the festivities. Pity."

Antoninus' smile vanished, and I tensed, for it seemed as if he was about to strike Father. After a long moment, Severus placed his cup down on the table. "Enough," was all he said. The musicians took up the tune again, and the guests all turned away back to their conversations, though I saw that the senators, and in particular Cassius Dio, were still watching carefully. Father and Antoninus glared at each other for a moment longer, then Father stalked off, rather unsteadily. I realized I had been holding my breath and exhaled. Suddenly, Antoninus' hand grabbed my arm and squeezed it so hard I thought it would break.

"Never interject into my business again," he said menacingly. "Or there will be consequences, Plautilla."

"Yes, husband," I gasped, tears springing into my eyes from the pain. Antoninus finally let go, and my hand flew up to my arm, where the flesh still throbbed. I glanced up, and for a moment, met Cassius Dio's eyes. Embarrassed, I quickly looked down. If any of the others around us had seen, they pretended not to notice.

* * *

The next month was dark indeed. I was once again encouraged to take my meals solely in my cubicula. The brothers vanished daily, and my slaves informed Antoninus was spending much time with his Praetorians. When I enquired where Geta was spending his hours, they did not know. I wrote to Mother and entreated her to keep an eye on Father, for I suspected that he had offended Antoninus greatly and I did not know what would happen. *Please, have Father apologize,* I wrote, though I did not know what Father should specifically apologize for.

Decembris arrived and heralded innumerable festivals, culminating in Saturnalia's three-day bacchanal. Palatine Hill was bursting with revelry that spilled from marble atriums to the streets as slaves and masters alike drank, ate, gambled, and exchanged gifts. Greenery was draped throughout homes and temples, a sign of life to ward off midwinter's chill. Slaves were waited on by their masters during various festivities, and I found it ironic that as an Augusta, I was treated with more disdain than the lowest slave at this time. Despite this, I once again demanded the finest fabrics for my stolas and bedecked myself in elaborate jewels. On the final night of the festival, I wore a simple mask over my finery. Satisfied that my identity was concealed, I released my slaves and told them the evening was theirs before heading to the culminating feast. The plebians and soldiers I encountered hopefully assumed I was merely a cosmetae slave dressed as her mistress as I passed by.

When I arrived at the grand atrium, it was difficult to determine who was who. Many other guests were also masked. I saw Geta in the corner of the room, surrounded by several women vying for his attention. He was dressed in a bright blue *synthesis*, a colorful short toga, and his laurels had been replaced by a *pilleus*, a cap symbolizing freedom that all the men wore on this night. Geta leaned forward and embraced one of the women while the others laughed, and I closed my eyes to blot out the sight, nearly knocking over a table of delicacies in result. Embarrassed, I ducked behind a pillar to gather myself.

Stop it, Plautilla, I thought. *It is no concern to you what Geta does on this night.* Yet my heart could not bear watching him seduce another, so I forced myself to start walking until I descended into the street. I had no idea where Antoninus was, and I didn't care. As I wove through crowds of sweaty, drunken men, I briefly thought of giving myself up to one of them in the hopes of conceiving again. Let some lowly ditch digger or shepherd plant their seed in my belly and become the true father of an heir to the imperial throne. That would be a sly Saturnalia trick indeed.

For hours, I drank and danced with strangers, seeking freedom but not truly finding it. Eventually, I returned to the palace, slipping into one of the side gates near the gardens. My feet hurt, and the night mist was starting to gather in tendrils far below near the river. As I trudged up the steps, I encountered men and women kissing, and in some cases, coupling in dark corners throughout the grounds. I thought of the schola and wondered if Geta had taken anyone there. What did it matter if he had? He was not mine. Yet I could not shake the thought of him lying with another. Boldly, I headed for his chambers instead of my own cubicula. The servants and guards were all too drunk to care, and I was still masked. My finery hid my true identity better than any tattered rag.

Geta's chamber was brightly lit with dozens of lamps illuminating him and two women laying on his bed. Various servants were also present, some drinking wine straight from the bottle. One of the women wore nothing but a green garland draped around her shoulders, and Geta was kissing her belly while the other played with the curls in his hair. As I watched from the doorway, I considered uttering a cutting remark but decided against it. The risk of being discovered was too great. As I turned to leave, I must have caught Geta's eye, for he raised his head and called out to me. "Another guest! Come, join us! Tonight, all servants are treated like royalty in my chamber." The women tittered as I turned back and stepped closer. Did Geta not recognize me, or was he playing a game?

"And what of royalty? How will they be treated?" I countered.

Geta's expression changed from lazy amusement to shock, then quickly to roguish.

"Let's find out together," he said, and leaned back, spreading his legs widely against his companions. It was a silent challenge and something inside me snapped as if I had been pulled. I stepped farther into the room. Geta never took his eyes off me as I walked toward the edge of the bed.

"Is there room for one more?"

Grudgingly, the women moved as I unfastened my stola and let it fall to the floor at my feet. I was fully naked save for the mask that hid my face and the gold on my hands, wrists, and neck. Geta's eyes traveled down my body and up to my eyes, and he held out his hand. As I crawled on top of him, I whispered, "I must stay hidden," and he nodded.

For the next hour, I watched Geta couple with the two

women next to me as I lay on the bed. Servants came and went. I never removed my mask, though it was hot against my face. The women moaned and wailed and made a show of enjoying Geta's efforts. At one point, I burst into laughter, and Geta looked at me, stricken, which caused me to laugh even harder. Finally, when both women appeared sated, Geta ordered his attendants to see them out and to leave the chamber. Once the servants departed and he ensured we were alone, he returned to the bed and stared as I slowly removed my mask. Geta then crawled forward and began to kiss my ankles, then knees, then thighs, belly, breasts, and neck. Finally, he was fully on top of me and kissed my forehead. "What inspired this boldness, Plautilla?" he whispered.

"You did," I answered, and then we were in each other's arms.

At first light, I tiptoed back to my cubicula past snoring guards and servants who had drunk themselves into a stupor. My hair ran loose down my back, and I was barefoot, dressed only in a simple shift taken from one of Geta's slaves. My steps were light, despite my tiredness. I could still smell Geta upon my fingers, and I knew his scent lingered between my breasts. I felt more content than I had in months and was already plotting how to be with him again. *For I will die without him.*

"I trust you had a good night?" Antoninus' voice echoed off the marble. I froze. Heavy footsteps approached, and my husband appeared, disheveled and wearing the remnants of a green synthesis. He was holding a bottle of wine, leaning sardonically against a pillar. "Were the festivities enjoyable?"

"They were," I said cautiously.

Antoninus lurched forward and circled around me before leaning into my face. I could smell the wine on his breath. "I am not angry you found your pleasures, Plautilla, but I trust you were discreet."

Fear snaked through me. Would he be able to determine where I had been? "I did not participate in any…activities, husband, even on this night, as we know that such wanton actions are beneath an Augusta," I said.

Antoninus contemplated me, then reached out and fingered one of the gold chains around my neck. The sensation of his thick fingers against my skin, so different from Geta's, gave me goosebumps. The silence stretched uncomfortably until he finally spoke. "You are a talented liar, Plautilla. I suspect you have inherited this skill from your father." He then marched off without another word, shattering whatever peace I had achieved.

* * *

Saturnalia was behind us, and soon it was the kalends of Ianuarius. One night, after I lay with Geta, I dreamt again of the eagle and serpent fighting above the city. This time, the snake fell onto the palace's grand atrium and slithered into the impluvium. As I was about to step naked into the pool, I shook myself awake in terror. Afterward, I lay in my bed for a long while. I wondered why the gods had decided to have this dream revisit my thoughts, and what they wanted me to dream of next. The next night, I dreamt of birds gyrating above a steep cliff. The following night, a single white albatross, gliding over ocean waves. The next morning, I made a small offering to Vesta, my first since I had lost the child. Cael fluttered off my shoulder and pecked at the lararium, as if he too were making an offering to the goddess.

The rain returned for a brief spell, followed by a few weeks that were clear and cool. I spent the better part of this time in the gardens, gazing at birds in the sky. I could not tell you if I marked auspices or not. Perhaps I could not bear the dark halls of the palace, where my husband seemed to be in a dark mood to match. I longed for Geta's embrace, but I was watched by guards and only felt Cael's light touch on my shoulder as I gazed over the rooftops of the city.

Once again, I cast off my finery for simple stolas and let my hair loose down my back. If I received disdainful glances and comments about my appearance, I no longer cared. I realized that I had only longed for finery because I thought it represented power. Now I understood that an Augusta was merely an ornament that reflected upon an Augustus. She held no power of her own. Perhaps in my own way, dressing simply was a rebellion, a plea to be seen as a person and not a figurehead. I was wearing such a garment when I unexpectedly saw Father arrive at the palace one morning, accompanied only by his personal servant. He looked pensive and did not see me until I was nearly upon him. "Father!" I ran the last few steps and threw myself into his arms.

"Plautilla, what is this? Are you ill?" Father stepped back, apprising my clothing. "What is the meaning of presenting yourself this way?"

"Prefect, we must not tarry," interrupted Father's servant. "The emperor awaits with his nummularius."

"I know the emperor awaits!" snapped Father. "But I will speak to my daughter. Tell Severus I will join them presently." He dismissed the servant with a wave of his hand. The man blanched, unwilling to be the messenger of this news, but acquiesced to Father's demand. It was a measure of Father's power that he could keep the emperor waiting without repercussion. I remembered the concerns I had shared with Gaius.

"Father, is everything all right? Why are you here? What is a nummularius?"

Father brushed off my question. "Of course everything is all right. A Nummularius is a money-changer. The emperor wishes to review a treasury matter, nothing more. Simple misunderstanding. I am more concerned that you do not wish to please your husband with your appearance, Plautilla."

I hung my head, suddenly ashamed. "I would hope that he would wish to please me." A year ago, I would have been concerned about angering Father by expressing the thought, but I was tired of not speaking my mind freely. Father sighed, but then he unexpectedly pulled me back toward him for another embrace. I closed my eyes and inhaled his familiar scent of leather and slightly bitter almond oil. For a moment, I was a child again, safe and protected from the world. Perhaps Father felt it too, for he murmured comforting words into my ear.

"I will speak to Severus about Antoninus, Plautilla. It does not go unnoticed that he treats you poorly. Bear with me for a bit longer."

"Father," I began, but I did get to finish my thought. I spied the emperor's personal guards approaching out of the corner of my eye.

Father quickly stepped back from our embrace and straight-ened his armor. He bowed his head in greeting as the guards approached. "Gaius Fulvius Plautianus. The emperor awaits."

Father gave my hand one last squeeze. "Chin up, Plautilla. We will speak again soon on this matter." And then he was gone.

* * *

Near the end of Ianuarius, the gods sent me a vivid dream of a peacock. It strutted about the halls of the palace, preening with its feathers spread wide for all to admire. As it passed by the impluvium, the snake slithered from the depths and struck the bird in the throat. I woke to the sound of shouting in the hallway, then the pounding footfalls of running guards. One of my slaves burst into my cubicula as I swung my legs onto the floor. "What is happening?" I asked. Cael was frantic, his wings beating at the bars of his cage. I quickly crossed over to release him, and he streaked past me and fluttered madly above my head before landing on my shoulder.

"Domina, come quickly," the slave entreated, and I hurriedly slipped on my shoes and followed her. Guards were rushing toward the emperor's library, swords drawn. Many were shouting, and I shrank closer to the wall as dozens pushed past us. Cael swooped ahead of me, hopping from statue to statue as we followed them. Before I could reach the entrance, two of Antoninus' personal guards exited and marched toward me, stopping on either side. "Augusta, come with us," one said. Before I realized that the soldier had commanded me instead of bowing his head, the other grabbed me roughly by the arm.

"How dare you! What is the meaning of this?" I demanded, but the guard simply dragged me toward the doorframe as if I were a child. I struggled to free myself, but the second guard held my other arm. They pulled me into the room and shoved me into the center of a circle of men. Looking around, I saw Antoninus, Severus, and several centurions. "Wha—" The word died on my lips as I spied Father's body on the marbled floor. His chest was covered in blood, and his vacant eyes were staring at the ceiling. He was dead.

I opened my mouth again to speak but no sound came out. All I could think was *Father is dead Father is dead Father is dead.* I stared at his body, willing him to rise. Finally, the enormity of what had happened sank into my bones: *Father is dead, and he cannot protect me.*

As if he could read my thoughts, Antoninus spoke. "Let all who are present mark this moment. Gaius Fulvius Plautianus was a liar and a traitor. He was plotting to overthrow the true and rightful emperor, Septimius Severus. These honest centurions uncovered his plot with this letter, which they brought to me to share with the emperor. When Plautianus was confronted with the evidence of his treason, he brandished his weapon against both the emperor and me, Rome's Augustus and heir. These brave centurions then performed their duty and killed him, striking him down in the moment of his blackest treachery."

"No," I whispered, but no one heard. Behind me, I heard a commotion, and Geta burst into the room, followed by his own guards. Antoninus crossed deliberately over to Severus as Geta stepped into the circle and stared at Father, his face unreadable. A sob escaped me at that moment, but I forced myself to be calm. Geta turned and nodded at Antoninus and Severus.

"So the rumors were true," he said. He did not look at me.

Antoninus laughed. "Always playing the part, brother. You will have to find another useful idiot to manipulate."

Geta calmly stepped closer to Antoninus and faced him squarely. "Your innate distrust of everyone and everything will be the end of you one day, *Caracalla*."

"What did you call me?" Antoninus growled, but the emperor raised his hand, silencing them both.

"I am aggrieved at the loss of my oldest friend, but his treachery was too much to bear," he said. "We have much to do, for the Praetoriate will need new prefects, ones who are utterly loyal to me. Geta, you must see to it." Antoninus opened his mouth to protest, but Severus silenced him with a look. "Antoninus, you must take up the affair with the consulate and Senate. I will have the imperial legio dispose of the body. There is also the matter of his family." At this, Severus gestured to me. Once again, my mouth opened, but seeing the looks on all their faces, I quickly shut it. "What is your course of action, Antoninus?"

All three regarded me then, and I was suddenly conscious that I was still wearing my short night tunic, and my unbraided hair still cascaded down my back. Severus bore no emotion in his expression. Geta's face was a mask of indifference, but I marked a deep furrow between his brows that indicated tension. Antoninus' stern visage suddenly broke into a tight smile. "Fulvia Plautilla, daughter of Gaius Fulvius Plautianus. We have been married for longer than a year, and you have not borne me a son. Your father's treachery runs deep, and I now disavow myself of any marriage bond. You are no longer an Augusta. Your treachery and your family's treachery will be severely punished."

Blow after blow, but I summoned my last shred of regal bearing and looked Antoninus directly in the eyes. "You speak lies," was all I said.

"You deserve to die, as does your entire family!" shouted Antoninus. He suddenly kicked Father's body and gestured to the centurions. "Throw his body in the street."

"No!" I screamed as the men stepped forward and hoisted Father as if he were a sack of cabbage. "No, please. Let us bury him, let us honor him—" My sobs returned, and I could not finish my thought. I was not afraid of dying at that moment, only of Father being disposed of like a dog. If he was not properly buried, he would be condemned to walk the streets for eternity instead of crossing over into the underworld. I took a step forward, but Antoninus swiftly unsheathed his sword and held it above his head, stopping me. His next words were aimed right at me. "I condemn this traitor to a *Damnatio Memorie*, a condemnation of memory. Let every statue and coin bearing his face be destroyed."

"No!" I screamed. Suddenly Cael descended from a light sconce. I had forgotten he was even there. He moved so quickly that he was only a dark blur as he swept into the circle and fluttered his wings in the guard's faces before circling Antoninus above his head.

"Silence!" Antoninus stepped thrashed at Cael with his sword before suddenly pointing the blade at my neck. The cold steel was sharp against my throat, and I gasped. Geta flinched, his hand reflexively reaching for the hilt of his own sword. Severus noticed this action before lifting his eyes and scrutinizing me. The air in the room was thick with tension. Cael dropped suddenly to the floor, next to the pool of blood that still marked the tile. For a few moments, the only sound was the faint scratch of Cael's talons on the floor as he paced frantically next to me.

Severus finally broke the silence. "Do not proceed, Antoninus." Antoninus was breathing heavily, his blade still pressing against my neck. The emperor reached over and forced

Antoninus to lower his arm. "This action is not befitting to an Augustus. Plautianus has betrayed us, but he served our family well." Antoninus opened his mouth to interject, but Severus gripped his forearm firmly. "The legio will bury him, and his family will not be put to death. Rather, we will exile them to Sicilia, where they shall live out their days. How they fare without the stolen riches of Plautianus is not of our concern. But I will not have their blood on mine or anyone's hands. Do you understand me, Antoninus?"

"Yes, Father," Antoninus said quietly before slowly sheathing his sword. Geta dropped his hand, flexing his fingers from tension. Cael squawked and pecked at Antoninus' feet, skittering out of the way as Antoninus attempted to kick him. Without another word, Antoninus spat on the floor and stalked away, followed by his guards. Geta remained still as a statue, staring at me, until Severus cleared his throat.

"Do not tarry, Geta," he commanded.

"Yes, Father," whispered Geta, and then he too walked out, followed by his own guards. Now it was just Cael and I with the emperor and a few members of his consul. I stretched out my fingers, and Cael flew into my hand. I stroked his soft feathers, trying to calm him but also myself.

"What happens now?" I asked timidly.

Severus did not even bother to look at me; he merely gestured to the remaining legionnaires. Two of them stepped forward to snap up my arms once again, launching Cael in the air. "Take her away, and that damn bird with her," he barked.

I never saw Septimius Severus again.

Part Three

SICILIA

XII.

We were deposited upon the rocky shore of Sicilia like unwanted cargo. The *Actuaria* did not even dock into the port; rather, the crew forced us to disembark into the shallow water, tossing our belongings after us. Gaius carried Aurelia to the shoreline, then hurried back to retrieve the few sacks we had hurriedly gathered before being forced from our homes. I held Mother's hand tightly, doing my best to guide her toward the beach. She clutched my hand, her head held high, but she did not speak.

I craned my head and squinted against the midday sun. Cael was flying above us, and he landed on a shrub nearby as we huddled on a rocky ledge. The city of Panormus was visible in the distance, perhaps an hour's walk if we were lucky. The heat radiated off the stone cliff above, and I felt the fabric of my stola sticking to my back. Despite the heat, Mother clutched her palla tightly around her shoulders. Aurelia wrung out the hem of her stola and shaded her eyes, looking toward the city in the distance. "Why didn't they dock at the harbor?" she asked. "Surely they will want to gather supplies for the journey back to Rome?"

I looked at Gaius, wondering how much he had told Aurelia about Sicilia, but he shook his head at me as a warning. "I'm sure they have other cargo to deliver before nightfall," he reassured Aurelia as soothingly as he could. "Come, let us make haste." Gaius lifted two heavy sacks over each shoulder, and we each took our own as we followed him down the slippery rock toward the path. I was exhausted, but I knew I needed to keep going, at least for Mother and Aurelia's sake. I knew Gaius was as terrified of what lay ahead as I was. But we had no choice but to press on.

As we walked, I remembered only fragments of what Father had mentioned about Sicilia. I was sure Gaius knew far more than I, but the little I did recall frightened me. Once, Sicilia had been a coveted prize, fought over by Carthage and Greece, until it eventually became a Roman province. The island was a fertile breadbasket that fed many in the empire. But it was a senatorial rather than an imperial province, hence there was no military protection for ships delivering cargo. Many patricians had built *latifundias,* or villas, on the island, but only lived there intermittently, leaving them vacant for long periods. Our fear was that the island was only a place for exiled Romans, thieves, and a few odd sects of those who did not worship the gods.

Mercifully, Severus had not prevented Lucius Aurelius Gallus from bequeathing his family's ancient latifundia for us. Of course, there would have been no Roman law to stop us from simply taking it by force. We had no idea what to expect, as the property had been abandoned for years, but it was a roof over our heads. Gallus had also pressed a few coins into Aurelia's hands as we had been loaded onto the ship. It was not much, but hopefully it would be enough to secure transportation into the countryside. As we trudged along the narrow path, I overheard Mother mumbling a prayer to

Juno in hopes of safe passage to our new home. I held myself back from a cutting remark. I was angry at the gods. They had not protected Father from Antoninus' lies. They had not protected me.

The path began to climb, and we soon fell into silence as we continued traversing the steep terrain. Despite our dire situation, I could not help but admire the landscape. Below rocky hillsides that featured various cacti and shrubs, the deep blue of the sea crashed into bleached rocks. Birds were everywhere, sailing above us on ocean breezes or diving into the waves below to catch fish. I searched again for Cael and spotted him floating on the wind above. The little bird had not left us from the moment our ship had set sail on the Tiber, keeping us company throughout the two days at sea. Even Mother had smiled when he'd hopped into my lap to peck at a few crumbs of stale bread.

My belly rumbled at the thought of bread. We had barely eaten over the past few days, only drinking sour wine and eating a few pieces of rancid meat and cheese on the ship. The bread had been deemed too hard by one of the other passengers, but Gaius had bartered for it before breaking apart with his knife. I hoped Gaius planned to use some of the coins to purchase food in Panormus, for I feared Aurelia would faint without it. Of all of us, she was taking our swift banishment the hardest. I felt for the poor girl. To be newly married and expecting a life of luxury one moment, only to be thrust into a harsh life of survival the next. She clung to Gaius, not even sleeping unless in his arms, which left the care of Mother to me.

I knew Mother was grieving Father and lamenting that he had not been given a proper funeral. We could only hope

Severus had kept his word that he would be buried. The loss of our home and all our belongings was hardest for her. I had never truly felt that Palatine Hill was my home, so the jewels I had accumulated meant little to me in the end. The bitter irony was not lost upon me. But my childhood home had been Mother's refuge. I felt rage about so many things, but the stripping of peace away from Mother angered me almost as much as the murder of Father. As we walked, I distracted myself from the ache in my feet with thoughts of killing Antoninus. I fantasized about slitting his throat while he slept, or releasing a snake into his bath, perhaps poisoning his wine. Eventually, my thoughts gave way to Geta, and my heart panged. I remembered the last night we had lain together, how his skin had shone in the dim candlelight. How my fingers had traveled along the soft lines from his collarbone to his belly, and eventually below, making him gasp.

I stumbled on a rock and nearly fell, catching myself at the last moment from tumbling down the hill. Mother shouted, and Gaius turned around quickly. His face was a mask of fear, and I felt guilty. "Sorry, I'll be more careful," I mumbled. My mind was a maelstrom of memories, but I needed to be present in my surroundings. I promised myself I would find a way to punish Antoninus if it was the last thing I ever did. But first, I needed to survive.

* * *

We entered the city at dusk. As we wandered the dusty streets, merchants were closing their stalls in the marketplace. We managed to secure a few pieces of oddly shaped fruit for two sestertii, as they would be too ripe the following morning.

The pears tasted like the sweetest nectar and quenched my thirst. I licked my fingers as Gaius asked the merchant where we could find passage into the hills. Unfortunately, we needed to wait for morning. We spent the night near the dock, curled together in an alley as Gaius kept watch. As Cael slept on my shoulder, I craned my head back and saw a few stars and eventually the new moon. *Diana, help me*, I prayed before I could stop myself. I had never prayed to Diana before, but I needed her strength. *Teach me to hunt*, I prayed. *Teach me to punish my enemies.*

The next morning, we spent our last few sestertii on bowls of what appeared to be fish stew. It was too salty, but it filled our bellies for the journey ahead. As Gaius departed to find a willing guide, we washed our feet in the sea and repacked our bundles. Finally, as the sun approached midday, Gaius returned with good news: he had found a man whose father used to work for Aurelia's family, and he would be willing to transport us in his cart to the villa.

"The family of the Aurelii still means something here," he said. "The gods are with us."

We journeyed up the hill to the stables and found the man, whose name was Cornelius. He nodded at us gruffly. "Do you have the money?" he asked. Gaius carefully handed him our last gold *aureus*. We were completely at the mercy of this stranger, who could lead us into the wilderness and slit our throats. Yet we had no choice but to trust him.

As we loaded our belongings onto Cornelius' small cart, he tethered a gray donkey to the front. Unlike the carts in Rome, this one only had two wheels and rose a bit higher off the ground. Gaius helped Aurelia and Mother into the cart before turning to me. "We will have to walk," he said. My heart sank at the thought of another day on my feet, but I smiled bravely. At least Mother could rest on the journey.

As we wheeled the cart through the city, a few stared at our party. Our stolas and Gaius' toga stood out against the simple tunics most people wore. Barefoot children were running everywhere, chasing dogs or fetching food from the markets for their mothers. Groups of men gathered in groups or hurried purposefully through the narrow streets. We saw no sign of Roman legions. It felt odd, to be without the constant presence of soldiers, but instead of creating disorder, people seemed to merely be going about their lives. Women passed by carrying baskets laden with goods, some even balanced on their heads. My mouth watered as we passed through a larger market that boasted stalls laden with fruit, meat, fish, and what looked like dried peppers. Suddenly I had a thought.

"Gaius," I whispered. "There won't be any food in the villa. We need supplies."

"I have spent our last coin, Plautilla," he said. "We'll have to hunt."

I huffed my breath out in exasperation. Of course that was Gaius' plan. As if he could bring down a boar with his ceremonial sword, after not eating properly for days and hiking for hours. I leaned over the cart and grabbed Mother's hand. "Give me your ring," I muttered urgently. Mother stared at me as if I had grown two heads. Her silver ring was one of her most prized possessions. Father had given it to her when they had become betrothed. I knew it was one of her last remaining talismans from Father, but we had to eat. "Please, Mother," I begged. Mother closed her eyes and let the ring slip from her finger into my palm. I did not want to think about how thin her fingers had become. Instead, I squeezed her hand in gratitude before hurrying up to Cornelius.

I tapped him on the shoulder and held the ring up in front of him. "My family needs to eat," I said. "Help us find provisions, and we will reward you well." I had no idea what other items I could trade, but I needed to convince him to help us now. "The gods will favor you if you do."

Cornelius laughed. "We make our own luck here. The sooner you learn that, the better." He gazed at me shrewdly but held out his hand. I dropped the ring into it, and it was tucked away in his purse before I had the chance to regret my actions. "Very well," Cornelius said. "Come now, for we must hurry." Before we passed out of the city, Cornelius secured a few sacks of flour, salt, and precious jugs of olive oil and sourdough. Best of all, we procured two freshly killed rabbits. Cornelius hung them on the rear of the cart, and we set off.

As we climbed, the paved road eventually transitioned to dirt. Despite the ache in my legs, I could not help but marvel at the countryside. Flowers bloomed all around, even sprouting from rocks. Some hillsides were entirely yellow or red with blooms. The warm breeze smelled of citrus. Olive trees were everywhere the eye could see. My heart gladdened a bit, for at least it seemed that we would be able to forage for olives, if nothing else. The trees reminded me of the garden in Campania, but the landscape was wilder. I felt an inexplicable urge to explore, forging new paths with Cael as my guide. Realizing I hadn't seen the bird in a while, I craned my neck for him but did not have to look far. Cael was following us, swooping from tree to tree as we wound through the hillsides. Eventually, Cornelius noticed as well.

"Is that a pet?" he asked.

"Yes," I replied. "I have raised him since he was a fledgling."

Cornelius grunted, and I wondered if he thought it extravagant to keep a pet in this way. On Sicilia, animals were clearly there for only two purposes: to work or be eaten. We fell into silence before entering a grove of olive trees. Gaius reached up and picked several, handing them to Mother and Aurelia as we passed underneath the silvery boughs. I lifted the hem of my stola and picked as many as I could find, spitting the seeds out as we continued to walk. Eventually, we came to a stream and halted for a bit as we drank. As I crouched to cup water between my hands, I heard an odd sound. I looked to my right and saw the donkey, slurping water just as thirstily as I. Suddenly, I could not stop laughing. Here was the exiled empress of Rome, drinking from a stream next to a donkey. Gaius too began to laugh at the sight, and I felt as if a weight had lifted from my chest. I knew then the gods were favoring us, even here.

We reached the villa in the late afternoon. It was built on the top of the hillside, presiding over a view that stretched along the northern coast of the island. The structure was large, spreading out over a sloping ridge that featured terraced levels below. Behind it grew a row of giant poplars. We passed a barn with a collapsed roof, next to what I suspected was a storehouse for grain. The front door was open, swinging in the breeze underneath a stone arch. Cornelius unloaded the cart as Gaius entered carefully, sword drawn. I followed closely behind. Together, we gazed at the large atrium, empty save for some broken pottery and cobwebs next to a pile of wood that might once have been a table. Cael suddenly swooped in and landed on the eve of a broken window. I heard footsteps behind me as Mother and Aurelia entered. The girl clapped her hand over her mouth, and Mother's shoulders sagged. Gaius looked at me, helpless. I sighed.

"Let's start a fire," I said.

With Cornelius' help, we found the kitchen. Luckily, the firepit was still usable, and Gaius set to work striking his blade against his flint stone, attempting to spark the wood. Mother and Aurelia gathered what little straw and branches there were to be found. Finally, the pile caught a spark, and Mother knelt to blow on the flames until they took. I asked (as I could no longer order) Cornelius to help Gaius carry in the broken table for firewood. Afterward, I thanked him for his service to us. "Perhaps you can return in a few days, as we will have some need of work," I suggested.

Cornelius cocked his head sideways. "How will you pay me, girl? You have just given me your last coin." I turned to Gaius to respond, but he looked stricken. His classical education had not prepared him for this. I thought of asking Mother to reason with the man but realized she would not be able to in her current state. Aurelia was too innocent to even try. It was up to me to convince this man to help us. I tried to remember how Father would persuade an adversary to take his side. Taking a deep breath, I smiled my most courteous smile—the same smile I would use to charm a particularly important guest at an imperial banquet.

"When this farm becomes fertile, someone will need to bring its bounty to market," I said sweetly. "Surely you would be willing to help us harvest these lands and partake in its riches."

Cornelius laughed then, a deep belly laugh. "You are bold, girl, I give you that," he chuckled. "Everyone on this island has a farm. It will take you years to cultivate this land. We have no need of your almonds or lemons."

My heart sank, but I pressed on. "What is valuable then?" I

asked. "What do people seek that they do not have?"

Cornelius shrugged. "I cannot speak for all, but many simply wish to live our lives in peace. Long ago, the Greeks came, then Carthage, then Rome, and there was bloodshed. War brought disease to this land. Now it has healed. Rome needs to leave us alone so we can farm and fish. Nothing more."

"Is it just war you fear?" I asked, an idea suddenly forming in my mind. My heart started beating very quickly and gooseflesh rose on my arms. "Do you not fear the gods?"

Cornelius shrugged. "The gods have little sway here."

"Do they not?" I queried, stepping even closer. I could sense I was making Cornelius uneasy, but I did not stop. I lifted my arm then, summoning Cael. The bird flew to my outstretched palm and turned his head toward Cornelius. In the darkened room, Cael's eyes were obsidian, and his feathers appeared as black as pitch. Cornelius took a small step back. I lifted my other arm and began to chant softly, my voice echoing off the ancient tile.

"The gods punish us with storms. They command the wind and the sea. They speak to all living things, encouraging them to either grow or die. I have worshiped at the altar of Faunus. I have seen the auspices. I have interpreted the gods' will. There is a value to that, old man. Ignore my gifts at your peril." At that moment, a cloud passed, and the windows went dark. I held my breath; it had to be a sign from the gods! Would Cornelius see?

Cornelius took another nervous step back. "You speak in riddles," he finally said. I smiled then, for I knew he was considering it.

"Bring me someone with a question, and the birds will answer," I ordered. "Tell all who seek knowledge that the auspices will be read. People will pay to learn their future."

Cornelius shifted his weight, but something must have convinced him. He bowed his head. "Yes, Domina," he said.

As we watched Cornelius ride the cart downhill, I knew he would return. I nodded at Gaius, who was regarding at me with an odd look on his face. I realized that I had stepped into a new role for my family: breadwinner.

* * *

It was Mother who skinned the rabbits and cut them up into pieces to lay on the fire. We pulled the charred meat out with sticks and ate it with burned fingers. Afterward, we curled up on the kitchen floor and slept next to the embers, warm and full for the first time in days.

The next morning, we woke at dawn and began the daunting task of repairing the villa so that it could be truly habitable. I sent Aurelia with Gaius to see if there was any fruit to pick, while Mother rekindled the fire with the last of the firewood. After they returned with a pitcher of olives and some almonds, Mother asked Gaius to fetch her a large flat stone. I gathered a few dead branches and managed to fashion a broom to sweep cobwebs while Mother carefully poured flour onto the stone and added the sourdough.

We decided to live primarily in the kitchen as we worked. As we slowly reclaimed the rooms, the domus came back to life. Gaius was excited to bring water back to the baths, and I was interested in cultivating the garden. Aurelia stayed close to Gaius as he wiped the walls with a damp cloth to reveal bright mosaics beneath. We were very lucky Mother maintained the fire, for if she had not, I don't believe we would have fared so well. The nights were colder than in Rome, as the fog from the sea rolled toward us at sunset, chilling the air and leaving droplets of water on the window ledges. Without any lamps, our fire was the only light at night. Gaius barricaded the windows with branches while we slept so that we did not have to fear any animals entering, though I know he was still more concerned about bandits. Yet we had seen no other people besides Cornelius.

I explored the hills with Cael and found a small mountain stream a fair distance away. Gaius and I took turns gathering water at daybreak and late afternoon, though I know he was keen to find the water source closer to the villa because he did not want to leave Aurelia for too long. Though she put on a brave face, our situation was harder on her than the rest of us. She was quiet and often wept when she spoke about missing her family and life in Rome. I tried not to feel impatient with her, but after three days, I wanted to shake her by the shoulders. That life was never coming back to us. If we wanted to survive, we needed to embrace this new one. Perhaps I was more like Father than I thought. I only wanted to move forward and claim my place in the world, stone by stone. When Aurelia started to sniffle about all she was missing, I whistled for Cael, and we escaped into the wild. To me, Sicilia felt like freedom. Though my belly was hungry and my clothes unkempt, my thoughts and wishes were my own for the first time in my life.

Ever the practical one, Mother asked Aurelia to assist with breadmaking to keep her mind occupied. The loaves we consumed gradually improved from being nearly impossible to chew to fragrant and soft. Our diet in those first days consisted of bread, olives, a few nuts, and lemons. We bathed in the stream and untangled each other's hair with Aurelia's comb, the one precious object she had carried with her from her villa. Luckily, there was enough olive oil to ensure that our skin remained clean and soft, though our hands were quickly becoming coarse from the rough work.

Of course, Mother insisted that we restore the lararium to ensure our continued survival. We prayed and made simple offerings to Vesta, thanking her for our new home. Mother would place a few embers from the fire upon the altar and pray for Father's soul to find his way to the underworld, where he could be at peace. It was only when she prayed that I saw her composure crumble and tears roll down her face. Gaius never mentioned Father in his own prayers to Apollo, but he sharpened his sword every night. I knew he too wished revenge on Antoninus. As for me, I only prayed to Diana, goddess of the hunt and wisdom. Nature was my altar, and Cael and I made offerings to her often. If we found a bird's egg on the ground, we placed it into the tree above. If we found fruit on the ground that was not edible, I split it open with a rock and arranged it for bees and animals to find. I tended to Diana's garden and prayed that she would provide me with her bounty.

On the morning our first flour sack was emptied, Cornelius returned with a woman. She was dressed in finer clothing than he was, and kept her face hidden with a colorful head covering that featured bold patterns. What little of her face revealed olive skin and eyes lined with dark kohl. As he stepped into the atrium, I observed Cornelius noticing the stacked firewood and clean floor. Gaius bowed his head in greeting, as if he were a magistrate or Senator arriving at our old domus. "Greetings, Cornelius, we are glad to see you," he said. "Can I offer you a cup of water?"

XII

Cornelius pointed to me. "We have come to see her," he said gruffly. "We seek knowledge from the gods. If she truly has the skills she spoke of, we will pay well for an answer."

I nodded. It was time to prove my worth. "This way." I led Cornelius and the woman to the rear portico facing the sea. I tried to recall the nine quadrants of the templum that Sulla had explained to me, and which ones were weak or strong. I reminded myself that the view was of the northern sky, so that any traditional interpretation of an auspice would need to be reversed. Facing north, bird movement to the right was auspicious, versus the left. If I did not sense the gods' will, I would need to fall back upon the classical interpretations of bird movement to provide an answer. I turned to the woman, who was studying me intently.

"What is your question?" I asked. Behind me, Mother, Gaius, and Aurelia had joined Cornelius. As they all stared, I felt my face flush hot. Cornelius turned and repeated my question to the woman in a language I recognized as Punic, the tongue of Leptis Magna. I had heard Father speak it to visiting cousins on occasion. I wished I had paid more attention to those conversations. Father had never taught Punic to Gaius or me, insisting we only learn Latin, as we were Romans first. Still, I recalled a few words. "Hello," I said haltingly. "Welcome." That was the extent of my knowledge, but the woman nodded her head in response. She spoke rapidly to Cornelius, and he turned back to me.

"This is Tasa. Her family has been here since the Punic wars. Like you, they have reclaimed villas that once belonged to others and worked to tame their land. Tasa asks if soldiers will return and force them to leave. There is an opportunity for her clan to return to Leptis Magna, but many want to remain here. You say you interpret the will of the gods. Should her family return, or stay?"

For a moment I almost laughed. I did not need the birds to tell me that Rome could not resist riches of any land for long. If wealth were being cultivated, increased taxes and the enforcement of legions would soon follow. But I said nothing as I stepped toward the edge of the portico and gazed at the sky. To my right lay a ridge of rocky cliffsides. To my left was a grove of trees that covered the sloping hills leading toward Panormus. In front of me was the sea, and above it, the bluest sky I had seen since arriving on Sicilia. The breeze had strengthened again, and the air smelled more strongly of salt. The trees danced in the wind as goosebumps rose on my arms. I sensed the auspice the moment before I saw it.

A gray dove took flight from one of the olive trees and headed toward the cliffs. As it swooped over the valley, a black dot on the horizon suddenly appeared and swiftly took the shape of an eagle. It was over before I even took a breath. The eagle snatched the dove and carried it to an impossible height before both birds disappeared into the clouds, one clutched in the talons of the other.

I turned to Tasa. "As long as Rome exists, there will never be peace. For it is against its nature. War will consume peace, just as the eagle consumes the dove. Return to Africa, for it is only a matter of time before the legions return."

Cornelius began to translate, but Tasa raised her hand and he stopped. She placed her hand over her heart, and I understood: she felt sorrow. After looking back at the sky, Tasa nodded at Cornelius. "What is my payment?" I asked.

Cornelius grunted. "You'll see." I followed them back through the atrium to his cart, which held a large basket in the back. Cornelius lifted it up and placed it on the ground at my feet. I knelt and lifted the lid to find four young chickens chirping at the bottom in a frenzied clump. It was the finest gift I had ever received—finer than any ornate jewelry—for it meant eggs, and eggs were life. I stood and bowed my head in gratitude.

As they drove off, Mother lifted one of the hens out of the basket. "Let's build a pen," she said, and we set to work.

Two days later, a man arrived, seeking to know when the best time would be to plant his wheat. I asked the auspices if the new moon was too soon, and flock of sparrows lifted from the hillside but then hastily retreated. I bade the man to wait until the next moon, and he thanked me and provided me with a large loaf of braided bread that smelled of rosemary. That night, we ate eggs roasted from the fire with the bread, and even Aurelia smiled. Two days after the new moon rose in the sky, heavy rains arrived. Rivulets of water streamed downhill and swept detritus down to the churning sea. As I sat listening to the raindrops pound the roof, I realized that my auspice had proved true. The man's wheat crop would have been lost had he not waited. I closed my eyes and thanked Diana for the powerful gift she had bestowed upon me.

Others soon followed. A woman who wanted to know if her child was to be a boy or a girl. The captain of a fishing boat sought the best routes for his catch. A Greek wanted to choose the direction in which to construct his domus. We received more eggs, a basket of freshly caught salted fish, and the sweetest peaches I had ever tasted. Eventually, the gifts included tools, cloth, and pottery. Mother never spoke to me about the items we received; she only nodded and incorporated them into our daily routine. Gaius had begun to hunt successfully, and our diet improved. Soon we had illumination at night with new lamps, and Gaius and Aurelia claimed the room on the far side of the atrium as their own. Mother chose to remain close to the fire and the lararium. I wondered if she felt closer to Father this way. For my part, I chose a tiny cubicula next to the kitchen, reminiscent of my room in Campania.

Occasionally at night, I overheard the sounds of Gaius coupling with Aurelia. It was only then that I allowed myself to think of Geta. I wondered where he was. I knew better than to hope that he was thinking of me. He had most likely found another woman (or women) to occupy his bed. Would he even still desire me, now that I was only a shadow of my former self with my wild ways? Or would he admire me anew? I was no longer a sad girl locked in a cage. I was free, an exile, a vessel for Diana's will with my own sacred bird by my side. Yet my body still hungered for the fire of his touch. My fingers found the sweet place between my legs as I whispered his name. *Please Diana*, I prayed. *Bring Geta to me once again.*

XIII.

Months passed, then a year. Through hard work and the favor of the gods, we survived. The villa was not fully restored, but it kept us housed and somewhat protected from weather. I cultivated a garden and added odd-shaped beans and melons to our diet. Gaius was able to hunt small game, and we foraged for abundant wild fruit and vegetables. Many times, it was Cael that helped us discover new fruits. He would flutter into the kitchen and deposit the remnants of something sweet before leading us back to the tree where he had found it. Mother and Aurelia continued to bake, though increasingly, it was Aurelia who rose and began the preparations for the day's loaves.

If the patricians who had known us in our previous life had seen us, they would hardly have recognized us. Our fine fabrics, glittering jewelry, and cosmetics were replaced by simple garb and faces that freckled in the sun. I could only imagine what my own hair looked like as I saw Aurelia's twisted haphazardly upon her head with only a twig to hold it into place. Gaius grew a beard, and his own locks had grown wild, though I was able to tame them with makeshift shears. Mother's hair had turned gray, and she often complained that her hands hurt after so much kneading. Her face had grown more careworn. She had begun to spend her days sitting by the fire or out in the garden sun, complaining of cold. I knew the gods were calling her to them, but I was not ready to lose her yet. I boiled water with lemon and nettles to help her ward off the chill. Cael often kept Mother company, hopping around the garden beds and bringing a rare smile to her face with his antics.

We heard little news of the outside world. Occasionally, Gaius accompanied Cornelius to Panormus to trade lemons or olives for fish, and he mentioned that the legions had indeed returned to the city. As exiles, we were of no interest to them. Our previous relationship with the imperial family was as distant as the misty islands far to the north of us. To these soldiers, we were part of the rogue's gallery of Sicilia: Exiles, Greeks, Carthaginians, and Judeans. All of us scratching for a living in the shadow of the empire. If the legions heard whispers of a woman augur who predicted the future, they most likely laughed it off as another superstitious tale.

One day in late Februarius, Gaius returned from the city with some real news: the imperial family had decamped to Baiae, a city on the coast, for the time being. Even though Baiae was on the other side of the *Mare Nostrum*, or northern sea, the thought of both Geta and Antoninus being somewhat closer made me restless. Antoninus could do nothing more to harm me than he already had, save killing me with a blade, but I felt a strange fear nonetheless. In my experience I knew that a sudden change of scenery was never a positive development for the imperial family. Most likely, the conflict between the brothers had become too obvious to ignore, so Julia Domna had demanded they transition to the countryside for restitution.

"Some things will never change," I commented wryly to Gaius as he draped yet another cloth around Mother's thin shoulders. "They'll tear each other apart no matter how beautiful the surroundings." We were seated by the fire after our evening meal, the flickering light illuminating our faces. Aurelia bit her lip, and I could see her brow furrow. Gaius noticed as well.

"What is it, my love?" he asked gently.

"It's just...if they are not in Rome, perhaps we could get a message to my father?" she asked timidly. "To let him know we are well? He must be very worried about us."

I felt a pang of guilt. Sometimes I forgot Aurelia still had family in Rome. Of course she must long to see them, just as I longed to see Geta. I turned toward Gaius. "Do you think it could be possible?"

Gaius sighed. "I don't know who we could trust to do it, though honestly, anyone would do. It's not breaking any laws to send a letter. We aren't petitioning for a reinstatement of our citizenship." I glanced at Mother to see if she had any counsel, but she was once again staring into the fire.

"Perhaps I could take an auspice to determine a course of action," I suggested. At this, Aurelia stiffened. She did not approve of my readings, even though the few comforts we enjoyed came from them. I had heard her mutter to both Mother and Gaius that they were sacrilegious against the gods and that I was courting their wrath. "Is there something you wish to say, Aurelia?" I asked pointedly.

Aurelia pouted. "No, Plautilla," she mumbled, and the subject was dropped. I knew Aurelia resented me for many reasons, not least of which was a belief that I was somehow responsible for Antoninus' hatred of our family. But I suspected it was also because she wanted to create her ideal home with Gaius, and a spinster sister and a mother-in-law were in her way. Perhaps she was right, but I had no time for her girlish foolishness. It was hard enough just to survive with what little we had. Just then, Cael hopped onto Mother's lap and pecked gently at her fingers, and we all laughed, breaking the tension.

The next morning, Gaius found me in the garden and knelt to help me turn over the damp earth. "I think I have found a way," he said. "I have traded often with one of the captains of a fishing vessel from Massilia. He travels to Ostia frequently from here. If we send a sealed parchment to Lucius Aurelius, it will reach him eventually."

"Can you trust him?" I asked.

"As much as anyone can be trusted," he replied. "And an Aureus wouldn't hurt." We had managed to save enough to possess two gold coins, hidden away underneath a loose stone in the kitchen. I nodded, giving my assent. Since Mother had become feebler, we had increasingly turned to each other for counsel.

"Do it, then," I said. "We'll manage without it, and some news from home may lift our spirits." *Or give us more reasons to stay hidden.* Gaius nodded and then went in search of Aurelia.

After much thought, a message was composed. Gaius spent days writing it with ink derived from crushed sumac berries onto a thin strip of animal vellum. Luckily, it did not cost us much to trade for the vellum. It was Martius before the vessel returned, and Gaius traveled with Cornelius to deliver the vellum to the ship along with payment. The captain agreed to deliver it to Ostia and ask a local slave to bring to Lucius Aurelius Gallus. We could only hope he would receive it before the end of the year.

While this was happening, Mother continued to fade in front of our eyes. I should have stayed by her side. But I could not bear it. That, in addition to the knowledge that Geta was just across the sea, caused me to increase my restless wandering. That spring, I would rise earlier than the others, bundle a bit of bread in a sack, and depart with Cael for hours. We hiked to the top of many cliffs, sharing the bread as we watched the clouds roll in over the sea. I found empty riverbeds with colorful stones, entire groves of citrus growing at an angle out of the mountainside. But I could not find peace.

After many weeks of this, I decided to cast an auspice for myself. I was facing southward toward the main part of the island, and it was an uncharacteristically cool and cloudy afternoon, threatening storms. Cael had settled on a rock close by, pecking at a shiny piece of flint with his beak. For a moment, I remembered the raven that had pecked at walnuts above me near the auguraculum. How long ago that had been. I wondered then, if I knew then what I knew now, would I still have agreed to marry Antoninus? Would Father still be alive if I hadn't? Yet a small nagging voice whispered to me: *his ambition was his downfall, Plautilla.* If I had not married Antoninus, I would never have fallen in love with Geta. But was it love, or merely infatuation? Had we only been two people trapped in a cage, seeking solace from one another because we could not escape?

These thoughts and more swirled through my head as I raised my arms and cast my auspice into the sky. I meant to ask how much time I had left with Mother. I truly did. But instead, I called out: "Will I see Geta again?"

Cael looked up and tilted his head sideways, as if to say *wrong question*. But I was lonely, in some ways as lonely as I had been in the palace. I had more to do each day, and a sense of purpose for the first time, but I still felt incomplete. I still wanted more. Was I too ambitious? Did I risk my own downfall? At that moment, I no longer cared. I only wanted the chance to see Geta once again. Closing my eyes, I tried to recall the sensation of my lips against his. My skin felt the charge in the air that comes before a storm, and the wind had completely died down. Even Cael made no sound. I opened my eyes to see only a dark blank sky. There was no sign of a bird, besides Cael, anywhere.

So that was what my auspice told me—that I could not have an answer. I didn't know whether to laugh or cry. Picking up a rock, I hurled it as hard as I could down the mountainside. I picked up another and threw it at the sky, daring the gods to strike. Cael bolted from his rock, narrowly avoiding the falling stone. I threw myself back down on the ground before dropping my head into my hands. After a few minutes, the soft flutter of wings caught my attention. Cael flew into my lap, as if my crossed legs were a nest. I petted his sleek head as he croaked softly. "I'm sorry," I told him, feeling guilty for my outburst. Cael ruffled his feathers and preened, a sign that he was content. Together, we watched the storm clouds approach.

I returned to the villa chastened and spent the rest of the evening ensuring we had enough vegetables for a stew before stoking the fire to keep Mother warm. Later, I sat by her as she slept and held her hand in the darkness.

* * *

It was the full bloom of summer when I heard the familiar sound of Cornelius' cart approaching. I was in the garden, gathering the first of what I hoped were many harvests, when I suddenly heard men's voices, one of them raised, followed by a shriek. I raced toward the front of the villa to find several Romans talking with Gaius and Cornelius. I then saw Aurelia fiercely hugging one of them and recognized Lucius Aurelius Gallus. My mouth hung open in shock. How was this possible?

A short while later, we gathered on the portico, drinking wine for the first time in many months as Lucius shared his story with us. As he spoke, I looked down at my dirty tunic and hands and felt a feeling I had not experienced in a long time—shame. But then I looked at Mother, who seemed to have remembered her patrician manners. She was sitting as straight as she could while holding her cup of wine, as if she were hosting the ex-consul in our old domus. I realized that I had nothing to be ashamed of and sat up straighter myself.

Good winds and a trustworthy slave had ensured our message had arrived by the Ides of Lunius. As soon as he had heard Aurelia was alive, he had traveled at once to see us. "It has been very hard on your mother," he said, gripping Aurelia's hand tightly. "And also for myself. When I received your message, it was as if the gods themselves had spoken to me." Aurelia burst into tears anew, and both Gaius and Lucius consoled her. I tried to temper my impatience, for I was anxious to hear news from home. Finally, Gaius spoke the question that had been on all of our minds.

"What news from Rome?" he asked. "We know nothing of the political situation since Plautianus was killed."

Lucius' mouth collapsed into a grim line. He then looked at me, and my heart sank, for I knew what he would say next.

"Antoninus has…been ruthless in his revenge," he muttered. "If not for our family's close relationship with Julia Domna's sister, I fear we too would have been a part of the purge."

"Purge?" I felt faint. I had never heard of a purge, but I knew it must be terrible.

"The execution of anyone who benefited from your father's patronage," Lucius said flatly. "Hundreds were put to death by Antoninus' legions. It was a dark time."

We fell into silence, contemplating this awful news. Finally, I asked the question that had pulled on me for months. "And now? Why have they traveled to Baiae?"

Lucius took another gulp of his wine. "I suspect to temper Antoninus' bloodlust, but also to send reinforcements to the *Legio II Augusta*. Severus has replaced many of their captains with his own, since they supported Albinus' claim to Britannia. But now that northern front has been overrun by barbarians, and the emperor may travel there to quell it himself, possibly with both Antoninus and Geta. The *Legio II Parthica* may join them."

The Legio II Parthica were an enormous force, loyal to the imperial family, that had once reported to Father. They were stationed just south of Rome. For Severus to consider sending them to Brittania, the situation must be dire indeed. My heart leapt at the thought of Antoninus facing such danger and then fell at the thought of Geta meeting it as well.

"This is shocking news," Gaius said. "Who will govern if Severus departs?"

"One of the prefects—Papinian or Laetus, unless they join the campaign," answered Lucius. "Though Julia Domna has taken over much of your father's administrative responsibilities, as well as his fortunes, which she has cleverly plied into the imperial coffers to help fund Severus' efforts. She has stationed several loyal ex-consuls in your old domus." At that, Mother let out a small sound, and we quickly changed the subject.

Shortly after, Lucius departed for Panormus, vowing to return the next morning with fresh supplies. More importantly, he planned to leave three servants with us to finish restoring the villa and harvest grapes from the northern hillsides. I knew these men would be of great help to us, but had only been sent only to support Aurelia and Gaius, not Mother or me. Aurelia would now be domina of the villa. Soon, she and Gaius would start a family, and we would be relegated to supporting their needs before our own.

Lucius' news only made me more restless. Geta would not remain in Baiae for long if plans were being made to decamp for Brittania. The brothers were too competitive, and both would need to command legions for them to have any future claim to the imperial throne. Of the two, Antoninus was further along after leading battles in Parthia and Africa. Geta would waste no opportunity to gain his own experience in hopes of also becoming an Augustus. If Antoninus were to die in battle, Geta would be the natural successor to Severus. He would need a wife, and to establish an heir of his own...

I was so lost in thought as I gathered firewood that I did not hear Gaius until he gently cleared his throat behind me. I turned swiftly and smiled, the thoughts of palace intrigue quickly receding. "Is your heart gladdened, brother?" I asked. "Surely the gods smile upon us, for our fortunes have turned for the better."

Gaius shifted his gaze out toward the hillsides, where the grape vines were illuminated in the golden light of the setting sun. "I am glad, though I know nothing about cultivating grapes. I suppose I will have to learn."

"We knew nothing about survival on our own, yet we managed," I said. "And you will have help. I trust Aurelia is pleased with the arrangement."

"She is," he said. I sensed he wanted to say more.

"Speak your mind, Gaius," I said gently.

"Why did you ask Lucius about the imperial family, Plautilla?" he asked.

My heart started to beat rapidly, and I knelt to deposit the wood I was holding.

"Only to determine whether their movements had any bearing on our safety," I said. "Antoninus is fearsome, as you well know, Gaius. I hoped to hear that his thoughts were no longer consumed with anger toward us. I am glad to hear that they most likely are not. He will be consumed with planning an invasion of Brittania, if Lucius speaks true. This is good news, surely."

Gaius sighed and knelt next to me before taking my hand in his own. He looked me straight in the eyes. "Do you still have feelings for Antoninus, Plautilla?" he asked.

I threw back my head and laughed. I laughed so hard I had to clutch my belly. Gaius chuckled as well, but I knew he was waiting for an answer. "By the gods, no," I gasped. "Unless you consider the desire to toss him off a cliff a feeling."

"And Geta?" Gaius asked softly.

"What?" I said, laughing no more. "Why would you ask that?"

"I'm not a fool, Plautilla," Gaius said. "And I have heard…of Geta's ways. It was well known on Palatine Hill that he used his considerable charms to lure a succession of women in his bed. Did he use them on you?"

I felt as if I had swallowed a stone. "Of course not," I said, perhaps too quickly. "I too am not a fool, Gaius. Geta's lewd behavior was well known at the palace. We jested about it. I was an Augusta. I would never have risked my life, or our family's position, to satisfy Geta's womanizing ways." I squeezed his hand in reassurance.

Gaius nodded, apparently satisfied. "Let's get this wood inside," he said. "Mother is waiting."

* * *

That night, I couldn't sleep. I kept ruminating about my conversation with Gaius. How long had he suspected? I wondered if his questions were really Aurelia's. Given her age, Aurelia would have been a potential match for Geta, and his behavior was indeed well known. I wondered if Aurelia knew something Gaius did not. Had someone seen us? Had Lucius found out and told Aurelia? If Antoninus knew, both Geta's and my life were in danger. I had to warn him somehow. But how?

I then thought of the vellum Gaius had used to transcribe his message. He had not used all of it, and the remnants had been rolled up and stored by the fireplace, to keep it dry. Could I get a message to Geta? Perhaps I could travel to Panormus and ask a soldier to deliver it? Perhaps I could ask one of Lucius' servants?

My nose tickled suddenly, and I sneezed, knocking sense back into my head. Of course, all of this was madness. I could never risk such a thing, especially not for Geta. Clearly, I was just another pawn in his endless game of seeking new partners for his pleasure. He had only convinced me there was more between us because he had been as desperate as I was to escape the confines of his family. I had been a dalliance, nothing more. I had meant nothing. This realization landed like a giant weight upon my chest, and I started to cry. I curled tightly into a little ball so that my sobs would not wake Mother.

Lucius returned the next day with his servants and a cart full of supplies. Over the next few days, our lives took a large step back toward the level of luxury we had enjoyed in Rome. With the servants' help, Gaius was finally able to repair the cistern next to the baths by installing new lead pipes, and at last we were able to bathe in the villa. Fresh water also filled the atrium pool, saving us hours of time, as water was now steps away instead of nearly a league. Once the furnace next to the bath had heated the water enough, I helped Mother bathe in the hot water for the first time in more than a year. Next it was my turn, before Gaius and Aurelia enjoyed the bath in private.

As the servants worked, Lucius met with Aurelia and Gaius and provided them with a few more gold coins, to ensure that we could purchase enough flour and fish not to starve. "I am amazed that you have fared so well," he said, "though Cornelius tells me that Plautilla has been taking auspices to help support you." With that, the three of them turned to face me as I swept up the ash from the fireplace. My cheeks flushed hot, and I hastily exited the kitchen to carry the ashes out to the garden.

As I scattered them into the soil, I heard steps approaching. Assuming it was one of the servants, I spoke without turning around. "You can lay your tools beyond the wall," I ordered. "Do not bring them in here, for you will muddy the tiles with them."

"Are you the witch who reads signs from the gods?" asked a harsh voice. I froze.

Gaius, Lucius, and Aurelia rapidly appeared as I rose to my feet and turned to see a *contubernium* of ten soldiers. A few of them had fanned out and stood between us and the gate, blocking the exit. The *decanus*, or leader, stepped closer to me, his hand on his sword. "Answer the question, woman."

My first thought was that Antoninus had found me. My second thought was that I was unafraid. "I am she who you seek," I said calmly. "What is your business here?"

The soldier shifted on his feet uncomfortably. "We have been sent to seek an answer from the gods," he said. The men behind him were silent. They were different than the Praetorians that had been a near constant presence on Palatine Hill. They were a bit rougher around the edges, and their uniforms were darker, distinguishing them as provincial *miles*, or foot soldiers. To a man, they were each taller than Gaius, and the one who was speaking had legs as thick as tree trunks. They could easily cut each of us to pieces within moments if they so chose.

Lucius stepped forward as if to speak but I held up my hand to stop him. "Who seeks this auspice?" I asked.

"Our *Prefectus classis*," he responded. "We have orders to transport to Tyrus. The seas are treacherous, and he seeks to know the most auspicious day to sail. He has heard of many shipwrecks from Sicilia that have killed good men." The soldier spat on the ground.

"Very well," I said. "This way."

I headed for the portico and the soldiers fell into line behind me. Behind them, Gaius, Aurelia, and Lucius cautiously followed. Today, much of the view was obscured by low clouds that were drifting in from the west.

"When do you wish to sail?" I asked the decanus.

"We are required to sail within a few days," he responded, glancing warily at the tree line, as if he expected a creature from the underworld to rise up from the fog.

"Who told you about her?" interjected Gaius, but I waved my hand impatiently.

"Not now, brother," I said. I could sense the auspice building in the cool mist. I took a few steps forward, as close to the edge of the portico as I could. I scanned the skies but could not see any birds in flight. I strained my ears but heard no calls. Behind me, the soldiers shuffled their feet impatiently. Ignoring them, I closed my eyes and fixated upon the feeling of energy along my skin. It was traveling up from my feet. Suddenly, I thought I heard a soft *cheep*. Opening my eyes, I looked down and saw a small brown bird hopping amongst the stones, scratching for food. I observed as it hopped cautiously onto a rock before hurriedly fluttering back to the safety of the bushes. I observed the bird do this three times before it vanished from view.

I had marked my first delaying bird, the bird who occupied the bottom center of the templum. This little fellow was cautioning the Centurio to wait. I turned back toward the decanus and bowed my head. "Tell your captain he must wait three days," I said. The decanus said nothing but simply pivoted and strode out to the gate, the others falling into line behind him. Soon, they broke into a rapid march. We gathered and observed them as they filed down the hill.

"I wonder if Cornelius has been speaking of you," Gaius mused.

"I would not be surprised," I said. "He receives payment as well when we have visitors."

"You need to be careful, Plautilla," Gaius chastised. "This is not a game. We do not wish to draw too much attention to ourselves, not when our fortunes have recently improved so much. Please be discreet. Perhaps…do not take an auspice for a while, while we enjoy Lucius' generosity."

I tried not to bristle at Gaius' words, for he spoke sense. Yet I felt aggrieved for some reason. Perhaps it was because I knew that if Lucius was able to provide for us, my skills would not be needed. What would become of me then?

* * *

Lucius returned to Rome the next day, claiming pressing business that required his attention. He vowed he would return before winter. "I leave you in good hands," he said to Aurelia, wiping the tears from her face. "You have my slaves, and I have ensured supplies will continue to be provided for you, my dearest daughter." Aurelia sobbed and hugged him, unwilling to let him go. I turned away, for her sorrow made me pang for Father. I was glad Mother was dozing by the fire and missing this spectacle.

After Lucius departed, life continued. The three slaves, Claudio, Felix, and Marcus, helped us finally repair the roof of the villa, ensuring no more leaks when it rained. The barn was restored and housed the chickens as well as the goat Lucius had procured for us. It fell to Marcus to milk it, and he would bring a jug of warm goatmilk into the kitchen every morning, while Felix tended the fire and Claudio gathered the eggs. Aurelia continued to bake, and I continued to clean and care for Mother. Gaius plotted out the hillsides with the slaves and turned over the earth, in anticipation of laying a winter crop. Cael acted as our sentinel, flying about the perimeter of the villa and swooping down at us from various vantage points on the roof.

During this time, I felt as if I was waiting for something, but what it was, I could not name. I watched the skies from the portico each night, as the stars marched across the sky. Were the gods watching as well?

One morning, Gaius told me what I had already suspected: Aurelia was with child. He told Mother as well, and she smiled, but my heart felt heavy. She was so frail that I worried she would not live to see it. This thought and others pushed me once again into the wild, and I set off on a long walk down the mountain. I hadn't planned on bringing Cael, but I noticed him swooping overhead shortly after I had reached the stream. He alighted on a rock and croaked at me as I dipped my feet into the cool water. "You don't have to follow me everywhere, little one," I chastised, splashing water at him gently with my fingers. Cael turned his head to the side and hopped to another stone, and I laughed.

Just then, Cael abruptly took flight, nearly grazing my head as he streaked to the edge of the tree line. "What is it?" I asked, the flesh on my arms rising into goosebumps. I stepped quickly out of the water and hurried after him. Suddenly, I heard hoofbeats. Someone was approaching on horseback. I hid behind one of the trees as I scanned to see whoever was coming. Before long, a Roman soldier appeared, his long cape draping off the side of a tawny brown horse. The man pulled the horse up short at the edge of the grove but did not dismount, and he peered into the trees as if he were searching for someone. Cael hopped onto a lower branch, and the soldier looked up, drawn by the movement. His features were rough, but his hair was neatly shorn, and his cape was a deep blue, clearly a symbol of high rank. This was no mere foot soldier. He carried himself as Father had, and his gold armor gleamed in the sun. I wondered why he was alone. Surely such someone of such rank would not travel without a guard? What was he doing here?

I stepped out from behind the tree and we scrutinized each other. The officer smiled.

"Fulvia Plautilla," he said. "I have been looking for you."

XIV.

His name was Primus Macarius Balbus, and he was a *Prefectus classis*, or commanding naval officer. He had recently been assigned to Drepanum, the large port city on the westernmost tip of Sicilia. He had served Septimius Severus during his campaigns in Africa, commanding vessels along the coast. He had drunk heavily with Antoninus many times, winning his favor, and they had enjoyed the pleasures of women in brothels dotted all along the coast of Leptis Magna. He told me all this casually as he cut up apples with his knife and stuffed the pieces into his mouth. His hair was oily, his fingernails were dirty, and the heavy rings he wore gleamed in the sun.

He told me quite matter-of-factly that I now worked for him. "I was very curious to hear tales of auspices on Sicilia. I knew your family had been banished here, but I didn't think it was you; perhaps a simple peasant spinning folk tales. I had my men seek you out, and when they marked a noble of Rome at your villa, I began to suspect the truth. I tested your auspice, by the way, and it came true. The ship that left on the first day foundered in the shallows off Messana. The ship that left on the second day remains lost at sea. And the ship that left on the third day? It arrived at Tyrus early, and my men were able to secure what they needed before our friends knew they were there. I knew then I had to find you, for what a wonderful opportunity your gift has presented."

As if to emphasize his point, he tossed an apple core casually at Cael, who pecked at it before darting quickly away. I sat under the shade of an olive tree as he prattled on, calm despite my mounting fear. I knew this man was dangerous, but whether to me alone or to all of us I was unsure. He had me trapped like a rabbit in a snare.

"What exactly do you think I will do?" I asked. Primus laughed, apple chunks still visible in the maw of his mouth. He pointed his knife at me.

"What I tell you to, girl. I want to know the opportune time to strike at every battle or set sail for any adventure. There are riches to be had in this land and many others. The element of surprise will benefit us both."

"Benefit?"

"You'll stay alive, and I'll get rich."

"Are you not rich enough, with the wages of a prefect?"

"There is never enough. Your own father knew that." His words landed like a blow, as I realized the truth of them. Father had accumulated his wealth in exactly this fashion. Despite all our patrician trappings, he had scratched his way up just as this fool was doing. I drew in my breath sharply.

"And if I refuse this demand?"

"I'll kill you," he said. "It will be like swatting a fly."

I fell silent. I knew better than to think he was bluffing. In truth, I cared little for my own fate, only that of Gaius and Aurelia. I had to protect them, so that they could protect Mother. But how? Suddenly, an idea came to me.

"It would be inconvenient, to be so far away," I suggested. "Perhaps I need to be closer to you, in order to perform auspices in a timely manner. In Rome, the auspices are taken daily, at sunrise, to ensure that the empire's business is not delayed." I waited while he digested this, along with the remnants of his apple. Finally, he nodded.

"Makes sense."

"Here are my demands," I said, and he tossed his head back and laughed.

"You get no demands, girl. You are mine to do with as I will."

"The gods favor me," I hissed. "You'll do best to remember that, or your men will suffer."

"Do they," he countered, amused. "Speak, then."

"My family will be protected," I said. "I will be allowed to see them when I wish. My Mother is frail and will not be long for this world. I will need to see her when it is time for her to cross over. Similarly, my brother's wife is with child. I will need to be there for the birth. You will provide transport for me when the time calls. In return, I will cast auspices for you daily, as you desire. I will read the signs, and I will make you rich."

He nodded, satisfied. "Very well."

"And I will be taken care of, as appropriate to my status."

Primus looked me up and down, observing my simple tunic and shawl and bare feet. "What status is that?" he asked sardonically.

"Priestess," I said. "I will be protected from men like you, or the visions will not come to me."

Primus nodded, suddenly solemn. "Understood. So we agree?"

It was a pleasant fiction, him giving me the choice, but I nodded, playing the part. I then reached out my hand and Cael flew to it. Together, we contemplated our new patron.

"We agree."

* * *

The ride back to the villa took only a few minutes. I dismounted from Primus' horse and entered the domus, looking for Mother. I encountered Gaius in the kitchen. He laughed when he saw me. "Where have you been, dinner is late—" He suddenly noticed Primus, and his smile vanished. "Who is this?" he asked, an edge to his voice. Aurelia entered the kitchen and clasped a hand over her mouth.

Primus bowed his head politely at both of them. "Primus Macarius Balbus, Prefectus Classis of the Legio III Augusta," he said briskly. "I have business with Plautilla."

"What?" Gaius said. "Is this true? Plautilla, what does he mean?"

"Let us find Mother, and I will explain," I said.

Naturally, both Gaius and Mother were distressed at my course of action (Aurelia was not but managed to hide it). I gripped both their hands, entreating them to understand. "I must serve him, so that you will not be forced to provide ruinous taxes. I have already pledged to return for the birth, and you will have enough help with Lucius' servants," I urged them. "The farther away I am, the safer you will all be from Antoninus' wrath should he decide to assassinate me." What I could not say was that I recognized Primus for what he was: an insatiable wolf who would stop at nothing to get what he wanted. I knew this because I had been married to one.

"She speaks sense, Gaius," urged Aurelia. "It is for the best." Gaius shook his head stubbornly, and Mother clutched my hand with all her remaining strength.

"It is only for a short while," I whispered. Behind us, Primus cleared his throat. A warning. Letting go of Mother, I kissed her on the forehead and nodded at Aurelia before turning to face the prefect. "I will gather my things," I said.

It did not take long to fold my few tunics into a sack, along with a small wooden carving of a bird Gaius had made for me. I accompanied Primus back to his horse, where he assisted me back into the saddle once again. I whistled for Cael and saw him perched upon the roof of the villa, waiting. Primus craned his neck to look at him as well.

"Does the bird always go with you?" he asked.

"Always," I replied.

Primus grunted, pulled on the reins, and we were off. I turned my head to look back at Gaius, Aurelia, and Mother, huddled together watching me, with the slaves behind them. I raised my arm and waved, and Gaius waved back. Then we descended farther into the valley, and they faded from view.

We rode swiftly, and the landscape passed by in a blur. Late-summer heat radiated from the cliffs in waves. I marked seabirds circling far ahead and smelled the salt in the air as we descended into a steep valley. Spread out ahead of us was the vista of the western sea, with the port of Drepanum located to the northwest, below the setting sun.

"Not much longer now," said Primus, and we traversed down the winding path into the city. As we rode through the cobbled streets, I saw townspeople going about their business as they had in Panormus, but oddly, none of them paid us much attention. A few times, I caught the eye of a young child before their parents quickly drew them away. It seemed that the people here were afraid of the army. After finally reaching the shoreline, Primus slowed the horse to a trot as we approached the archway leading to the harbor.

"The barracks are along here." Primus pointed to them, as if I were an official guest. "We have several dozen ships in states of repair in the harbor. Most of the other visiting legions are housed at the top of the valley." He indicated the direction from which we had ridden with his head.

"Where am I to stay?" I asked.

"With me, for the time being. Fear not, girl. Your honor is safe with me. Marcus Aurelius Antoninus may have exiled you, but I know better than to meddle in any Augustus' business. You'll remain intact." Though his words were crass, I closed my eyes and offered up a silent prayer in thanks to Diana for protecting me. Opening my eyes, I searched for Cael, but it had grown harder to see him once the sun had set. Yet I knew he was there. The horse slowed, and we pulled up to a large structure located just off the water. Primus whistled, and two guards hurried forward to greet him. He turned back toward me, and I smelled his rank breath. "Welcome to your new home," he said.

After dismounting, Primus strode into the building without looking back. I quickly observed the surroundings before dismounting the horse. Behind us was the dock, where several ships were tethered in a row, bobbing up and down in the evening breeze. Above us sloped the city, and at the very top of the mountain ridge, I saw lights. This was where I presumed the rest of the legions were stationed. No wonder the citizens of Drepanum were wary. They were hemmed in by garrisons of soldiers on both sides.

I scanned the night sky for a sign of Cael but found none. Reluctantly, I followed the guards inside and was led down a narrow, dimly lit passage. We passed by what I took to be the kitchens and entered Primus' chambers in the rear of the building. It was a large room with a table at the center that held various maps and models of ships. Along the wall were several chairs and a desk. A rear door led to a sleeping quarter. Primus pointed toward another door that was closer to the hall, and the guard opened it to reveal a tiny room with a small cot and table. This was a servant's berth, conveniently placed to be at their master's beck and call. I placed my bundle upon the cot and leaned against the doorframe, suddenly feeling exhausted. I had no idea where Cael was, I hadn't eaten in hours, and I was now in the lair of a wolf. It was all too much.

"Drink?" Primus asked casually, pouring a cup of wine. Despite everything, I nodded before accepting the cup. Raising his glass, he made a toast. "To auspices."

"To the gods," I countered, and we both drank.

"Right," he said, all business. "Food and rest. Tomorrow, I will show you where you will cast your omens." I nodded again, too tired to argue, even though I knew the auspices needed a clear view of the sky in all directions—something I wasn't sure would be available here at the docks. Primus glanced at me again and pointed to one of the chairs. "Sit," he commanded, and I did. Shortly thereafter, a guard brought me a bowl of fish stew with a crust of coarse bread. I devoured both before crawling onto the cot and falling into a dreamless sleep.

* * *

I woke to the sound of men shouting. For a few moments, I thought I was back on Palatine Hill. Disoriented, I rubbed my eyes and sat up, nearly hitting my head on the low ceiling above the cot. Shadows were flickering over the crack of light underneath the small door, and I realized that servants were moving about Primus' chambers. I slowly rose and opened the door only to find three men chasing Cael with sticks. The little bird was fluttering wildly from one side of the chamber to the other. One of the men shouted as his stick nearly grazed Cael's tailfeathers as he swooped overhead.

"That is enough!" I yelled, and all three turned toward me in astonishment. For a moment, I was an Augusta once again. "You!" I pointed to the nearest slave. "Fetch me a pitcher of fresh water and a cloth. And you!" I pointed to the next. "Fetch my breakfast. I will catch the bird. Now leave this chamber at once." I glared at all three of them, as they looked at each other before bowing their heads in submission. Mercifully, they departed, leaving the chamber to Cael and myself. I whistled softly and he flew to my shoulder, squawking softly into my ear. "Were you looking for me, little one?" I whispered. "Stay close."

The first slave quickly returned with the pitcher and cloth, followed by the second holding a bowl of *puls*. My mouth watered at the smell of it, and I snatched the bowl from the slave's hands and began to quickly spoon the savory porridge into my mouth, scalding my tongue with the hot gruel. "Thank you," I said gruffly, and the man nodded, glancing warily at Cael, who had landed on the table. I held my spoon out to Cael, and he dipped his beak at it, taking a small portion of the porridge for himself.

"I can see that you are having a good morning!" Primus entered the chamber, already dressed in full armor. He brushed Cael aside from the table and spread out a new map upon it. "We shall depart soon, for there is much business to contend with today."

"I will need to wash first," I said haughtily, though I continued to stuff porridge into my mouth as if I were a street urchin.

"Do not tarry," Primus admonished lightly, though I sensed the impatience underneath. I nodded and quickly finished the bowl before taking the pitcher and cloth back into my small room. After washing and changing into a new stola, I gathered my hair into a loose braid and put on my sandals. Finally, I placed the bird carving into a small pouch and placed it around my neck, for luck. Once I was finished, I whistled softly for Cael, and we set off.

A short while later, we were once again on horseback, heading for the barracks that overlooked the city. It seemed that Primus knew enough to provide me with a proper location to see the entire sky. As we slowly climbed, the air grew cooler, and I wished that I had brought my shawl. This time, we were accompanied by two additional centurions, who rode in front of us. Once again, Cael flew above. I kept squinting up to find him, comforted each time I saw his dark shape outlined against the light of the sun.

At the crest of the mountain, the stone walls of the outpost slowly came into view. It was massive, running along the entire mountaintop, and there were three roads that seemed to wind their way toward the summit from the north, south, and west. As the centurions approached the gate, Primus saluted the lookouts above, and they signaled to open the heavy doors to let us through.

Once inside, we passed several large buildings before turning a corner, revealing an enormous temple looming over the center of the fortress. It was as grand as the ones in Rome, though it was far older, with some of its columns beginning to crack underneath the edge of the roof. "By the gods," I uttered in surprise. "What temple is this?"

"It was dedicated to Venus. It was here for hundreds of years before we even arrived," answered Primus. "But now it will finally have a purpose that suits us." We halted as I stared at the graceful columns that rose imposingly overhead. I shuddered, once again feeling the cold against my shoulders. This was a sacred place, and one that did not welcome us. Slowly, I took Primus' hand as he helped me to dismount, and we walked purposefully up the stairs onto the vast portico. I turned to face the landscape and caught my breath as the entire western vista of Sicilia spread out below. In the distance, I could mark three islands to the north.

"What islands are those?" I asked, pointing to the most distant one.

Primus shielded his eyes from the sun. "Ah. Cala Rossa, the Red Cove. A great naval battle was fought there. Ten thousand bodies washed ashore. It was the victory that finally defeated Carthage. You have good eyes, Plautilla."

"Thank you," I said, for I could not think of anything else to say. The thought of 10,000 men dying was clearly not upsetting to Primus, but it filled me with sorrow. So much bloodshed. And for what? Another league of rocky land. Another island to add to Rome's empire. I was so tired of bearing the crushing weight of men's ambition, and I mourned the countless lives that were lost in the name of glory. No wonder the goddess of love and beauty was displeased.

Primus leaned toward me. "Is it not satisfactory for your needs?"

"It's perfect," I replied. I knew the power of Venus would

allow for strong auspices to be cast. I doubted, however, that Primus would readily accept the truth of them.

"Good," he said. "Then let us begin." He took a step back expectantly.

Slowly, I turned again in a circle, observing the faint mosaic on the ceiling of the portico above that illustrated a sky and clouds. As I glanced back toward the entrance of the temple, I saw candles lit below a statue of the goddess. "One moment," I said, and walked quickly into the main chamber. I needed a moment to gather my thoughts away from Primus, and I needed to show respect to the goddess.

As I approached the giant statue rising above the chamber, I knelt and carefully placed Gaius' small bird carving onto the altar. "Please, goddess of love, please help me read the auspices so that I may honor your wisdom and grace. Please help me to protect your people. Please, bring me love and kindness, not death and war," I prayed. I bowed my head in deference, and for a moment, I saw Geta in my memories, laughing as we fed Cael together. Was the goddess telling me something?

I heard heavy footsteps behind me and realized that Primus had entered the chamber. I knew I could tarry no longer. Rising, I turned to him and clasped my hands in front of me. "Speak your question," I intoned.

Primus glanced up at the statue, and then back to me. "For more than 100 years, the navy maintained these waters and protected the empire from pirates. Yet in the last twenty, pirates have returned. I need to find these ships and destroy them. You helped my men find one of these ships on Tyrus. Help them find another, so that news of our accomplishments reaches Rome."

Something prickled on the back of my neck. "To what

purpose?" I asked, though I suspected I already knew the answer.

"So that the emperor will appoint me Admiral of Mare Nostrum," answered Primus. "You will help me secure my place in the imperial court, girl. Now are you capable of this, or not? We are wasting time." He took a step forward and his mouth folded into a grim line.

"I am capable," I said. "Now I need silence."

I walked calmly toward the portico, though my mind was racing. Primus must have a direct way to communicate to Severus, or he would not be so confident in his ability to impress the emperor of his exploits. If I were to succeed, there may be a way to truly get a message to Geta. It was this thought that propelled me forward. Geta was closer to me than he had been in more than a year. I could nearly taste his kisses on my tongue. The physical longing for him was so strong I nearly swooned. For a moment, it seemed as if the candles placed alongside the walls of the temple flared, and I closed my eyes. *Cease this, Plautilla. Think of the task at hand. Interpret the signs, and Geta will return to you.* Whether the voice inside my mind was mine or Venus', I could not tell. But I needed to heed it.

I stepped outside into the cool sunshine. The sun had climbed higher into the sky, and sunbeams were rippling along the surface of the sea. I stared at the water for a moment, entranced by the beauty of the light. In the distance, the three islands shimmered. I considered Primus' request. Where did these invaders hide? Perhaps they returned to exotic homelands. I thought for a moment of migrating birds, who traveled vast distances, signaling the change in seasons. Suddenly, the skin along my arms prickled, and I knew the auspice was imminent. I stared into the distance, scanning for birds. But the shore was too far away to mark any. I glanced up toward the roof, to see if any bird fluttered above, but only saw Cael perched on a ledge next to one of the columns. He was preening his feathers, seemingly unconcerned of the surroundings. I glanced quickly back toward the water, and the light flashed against my eyes, blinding them temporarily.

My eyes watered, and I quickly closed them, the image of the light still imprinted against my eyelids. Suddenly, the image began to morph into a different shape. I was alarmed, as this had never happened before. Was the goddess providing me with a vision? I realized I was holding my breath and tried to calm myself by exhaling slowly. Behind my eyelids, the golden image gradually transformed into the outline of thousands of birds, floating on the surface of a river. They drifted together on the until the river met the sea before suddenly rising as one and scattering to the wind. The image then faded.

Blinking my eyes open, I stared out at the seemingly calm water. What was the auspice telling me? I sensed Primus waiting impatiently in the shadow of the columns. "How do your men chart the tides?" I asked.

Primus stepped carefully toward me. "By the position of the moon," he answered. "Why do you ask?"

"But surely you navigate the rivers as well?" I said, gesturing to the sea below. "Surely you know where they meet the sea and create their own tides?" Suddenly, a memory surfaced in my mind: I had climbed up to the top of the Actuaria ship that had carried us to Sicilia to breathe fresh air and escape the sorrow of the slave quarters underneath. I had clung to the edge, seasick, and had marked two pelicans soaring next to the ship. They had seemed to float effortlessly on the wind while the small ship continued to crash headlong into the oncoming waves.

"Go on," Primus said.

"These pirates know every hidden crevice and cave, and when the tides can carry a ship out of sight," I said. "Map the river flows, and you will find them." With that, I turned and went back into the temple, leaving Primus to contemplate my words.

* * *

The next day, Primus had me brought to the temple at sunrise, where I took an auspice on whether to send a patrol to the Syracuse, the port located on the southeastern tip of Sicilia. As I raised my arms, a white dove flew out of a thicket and streaked to my left, heading southeast. The patrol was then sent, catching a pirate boat unawares as they rounded the coast near Selinus.

The following day, I took an auspice of whether to build a barracks on the cliffs directly overlooking Panormus, near where I had first stepped foot onto Sicilia. When I stepped out onto the portico, I marked two vultures flying northeast. I sent word to refrain from building there. Within a week, the earth shifted, causing much of the land at the pinnacle of the cliff to slide into the sea. The week after, Primus mapped out a simple tidal map with the help of local fishermen and found another pirate vessel floating on the current along the route to Messana.

Thus it went as the days grew shorter. With each auspice I read, Primus' power grew. The spoils of these conquests filled his coffers, and he was lauded with accolades, and soon, finer quarters in a domus located on a hill above the city. For my part, I once again had stolas spun from the finest cloth Primus could acquire, and a chamber and bath of my own. I ate the finest food and was given the finest wine, at least by the standards of Sicilia. But I knew that it could all be stripped away at a moment's notice. One misread auspice, and Primus would have me tossed off one of the cliffs at the edge of the island, like they did with thieves. I was his pet, to do with what he saw fit.

We never dined together, but he would sometimes have me brought to his chambers to pore over tidal maps or discuss upcoming campaigns. Though I detested him, part of me warmed to the fact that he sought my counsel on some of his planned expeditions. Even Gaius had never consulted me in this way. True to his word, I had protection against any lewd advances from his men. I was once again under guard when I traveled to and from the temple. However, this monitoring did not prevent the occasional villager or fishwife from traveling to the fort to seek out auspices of their own. Once I cast the day's first auspice for Primus, my guards would depart to inform him of the day's decision, leaving me at the temple for a few hours. During this time, I would sometimes cast additional auspices, answering questions regarding fortuitous dates for weddings, funerals, and even business arrangements. The payments were meager, but I was eventually able to send a small number of coins to Gaius, along with a message that I was in no immediate harm.

On the kalends of Mensis December, I received an urgent message in return from Gaius: Mother was growing weaker and was unlikely live out the month. I received this news early in the morning as I was departing the barracks, and I ordered the guards to ride directly to Primus' villa. Cael, who had been waiting dutifully on the gate, sensed my agitation and croaked loudly as we set off. The sun was barely past the horizon as we pulled up to the gates, intercepting Primus as he was about to ride to the docks. I slid off the back of the guard's horse and ran forward to grab the stirrups of Primus' horse, nearly getting trampled by both in the process.

"What is the meaning of this?" he demanded.

"My mother is dying," I begged, entreating him. "Please, you promised me you would let me go to her. I must leave at once."

Primus contemplated me for a moment, his mouth held in taught line. It was an expression I had come to recognize as one he made when he was forced to make a difficult decision. Finally, he reached down and pulled me up behind him in the saddle. "I'll take you," was all he said. We set off immediately at a gallop, followed by our guards.

The landscape rushed past us as the early morning mist clung to the cliffs. As always, Cael flew above us, a black sentinel against the gray sky. Within a few hours of hard riding, we reached the villa. The sound of our hoofbeats had alerted Gaius, and he was waiting for us as we approached. Primus' horse had barely come to a halt before I slid off once again. I barely greeted Gaius, even though I marked his full beard and the strong muscles in his arms. My brother was fully mature and held himself like a true master of the domus.

"Where is she?" I asked urgently. I grabbed his hand, fearful of the worst. Gaius squeezed my fingers, a reassuring sign that I was not too late. I silently offered thanks to Venus, Vesta, and Diana for allowing me to return to my family in time.

"This way," Gaius said. He led me back into the kitchen. I barely took note of the freshly painted walls, or of Aurelia, sitting near the fire clutching her belly as if to protect her child from impending death. At the sight of Cael perched upon my shoulder, her brow furrowed. Gaius guided me to the small room I had previously occupied. There, on my old cot, lay Mother. She was so frail it was if half of her body had disappeared. She was huddled under several blankets, and a fur skin covered her feet. Next to her was a pot of hot embers being tended to by one of the slaves. The air in the room was stuffy and overly warm, yet Mother was shivering.

I gently touched the slave on the shoulder and he stood, letting me sit on the stool next to the bed. Carefully, I took Mother's hand into my own. Her fingers were so light I barely felt them. "Mother, I have returned," I whispered. "I have missed you." Mother did not seem to hear me, but her fingers twitched in my palm.

For the next two days and nights, I barely left Mother's side. Primus had reluctantly agreed to let me stay at the villa, and I had promised I would send for his guard when it was time for me to return. I suspected that our family's clear markers of wealth, proof of Lucius' continued patronage from Rome, had been a factor in his decision. Perhaps money had exchanged hands, though Gaius never said anything about it to me. Primus had ordered a guard to wait for me in Panormus.

On the second night, when Cael and I escaped to the garden to gulp fresh night air, Gaius joined us. I was grateful for his calm presence. For a while, we simply sat, contemplating the stars as we held hands. "Do you think Father is waiting for her?" I suddenly whispered. Sometimes I still woke from nightmares in which he was wandering the streets, seeking passage to the underworld.

"I think so," Gaius whispered back. "If he hoarded half as

much wealth as people said, he must have had enough coin to pay the boatman." I smiled at this thought, my heart slightly gladdened. I had to admit, Gaius had a point.

On the morning of the third day, Mother awoke gasping for breath, running her tongue repeatedly over her lips. We tried to give her water, but she waved off the spoon. Gaius and I then sat with her, each holding a hand as we listened to the rattle of her breath slowly fade. At the end, she crossed over with dignity, a patrician domina to the last. Cael fluttered over to the window, as if to guide her spirit into the fresh air. Aurelia then came into the room to pay her respects and squeeze her hand one last time.

Together, the three of us bathed her body and wrapped her in clean cloth. I kissed her forehead gently and Gaius carefully placed two coins on her eyes and pressed another into her palm. As the sun set, the slaves dug a hole near a large lemon tree she had favored, and we laid her to rest. I tried not to think of our family vault along Appian Way, where Mother's ancestors were buried in an ornate tomb alongside the rest of patrician Rome. I prayed to the gods that she would be accepted into a grand afterlife with the meager coins we had provided. I prayed that Father was there to show her the way. We made an offering of a slain rabbit to Vesta in her honor, and the slaves joined us in prayer. Afterward, we cooked another rabbit and ate it with our fingers, reminiscing about the first night we had eaten in the villa.

As the fire flickered, I finally had a moment to take in the furnishings in the room. There was a new rug on the floor, and Aurelia, like me, was dressed in finer fabric. "How goes the planting, brother?" I asked. "How many months until Aurelia is due?"

"Both are progressing well," Gaius said. "The hillsides are fully planted, and we expect a robust crop in the spring. The child is due in Martius."

Aurelia smiled, snuggling into Gaius. "Our home has been blessed by Vesta," she said sweetly. "Our only regret is that neither Mother nor my father will be here to greet the child when it arrives."

I could not help but notice that I had not been included in this thought. "Who will help you to manage the birth?" I asked her.

"We have arranged for midwives from Panormus to assist. Cornelius has been helpful in this. He has found one who has aided in many births and has several of her own. Clearly her hands are blessed with abundance."

I flinched at the implication that the loss of my own child was enough to taint Aurelia's birthing experience. I wondered if this was the result of yet another cruel piece of gossip from Palatine Hill. I dared not look at Gaius, but instead rose and stirred the fire, hiding my face as unfallen tears stung my eyes. I knew then that I would not return to the villa for the birth. Never had I expected to feel like an outsider in my own family, but with Mother and Father gone, the roles of patriarch and domina fell to Gaius and Aurelia, and I no longer belonged here. My place was now in the temple, serving Primus' ambition. I was no longer a daughter, nor a wife, nor a lover. I was only an augur, a vessel of the gods. I glanced at Cael, who was perched on the lararium, and for a moment, it seemed his eyes glittered in understanding.

* * *

The next morning, as promised, I sent one of the slaves to inform Cornelius I was ready to return to the Temple of Venus. By nightfall, a guard arrived to bring me back to Drepanum. As I turned to bid farewell to Gaius, I hugged him tightly. "Be well, brother," I said. "I look forward to meeting the babe when Aurelia deems the time is right."

"I'm sorry, Plautilla," Gaius said gently. "It's what she wants. She is terrified of losing it."

"I understand," I said in a small voice. "It is the loneliest feeling in the world." I then climbed onto the horse without another word.

As I rode through the darkness, I mourned what my family had lost. Our wealth, home, security—all scattered to the wind. Yet we had gained something back through hard work. Despite my sorrow, I was proud that we had managed to give Mother some stability and hopefully peace in her last days. I felt confident that Gaius and Aurelia would thrive, especially now that Lucius was helping them. Without me, their growing family was more likely to be secure. My heart was heavy with the realization.

XV.

I continued to take auspices after my return to Drepanum, and Primus continued to benefit. Word spread among the local folk, so much so that I even began to cast auspices for fishermen in the early morning before I would journey to the temple. I would stand on the edge of the dock and view the sea, watching the seagulls, and predict which coves or banks held the day's strongest catch. I never learned whether these auspices were truly accurate, but the fishermen continued to ask for them, so I assumed that my predictions were correct more often than not.

I was so preoccupied during this time with grief that I had forgotten about my desire to send a message to Geta. Things changed one night in early Februarius. Primus sent for me in the evening, as was his habit, and I was drinking posca with him and his officers when talk turned to the impending campaign in Britannia. By now, the men were used to discussing tactics while I was present in the room, and I used that to my advantage, learning more about the navy's movements than they intended. Tonight, we were joined by Androcles Cassius Sibylla, a prefect from the Legio II Parthica, the legion Father had once commanded. I was sure Primus enjoyed the irony of my audience, though Sibylla seemed uncomfortable with it.

"When do they intend to arrive in Britannia?" asked Primus.

"Preparations have already begun," answered Sibylla. "Severus plans to command the entire empire from there. All his consuls and even his family are joining him, for they expect to be there for years. Antoninus has already traveled ahead to ready the Classis Britannica. Once the legions are marshalled, they will sail to Britannia in the spring."

My ears pricked up at this vital piece of information. Antoninus had traveled far to the north. Where was Geta? Had he too been sent? Luckily, the whereabouts of the imperial family were of interest to everyone, and Primus asked the question.

"What of Geta? Will he remain in Rome and govern in Severus' absence?"

"No," sniffed Sibylla, pouring himself another draught of wine. It was evident that he did not hold Geta in as high a regard as Antoninus. "Geta remains in Campania, marshalling the Legio II Parthica to prepare them for the sea voyage. It will be a treacherous journey. We will sail via the Mare Nostrum around Hispania to reach Britannia by high summer. The emperor will require nearly the entire fleet."

My heart started to beat nearly through my chest. Would Geta sail to Sicilia? I wished I had paid more attention to the maps Primus had shown me. Luckily, Primus unfurled one along the table and studied it intently, pondering this new information. "Sail through the Fretum Gaditanum?" he asked. "How many ships will you need from us?"

"As many as you can spare," said Sibylla. "It unusual for legions to travel this way, but Severus insisted. Do you anticipate any significant risk?"

"There is no longer a viable military threat against our navy. But we will still need to be clever in our approach." Primus looked at me, and I felt goosebumps along the back of my neck. I would need to cast auspices to ensure that Geta survived this journey. Sibylla turned and gazed at me, suspicious.

"Who is she?" he asked.

"She is our oracle, Sibylla, and our key to a safe passage. Send word to Severus that I can ensure his fleet will survive the journey."

Sibylla grunted, though I still observed suspicion on his face. To him, I appeared to be nothing more than a simple girl. What power could I hold over the mighty sea? Finally, he nodded, tossed his head back, and drained his cup. "Very well."

"Excellent." Primus looked pleased at the opportunity to further demonstrate his usefulness to Severus. "When do we start?"

Sibylla plunked his cup down upon the table and wiped his mouth with the back of his hand. "Tomorrow."

* * *

Unexpectedly, when I woke the next morning, Primus instructed me not to cast any auspices until plans for the voyage were complete. Primus was to sail to Ostia and ferry the legions to Britannia, but the journey would require many stages and fortifications along the coasts of Sicilia, Corsica, and Africa. He anticipated returning within the month. "Prepare yourself, Plautilla, for when I call on you, you must interpret the gods' will as accurately as you ever have," he said. "Do not fail me." He was facing away from me, admiring the additional *armillae*, or gold armbands, upon his uniform in the clouded mirror of his chamber.

"You mean, do not fail Rome," I responded waspishly. "Surely the emperor will be gratified to learn his exiled daughter-in-law is still serving the empire?"

Primus twisted toward me. His expression was a warning. "Remember your place, *Augusta*," he said menacingly, and his emphasis on my former title caused me to shiver. "You serve at my command, and your reward is your life." He turned back to his reflection, dismissing me. My cheeks burned, but I suddenly realized that I was no longer afraid of this peevish little man. When Primus had brought me to Drepanum, I had not fully trusted my abilities. But after taking hundreds of auspices over the past few months, my confidence had grown. I rose from my cot and walked toward him until I was also caught in the mirror.

"Careful, Primus," I whispered. "Your glory will collapse into a hill of sand if you do not have the ear of the gods. You know this. If my life is forfeit, then so is your ambition. You need me as much as I need you. I promised to bring you riches, and I have done so. Now you must promise something to me." My heart was once again racing at the sound of my words, for I spoke with a bravery that I did not feel. Yet I could not stop.

Primus continued to gaze into the mirror. I could sense he was angry, but he did not raise his voice. Instead, he asked coolly, "What is it that you seek?"

"I need to send a letter to Caesar."

Primus turned around with a look of amusement. "A letter? To Caesar himself?"

"Yes," I said, suddenly desperate. "And it must be sealed and only opened by him."

"I see," Primus said wryly. "What could be so important that it requires a message to Caesar in this fashion?"

"The end of my family's banishment," I responded simply. "I seek entreaty for them only, not myself. You will not lose your augur. I have no desire ever to see Antoninus again."

Primus digested this unexpected information. "Very well," he eventually said. "I will compose a letter for you this evening when I return."

"No," I said. "Please, it must be written by my own hand. And you must deliver it to him directly. Please, Primus, I will ask for nothing else but this." We were almost nose to nose, but I did not back away. If I could not accomplish this now, there would never be another chance. If I could not write to Geta, I would cast myself off the cliffs by my own accord. I had to try.

I held my breath as Primus contemplated my request, but finally he nodded. "I will give you what you seek, Plautilla, but write quickly. I leave for Ostia in two days. And I will hold you to your word that you will remain my augur, regardless of what fate befalls your family."

I nodded solemnly in agreement. "I will not seek reestablishment for myself," I said honestly. What I did not tell him was that if Geta learned that I was alive, he could very possibly seek my reestablishment of his own accord, killing anyone who stood in the way.

Though I had been taught to read and write, it took almost the entire two days to compose the letter. I labored over the words and wrote and rewrote them again, tossing ink-stained vellum drafts at Cael before casting them into the fire. Every pent-up emotion I had been feeling for the past four years sought to pour onto the page, but I needed to be circumspect lest the message fall into the wrong hands. Though I trusted Primus to deliver it, there was no guarantee that he would not perish on the journey, or that Geta would instruct one of his consuls to read it first. It had to be plausibly cordial and not draw suspicion. Finally, before dawn, it was finished. I reread it by the light of my dim lamp one last time:

Publius Septimius Geta, I trust you are well. I am residing in Drepanum, where I serve Rome still, aiding the navy and its Prefectus, Primus Macarius Balbus. I have been taking auspices in the Temple of Venus above the city and have had much success. My family is faring well in the hills above Panormus. If your travels bring you to Sicilia, I will make an offering to the gods, to ensure your continued health. I wish you a safe journey and the blessings of Jupiter and Neptune in your travels.

I hoped that it conveyed what I needed it to, namely that I was alive and in Drepanum, and that I would wait for him if he chose to travel here. At the last moment, I added *you are in my thoughts* before signing it *Fulvia Plautilla Augusta.* I sealed the letter with wax from the candle before laying down with it held against my heart until it was time to give it to Primus.

* * *

The morning of Primus' departure, I took an auspice foretelling that the passage was safe and that his ship had departed for Ostia. For the first time since I could remember, I was not responsible to anyone but myself. Primus was not due to return for three weeks. I spent many of these days in the Temple of Venus, tending to its garden and gazing out at the view from the portico. Cael would perch on my shoulder until I lifted him and launched him into the sky, where he would float on the breeze above the cliff. Sometimes the little bird flew so high he was a mere speck against the crisp blue canopy above.

One day, I devoted some time to contemplating the statue of Venus located above the altar. Like many similar statues, the goddess was depicted in the nude, her shawl draped almost casually around her arms. She held her right hand over her sex and her left against her heart. She was alone, unaccompanied by a cupid or animal. Her head was tilted slightly to the side. I decided that the statue depicted her in an unguarded moment, as if she had been captured before she was about to bathe. Perhaps she, like I, had not asked for the power to determine the choices of others—only for the power to make the right choices for herself. Perhaps she merely wanted to live until she was cast forever in stone, destined to gaze out over the vast expanse of the sea.

The next morning, I took a walk along the path underneath the cliffs overlooking the harbor. As I ascended, I saw an opening in the rock that led to a shallow cave. I cautiously entered it before turning to view the sea from this new vantage point. The tip of the island was perfectly framed in its mouth like moving fresco. Fishing boats were sailing out of the shallow bay, seeking the day's catch. The sun's rays sparkled along the surface of the rolling waves. I sat on a large rock and watched the boats, feeling a sense of calm I had not felt in a long time. It was a slightly melancholy feeling. I thought of Father and Mother, both gone but hopefully together and in a better place. I realized that I no longer had to worry about anyone but myself. While my current situation was not ideal, I was no longer fearful of loved ones being harmed due to my actions.

I scraped up a handful of pebbles and tossed them out of the cave, watching them roll down the hill. As I let go of each stone, I thought of all the things I had cast off—my girlhood, my childhood home, my marriage, my pregnancy, my status in the imperial family, and finally, my role as caretaker of my family. Each stone was an identity I no longer possessed. What was left of me now? What would happen once the birds no longer spoke to me? Once again, my thoughts turned to Geta. Had he received my message? Had he held it close? Then a new thought arose: *what has Geta cast away?*

By habit, I looked at the sky, the question reverberating in my mind. Once again, I saw no birds. Why did the gods choose to hide Geta from me? Why couldn't I let the thought of him go, like I had let go of so much from my old life? Just then, something caught my eye on the horizon below. It was a large white swan, swimming placidly in the shallow lagoon at the edge of the harbor. Slowly, I stood and stepped forward, watching as it glided slowly toward a flock of smaller birds, who scattered as it approached. The swan preened, extending its long neck and nattering at its grand feathers. I held my breath, gazing at its ethereal beauty. It was surrounded by lesser birds, yet it was fragile and outnumbered. I felt a shiver rise on the back of my neck. The gods were providing an answer to my question, yet I could not understand what it meant.

A week later, I was awoken by the sound of men's loud voices. Dressing hurriedly, I exited my room to find servants scurrying about.

"Ships in port!" shouted one.

"Look alive, our master will be here quickly!" shouted another. I glanced out the window and observed dozens of ships underneath an overcast sky. Primus had returned. I quickly bound up my hair and arranged my shawl around my stola as the servants set out jugs of watered wine and dishes of olives, fruit, and bread. Before long, Primus strode into the chamber, followed by Sibylla and several officers wearing the emblem of the Legio II. Primus marched to the table and poured himself a draught of wine, tossing his head back and drinking deeply. The others followed suit.

I stepped forward, out of the shadows. "Good morning," I greeted them courteously. "Welcome back to Drepanum. I trust your voyage was pleasant?"

Primus did not respond, but one of the officers turned to look at me, his mouth full of olives. "About as pleasant as an invasion can be," he retorted, and the men laughed.

Primus finally glanced up at me, all business. "Get to the temple," he ordered. "I will be there soon. I trust you are rested, Plautilla." With that, he turned his attention to the table, dismissing me as he signaled to one of the captains to unroll a map. I bowed my head again, even though Primus was no longer watching me. As I looked up, I saw an officer of the Legio Parthica observing me. I realized that I recognized him; his name was Vel Papinus Betto, and he had often attended meetings in the palace with Father. I coolly nodded my head in greeting, though my heart was thudding in my chest. I passed by them without another word, Cael perched upon my fingers.

It was not until midday when Primus rode up to the temple. I was kneeling before the altar, once again contemplating the goddess' statue, when I heard the pounding of hoofs. I walked to the portico and waited until he came into view. Dismounting his horse, he gestured for his guards to wait outside before bounding up the steps. "Inside," he ordered. I followed. Primus strode toward the altar, giving Venus a cursory nod of his head before swiveling back to me. "We have much to do," he declared, setting his helmet upon the altar. "More ships will be arriving over the next few days. The fleet will sail to Septa to gather reinforcements from Mauritania and Numidia before journeying through the passage of *Fretum Herculeum*. The currents are very tricky, and with so many ships, we must time it precisely. You will need to ask the gods for the most auspicious time to set sail."

"I see," I replied. "Do I need to cast this auspice today? Or can I wait until dawn, when the signs are clearest?"

"You have three days," Primus said. "You must cast for departure from Drepanum and also Septa. We are still trying to determine which port in Gallia province to depart from after that."

"Perhaps I need to go with you," I jested.

"This is not a game, Plautilla!" Primus shouted, slamming his fist onto the altar. His helmet teetered next to several lamps, threatening to spill them over. "Cast the auspices, or I shall cast you over these cliffs myself!"

I took a deep breath. Clearly, much was riding on the success of this endeavor, not least of which was Primus' political career. I needed to mollify him, for I was desperate to know if he had delivered my message. I bowed deeply. "Forgive me, Prefectus," I said sincerely. "I do not take these matters lightly. I will cast the auspices you seek with sincerity and intent. I will make an offering to Venus. I will fast and pray in the temple tonight in penance, so that my mind will be clear." This seemed to mollify Primus, and he nodded his head in approval. Picking up his helmet, he adjusted his cloak, and I saw an additional armband upon his uniform.

"I see you have received more accolades. I compliment you on your continued service to Rome. Was it granted to you by Ceasar himself?" I tried to keep my voice neutral, gathering my shawl around my arms, momentarily resembling the statue above. Primus gazed at me shrewdly.

"I see Caesar remains in your thoughts," he said, and my cheeks burned. "I delivered your message to Geta's consul, who swore to me he would deliver it with his own hand. I do not know if he read it, for he appeared quite busy when I saw him. It seemed the business at hand ordered by the emperor himself needed to wait until the festival of *Parentalia* was celebrated. While we were concerned that Caesar would miss his family during this revel, it seemed he had plenty of company." Primus' smirk told me all I needed to know about what type of company he meant.

The redness in my cheeks spread to my chest as the anger coiled in my belly. Geta had forgotten me, and once again his bed was occupied by others. All the longing I had felt over these difficult months was mine alone. The world faded to gray, and I staggered slightly, grasping at the toes of Venus to right my balance. Primus marked this, but to his credit, said nothing. I was still breathing heavily, fighting back unwanted tears, when he leaned forward and whispered into my ear. "Clear your mind of earthly pursuits and speak only to the gods. I will arrange for food and wine and the comforts of home to be brought to you. Make your penance, for when I call upon you the third day, you will guide me to glory." With that, he departed, leaving me to my anguish.

XV.

Praying in the temple at night was a different experience. The flickering of the lamps cast strange shadows on Venus' face, and I felt uneasy in the silence. Even Cael behaved differently in the temple, keeping to himself in one of the crevices at the top of the columns. I was alone with my thoughts in this marble mausoleum. Determined, I made offerings of fruit and meat, burned *myrtus*, and prayed to Venus, Diana, Jupiter, Neptune, and whoever else might hear. I begged Father and Mother to entreat the gods to listen in the afterworld. I even said a prayer for Antoninus, just for good measure.

Outside, the garrison was filled with men, but I felt as if I were truly alone, with only the gods to witness my sorrow. After eating my simple meal of olives and cured meat, I proceeded to drink almost an entire jug of wine. Soon, memories of Geta came unbidden. I cried, then screamed, then cried some more. I tore off my stola and thrashed the garment underneath my feet. I smeared oil and ash on my face. I even ignored Cael, who kept an eye on me from high above. Finally, I gathered myself into a ball near the flame pit on the side of the temple, falling into a dreamless sleep. Even my dreams were empty.

I woke the next morning covered in sweat and filth, my

mouth sticky and dry. Gathering the remains of my stola, I crept out onto the portico. It was still night, and the evening star was sitting low on the western horizon. It would be dawn within the hour. I quickly hurried to the bathhouse and dunked myself in the scalding water before donning a clean stola. I braided my wet hair and tiptoed back to the temple, the mosaic tiles cold against my bare feet. I added more fuel to the eternal fire until the flames were flickering high against the wall, helping to ward off the chill in my bones. Cael squawked softly, and I knew it was time to cast the first auspice.

I stepped out onto the portico and closed my eyes, calming myself. I concentrated fiercely on the question, more fiercely than I had since arriving in Drepanum. *What is the most auspicious time for the legions to set sail?* I asked. In my mind's eye, I pictured the city, the harbor, and the islands off to the distance. I intended to cast the auspice for Drepanum today and the one for Septa the following day. Opening my eyes, I raised my arms and waited. I scanned the clouds but saw no birds. The sky was turning orange and pink, and the sun's rays were appearing in front of me as it rose over the mountains above the valley.

Suddenly, I marked two seabirds flying above, passing over the temple from the east. They were heading to the shoreline. I was waiting to see which direction they would take when I heard Cael emit a loud *caw* and take flight after them. I froze in shock, as Cael had never interfered with an auspice before. "Cael, no!" I called after him. What was he doing? Would this subvert the gods' will? Cael swiftly overtook the two gulls, buzzing at them and swooping around their wings. The first gull dove to avoid him, and the second followed suit. Cael continued to swirl around them until the birds disappeared, flying nearly straight down the center of my view.

I waited, holding my breath, but they did not return. Cael reappeared and flew onto the portico, landing at my feet. Flapping his wings, he let out another loud *caw*. I bent down and he hopped into my hand. I lifted him up until his dark eyes were level with mine. "What was that?" I asked, though I was not angry. Cael fluffed out his feathers and emitted a quieter *awk*. I stroked his beak, considering. The two birds diving straight down past the ground meant delaying. The ships needed to depart Drepanum in two days' time. "I hope you know what you're doing," I muttered, though whether it was to Cael or myself, I was not sure. I went off in search of the guards to get the message to Primus.

* * *

That night, it began to rain. The sound of the droplets was steady against the roof of the temple. I stoked the fire again and sat with my feet tucked underneath me, thinking about the day's auspice. I wondered if I should have cast it again. Perhaps it would be prudent to do so in the morning. Cael, for his part, had retreated to the shadows above. I was deep in thought when I heard the sound of hoofbeats through the rain. At first, I thought nothing of it, as I assumed the soldiers were carrying out their evening tasks. But then I heard more. It sounded as if an entire legion was riding into the fort.

I strained my ears and heard a few voices, but eventually they faded. They were probably housing some of the legions who had traveled on the ships. I was not concerned about any soldiers entering the temple. Primus had given orders that I remain undisturbed. It grew quiet again, and I decided to add more oil to the lamps at the base of the statue. I drifted back toward the altar, and soon the cella was glowing with soft yellow light. I was lighting another bundle of myrtus when I heard the creak of the giant door opening and the sound of footsteps echoing across the tile. I whirled around to face the intruder, whose face remained in shadow. I was trying to ascertain if I was in danger when he spoke softly: "You are just as I remembered."

My heart stopped. Slowly, the figure approached, and Geta's delicate features were illuminated in the lamplight. He stopped a few paces short of me, his armor dripping from the rain. He was without laurels and wore only a simple cloak.

I stared at him, not comprehending how he could be here. For a moment, I wondered if he was dead, and this was a trick of the gods—or worse, my own mind. Finally, my wits returned, and I bowed my head in greeting. "Ceasar," I began haltingly. I felt, rather than saw, Geta rushing toward me, and we were in each other's arms again at last. I threw my arms around his shoulders (*so thin, when did they become so thin*) and held him with all my strength, not caring that the fabric of my stola was becoming damp. "Geta," I choked, but I couldn't say any more, because I was crying.

"Shhhh," he whispered, his lips gently pressing against my cheeks, my eyelids, my neck.

"Geta," I panted again, urgent. And then we were devouring each other, as we had on that fateful morning long ago.

The world shrank. Geta filled my senses—the cold metal of the cuirass that surrounded his torso pressing against my chest, the smell of the leather bound around his wrists, the stubble of his beard and clammy skin against my cheeks, the hot sharp thrill of his tongue wresting with mine. His hands were roaming through my hair and pressing on my neck, pushing me farther into him. I stood on my tiptoes, thrusting my hips into his. Suddenly terrified, I pulled away.

"We will be discovered, we will be found out—"

"Plautilla," Geta pressed his finger against my lips, silencing me. "I have traveled far, and will travel farther still. We don't have much time."

"But—"

"Antoninus is in Germania, marching to the coast. Father and Mother have departed for Lugdunum. I am Caesar, and I will do what I please. You are no longer Antoninus' wife, Plautilla."

Hearing these facts said so plainly jolted me out of my reverie. I examined his face, more angular than I remembered. There was furrow of worry between his brows that made him appear to be scowling. His eyes looked darker, almost black, and I saw the glint of an emotion I could not name. The past two years had been hard on him as well.

"What do you want, Geta?" I asked. "Why have you come?"

Geta sighed, and I felt the weight of all he had been carrying on his thin shoulders. "I want to forget about war, politics, and my family, for one night. I want to rediscover you." He lifted my fingers to his lips.

"Rediscover as you have so many others?" The jealous words tumbled out of my mouth before I could stop them. Geta stared at me, offended.

"I never thought I would see you again, Plautilla. When your message arrived, I felt as if Venus herself caressed me with your words."

I turned to look up at the statue of the goddess, a silent

witness to our conversation. "Do you swear, upon the goddess herself, in her temple, at her altar, that you love me?" I clasped his hand and knelt, pulling him down next to me. Tears streamed from my eyes, but I did nothing to stem them. "Do you swear it, Geta? That your love has survived over two years, and that it survives still? For I am not the girl you knew. I have suffered hunger and thirst, I have protected my family, I have buried my mother. I have endured the exile your brother so cruelly imposed upon us. I am now a slave to one of your commanders, interpreting the will of the gods on his behalf. The only thought that has carried me through is the thought of you, of one day seeing you again. I swear, before the goddess and all that is good in this world, that I love you, with all my heart. Can you do the same?"

Geta stared at me, his eyes wide. I stared back. He reached forward and touched one of my tears with his fingertip. He then gazed up at Venus, her head forever tilted in a tribute to the power of love and desire. Geta clutched my hand tightly and closed his eyes. The sound of the rain intensified, and the sweet smell of burning myrtus filled our nostrils. The lamps flickered, casting shadows on his careworn face as he breathed deeply. Slowly, the tension left his body, and he opened his eyes. "I swear." He leaned forward and kissed me. "I am not the boy you knew either. I have lived under the growing shadow of certain death every day. I have learned how fragile life is, and how quickly fortunes can change. We are all on borrowed time, Plautilla." He shook his head, a sad smile on his face, as he squeezed my fingers. Slowly, he stood and pulled me up into an embrace. I laid my head his chest, feeling almost more than hearing his oath: "On my life, by the goddess of love and beauty, I swear."

XV.

* * *

We coupled underneath the altar, worshipping Venus together. I welcomed all of it, the pleasure and the momentary pain, for it had been so long. We stared at each other as we joined slowly, and I gathered all of him into my heart once again. Later, he took me from below, drinking in the sight of me. "You are Venus incarnate," he moaned, his hands reaching up to caress my breasts, my nipples swollen from the ministrations of his tongue. I leaned down and returned the favor.

I had been many things, but I had never felt more like a woman than I did with Geta. Every secret part of my body, soul, and mind was laid bare in his hands. He gave rise to everything divine in me. I was grateful for the passing storm, for the deluge muffled my screams as Geta brought forth the sharp sweetness between my legs with his tongue. He was insatiable, even taking me from behind as my hands gripped the altar, biting my neck as he thrust savagely up into me. We spent the night drawing pleasure from one another, until we lay spent, thirsty, and sleepy in the dying light of the lamps.

"I will need to cast an auspice soon," I murmured, running my fingers along the curve of his chin. I did not want to spend a moment without touching some part of him, even as I lay encircled in his arms. "I must ask the gods which is the most auspicious day for you to depart Septa after you arrive."

"What if it's the same day?" Geta jested sleepily.

"Then the gods are capricious."

"I know that already." Geta pulled me back toward him, and we kissed again.

I was drifting off to sleep when I saw movement out of the corner of my eye. Cael was hopping between the lamps on the altar, making gentle chirping sounds. Once again, the little bird served as our sentinel, alerting us to the cruel arrival of the new day. Groggily, I sat up and put on my stola, running my fingers through my tangled hair. There was not enough time to bathe. Geta was dozing, snoring softly. I shook him awake.

"It is nearly dawn, my love. I need to prepare for the day's auspice."

Geta blinked his eyes blearily and nodded, sitting up as well. I tried not to notice how prominent his ribs were. "I should cook for you," I jested, kissing his shoulder gently.

"I would like that," Geta said softly. "I would like to just eat a simple meal with you, Plautilla." For a moment my heart panged at the sorrow in his voice. If only we could have been born into other families; how our lives would have been different.

"Bathe," I told him. "Your men will wake to find you there and not ask where you slept. Primus will return before noon to hear today's auspice. I told him the ships need to depart Drepanum tomorrow."

"I know," said Geta. "The lead ship is mine."

I could not respond due to the lump in my throat.

A short while later, I stood on the portico once again, greeting the dawn in anticipation. The rains had departed, leaving a clear, bright morning. How different I felt today compared to yesterday, and not just because of our coupling and lack of sleep. For the first time, a quiet knowledge sat in my heart: *Geta loves me. He swore it*. No matter what happened from this day forth, I knew that knowledge would carry me for the rest of my life. I loved and was loved in return.

I raised my arms and closed my eyes, asking the question:

what day is the most auspicious to depart Septa? I held my breath as I opened my eyes. Today, the auspice was immediate. A group of seven geese flew in formation, moving from north to south, or right to left, in the most auspicious direction. They formed a "V" together, and it looked like an arrow pointing directly in the direction of Africa. The meaning was as clear as daylight.

By the time Primus arrived with his officers on horseback, Geta's legions were already amassed in formation in front of the temple. Geta appeared, his armor shining brightly and laurels once again in his hair. I stood underneath the columns of the portico, observing Primus bow obsequiously, his oily thick hair shining in the sun. Sibylla and Betto accompanied Geta. Primus then gestured to the temple, squinting up at me.

"My Imperator, here is our seer. You may know her as—"

"I know her," Geta cut him off, the very model of a bored prince. "You forget she was my sister-in-law, Primus."

Primus stumbled. "Of course," he said, and I could practically see the mental calculations in his head as he tried to discern whether enslaving me to do his will was a politically positive move. "Yes, well, er, she has a way with birds—"

I could not bear another moment of this, reverting temporarily back to my patrician upbringing. "It is an honor to see you again, Caesar. I trust you are well. I am pleased to serve Rome again in this fashion, regardless of my status as an ex-citizen."

Geta bowed his head politely. I tried not to peer at his neck, to see if my bite marks were still visible. He lifted his head and responded. "Greetings, Plautilla. I am heartened to see you as well. I have heard you have been successful in your taking of auspices."

"She has, Caesar," interjected Primus. "She has cast for our departure from Drepanum and from Septa."

"Indeed," I said. "You must depart Drepanum tomorrow, and once you arrive in Septa, you must depart on the seventh day. These are the most auspicious days to ensure that the fleet arrives safely to its destination."

"You are sure of this?" asked Primus, for show.

"Yes," I said, directing my response to Geta, and Geta alone. "The gods have spoken."

"Then let us dine together this last night before we depart," said Geta. "I wish to express my gratitude, not only to you, but the gods as well."

There was silence as we regarded each other. I felt the curious looks of the men keenly. We were courting danger, the two of us. Perhaps it was our exhaustion, or exhilaration in finding each other again, that led us to behave openly in this way. In retrospect, it was unwise. But in the moment, it felt suitable. I could see Primus watching us shrewdly. "Of course," he said. "We shall dine together this evening. Plautilla, please, use my personal bath." Suddenly, I was a favored guest instead of an indentured servant.

"I would be delighted," I responded.

* * *

Dinner was subdued. We squeezed around the map table in Primus' chambers, hurriedly rearranged for this purpose. I sat between Geta and Primus, across from Sibylla and Betto. We were served a meal of bread, cured meat, olives, cheese, fish stew, and wine. A simple meal. I exchanged a knowing look with Geta, and his knee brushed mine in response. I had bathed and even braided my hair to the top of my head in a nod to how I used to wear it in the palace, but tendrils kept drifting down toward my neck. I saw Geta's fingers twitch as one landed on my back, and I knew he longed to touch them.

Talk was mainly about the invasion and planned campaign in Britannia. Severus intended to reestablish Roman control in the Caledonian region. He planned to install several legions who had decamped to Gaul back in the area and address the raids that had troubled the province south of Hadrian's Wall. It was to be a difficult business and would most likely take more than a year to complete. I tried not to show my anguish at losing Geta so soon after seeing him again.

"I will be working with Augustus as well," said Geta. "We are to share the responsibilities of the army. Antoninus will command the Legions, and I will ensure smooth logistics in support." *I wonder how that will fare*, I thought. I knew both brothers well enough to know they could not work together for long, even in battle.

"Our navy will be at your disposal," said Primus. "We look forward to ensuring Roman victory yet again." His eyes darted from Geta to me.

"I understand that you have had a string of successes in rooting out pirates in the region," Geta said coolly. "It is most impressive."

Primus puffed up faster than a peacock could spread its tailfeathers. "Thank you, Caesar," he said. "We are grateful to continue to fill the empire's coffers with these conquests."

"And your own, no doubt," said Geta. Primus nearly choked on an olive, and Geta laughed. My chest warmed, as for a moment, I saw a glimpse of the old Geta, the mischievous youth who had teased me in the palace. "Fear not, Primus, I completely understand. Sicilia has been governed well. A few extra coins falling into the local purse is none of our concern." Primus nodded meekly and reached forward to gulp another cup of wine.

"Thank you, Caesar," he said again, less assured this time.

"I am, however, curious what you will do with Plautilla, once you have embarked on the voyage," said Geta. "Surely you do not expect her to remain here, away from her family for many months while you have no need of her?" I looked at Geta, surprised. He was reclining in his chair, holding his wine, the picture of easy authority. *Being away from his family suits him,* I thought.

Primus swallowed heavily. "I had not…considered it, My Imperator Caesar." I noted his elevated use of title, intended to curry favor. "I suppose I would have Plautilla continue to reside in the temple, where she can continue to commune with the gods."

"She is not a Vestal Virgin," Geta countered drily. I nearly spit out my wine. "Consider something else." He gave Primus a stern look. Once again, we were the center of attention. My cheeks burned, and I did not dare look at either.

"I suppose Plautilla can spend this time with her family," said Primus weakly. I looked up in surprise at this. I had not considered the thought of returning to Gaius and Aurelia. Perhaps I would be able to be present before the birth after all.

"I think it's the least we can do, to thank her for her dedication to Rome," said Geta. He then raised his cup. "To Fulvia Plautilla Augusta, Augur of Rome." This too, was deliberate, uttering the title after Antoninus had officially stripped it away. Geta tossed his head back and drank deeply.

The others raised their glasses and drank, though I saw a look pass between Sibylla and Primus.

"You are too kind, Caesar," I said politely. I turned to Primus. "I will wait out these months with my family, but I will continue my service to you when you return. I will keep my word to help Rome's navy, as I promised." This seemed to mollify Primus, and he nodded his head gruffly in thanks.

Geta took his leave shortly afterward. We did not have a moment to speak privately, but he turned to look at me once more before departing. "I will see you on the shore," he said.

"Yes, Caesar," I bowed. "Good night."

Later, as I was preparing for sleep, there was a soft knock on my door. I opened it to find Primus staring at me uncomfortably. "I am sorry to intrude, Plautilla, but I want to ensure that your comfort has always been my priority, and I never—"

"He is leaving, Primus," I said, perhaps too crossly, for my body was longing for sleep. "Things will revert to normal once you return."

Primus titled his head quizzically and gave me an almost half-bow. "Perhaps," he said, before shutting the door once again. I lay down on my cot, too exhausted to remove my clothes, and fell asleep to the sound of Primus retreating to his bed chamber.

The next morning, I stood at the edge of the harbor, watching the tender boats ferry the legions back to the ships. I was joined by several children of local fishermen who held flower garlands in their hands to lay upon the necks of the commanders for good luck. I had woken early, anxious to cast another auspice if needed, (and to keep Geta near) but the seas were calm with a slight westerly breeze—perfect weather for sailing to Septa. I silently thanked Cael for ensuring this auspice, for though I did not want Geta to depart, I needed to do all within my power to keep him alive.

Geta and Primus approached, and several children ran forward to lay the garlands around their necks. Geta then stepped in front of me and I bowed. "Farewell, Plautilla," he said, and stopped. The sun brought out the freckles upon his cheeks, and he smiled. I smiled in return, unable to help myself.

"Be safe in your travels, Publius Septimius Geta," I said softly. "You are in my prayers."

"And you are in mine," answered Geta. He leaned forward, and I thought for a wild moment that he meant to kiss me in front of the entire Legio II Parthica. Instead, he grazed my cheek with his as he whispered into my ear. "This is not the last time we will see each other, I swear it. Hold fast, Plautilla."

"I will," I murmured. The urge to throw my arms around him and kiss him fiercely was so overpowering I had to ball up my fists. Geta stared at me as well, and we kissed with our eyes before he strode forward and boarded the boat, followed by Sibylla and Betto. Primus stepped in front of me next.

"I will have my men return you to your villa," he said. "But do not forget: I will call upon you when I return."

"I understand," I said. "Safe travels, Primus."

Primus nodded and followed the others into the boat. Soon, the massive *naves onerariae* ships unmoored and lumbered toward the mouth of the harbor, powered by the dozens of men rowing in their bowels. Once at the mouth, they unfurled their sails, one by one, and picked up speed as they headed toward the horizon. Within a few minutes, they were gone.

"Come back to me, my love," I whispered. "Come back."

Part Four

LIPARA

XVI.

Not a day went by when I didn't think of Geta. It was hardest in the beginning, losing him so soon after reuniting with him again. It felt the gods were playing a cruel trick on me. But over time, as I returned to the villa and took over my old tasks, the pain faded into a soft ache. I often wondered where he was and what the landscape of Britannia looked like. I knew it was colder than Sicilia. Was he near the ocean? Did he wake early to look at the predawn sky? Did my absence feel like a physical pain to his body, as his did to mine?

Gaius gladly welcomed me back into the household; Aurelia less so. Though she was cool in the beginning, she was grateful that I arrived in time to assist her during her labor. She gave birth to a beautiful, healthy girl. Gaius named her Hortensia, after Mother. I was terrified to hold her at first, worried that my own ill luck would somehow taint my love for the baby, but one look at her tiny face put an end to any concern. I adored her and was more than happy to rock her in my arms in the early morning hours, allowing Aurelia a chance to rest. By then, Lucius had sent two additional kitchen slaves to attend to us, and the villa soon acquired the smooth rhythm of any Patrician domus in the city.

Gaius was having middling success with the vineyard, so

I returned to casting auspices for the local fisherman and other countryfolk to help provide for the family. The birds continued to reveal themselves to me. Cael was now much more active in his interactions with the various gulls, hawks, sparrows, jays, and other fowl that flew about the rocky hillsides. Sometimes folk asked if he was a fledgling, and when told them he was nearly seven, they would not believe it. Like me, Cael seemed held in amber by the gods' will, neither young nor old. I felt suspended between my old life and the next, waiting for news about Geta and Primus. About once a month, a courier would arrive from Drepanum, and for the price of a fresh meal would inform me of the navy's whereabouts. Primus intended to return at the earliest opportunity, but Emperor Severus insisted that he remain in Britannia and ferry troops from Gaul. Still, it was expected that the navy would return once the campaign was complete.

A year passed, then another, then a third. Hortensia grew like a weed, and the rugged countryside was her own little empire. She often played with Cael, making mud pies with flowers, and he hopped over them and placed various shells and rocks into a pile near her feet, delighting her. Aurelia and Gaius tried for another child, but the gods did not seem to favor them this time. Aurelia grew ever more religious, praying to Vesta both morning and night for a son. I knew it was only a matter of time before she accused me of angering the gods. I needed to leave again to bring peace back to the household, yet Primus had still not returned to call me back to my duties.

One day in early Junius, a few weeks after Hortensia's third birthday, a courier arrived with a letter from Geta. He spoke with a strange accent and told me he had been stationed with the Legio VI Victrix in Eboracum for nearly a decade. It had taken him nearly six months to deliver it to Sicilia. I took the letter with trembling hands. "He intended it only to be read by your eyes, Domina," he said. "It has traveled far."

"Thank you," I said in a wavering voice. I clutched the vellum in my fingers, careful not to crush it too much. The crinkling of the delicate parchment sounded like whispers.

"I have been ordered to remain with you until a response is composed," the courier said. "On orders of Augustus himself."

My blood turned cold. "Augustus?" I said, not comprehending. Had Antoninus found out about Geta and I? Was this a message proclaiming his death?

"My apologies for the confusion, Domina. There are now two who bear the title of Augustus. Emperor Severus declared Publius Septimius Geta as co-Augustus to Marcus Aurelius Antoninus last winter. The emperor remains in Eboracum, for he is in ill health. He intends for both sons to co-rule once he departs to the underworld. The message is from Augustus Geta."

My mind reeled, as this was shocking news. "Come, join us," I entreated. "We will make arrangements for your stay."

Later, we ate our midday cena in silence, taking respite from the heat. Hortensia was dropping slivers of apricot on the floor for Cael to snatch, hoping we weren't going to notice.

"Aren't you going to read it?" asked Aurelia, curious. Gaius said nothing, but he sipped his wine, his mouth set in a hard line.

"Not yet," I said. "Tomorrow."

I retired to my room and held the vellum close to my chest, the way I had held my own message years ago. Thoughts of Geta flooded my head as I spent a sleepless night listening to the snores of the courier by the kitchen fireplace. Before dawn, I slipped out, Cael on my shoulder, and headed down the ravine to my favorite spot near the stream. Sitting on the rock, I waited until the sun's rays were high enough to illuminate the ink on the thin paper and unsealed it to read.

My love, I think about you every day. The memory of you is my only warmth in this cursed place. I remain in Eboracum while Antoninus campaigns against the Maeatae and Calendonian tribes in the north. It is a difficult business. I have been tasked with administration of the empire while Antoninus is tasked with leading the Legions. Father intends for us to co-rule, and he was persuaded to grant me the title of Augustus by his advisors, who fear for his health. Antoninus was enraged, as he was assumed the heir to the empire. Mother is advocating for us to make amends before Father dies, for he will not live out the year. Once he is gone, we will leave this damned country to the barbarians and return to Rome.

I do not know if Antoninus and I can truly co-rule. We both have guards that are loyal only to us, and we do not travel anywhere without them. At some point, both of us will need to bear children, though the thought of extending this wretched family another fifty years is a cruel joke. I cannot share too much in a letter, but I think of the time we spent together and know it is you I want to bear my children. When I return to Rome, I will arrange to meet you, and we will rediscover ourselves again my love. You are always and forever my empress.

Geta

When I looked up from reading, I tasted the salt from my silent tears. Here was incontrovertible proof that Geta felt as I did. I read the letter dozens of times, until I memorized every word. It was the most precious gift I could ever have been given. I knew I needed to burn it so that we would not be found out, but I could not bear to destroy it. I held in my hands the most tangible proof of love I had ever received.

I returned to the villa and tucked the letter underneath my mattress. I needed to compose a response quickly to give to the courier. The longer he remained with us, the more questions he would draw from Aurelia and Gaius. I located Gaius' vellum and ink and set to work, writing feverishly by the faint light of my lamp:

My dearest Geta, I am heartened to hear that Severus has elevated you to Augustus. It is well deserved. I am prospering and overjoyed to hear from you. I remain at my villa as Primus has not returned. I miss you with all my heart and cannot wait to see you again. I shall pray for your safe return to Rome.

Plautilla

I longed to say so much more, but it would have to do. I quickly sealed the letter and went in search of the courier. I felt a sense of renewed purpose, for there was hope that I would see Geta within the year.

* * *

The summer came and went. Gaius and Aurelia never spoke of the courier and his letter to me, but I know they spoke about it to themselves, for I heard the hushed tones of their conversations that would cease as soon as I entered the room. Soon after the courier departed, Aurelia sent her own letter to her father, Lucius, entreating him to visit again. She began to teach Hortensia to behave like a dutiful patrician daughter, to curb her wild ways, and limit her time with me. Unfortunately, a child who had learned how to run in the fragrant sunshine did not take well to the idea of sitting still and learning how to weave or tend to the altar of Vesta. Hortensia was a creature of the wild, and I realized she took after me in this respect. However, I held my tongue as Aurelia fought to tame her spirit. As the days grew shorter, the villa began to feel as stifling as Palatine Hill, and when Primus sent word that he had returned to Drepanum, I went gladly. "I'll visit as soon as I can," I told a tearful Hortensia and stoic Gaius, but I did not look back.

When I arrived on the kalends of Septem, I discovered that Primus had installed larger quarters for me farther from his chambers, in a room that faced toward the sea. Cael settled in immediately in the window, pecking his beak against the thick glass. We returned to the temple and tended to the altar, which had fallen into disrepair during my absence. I cast auspices for local fisherman and also a few landowners who had returned to the villas that had sprouted up along the hillsides. Primus' success in rooting out pirates had resulted in more landowners returning to Sicilia. Their prosperity flowed into Drepanum, and I noticed more sellers in the marketplace and more buildings being constructed on the edge of the city.

A few nights later, I dined with Primus, who had finally achieved the coveted title of admiral. I learned that it was Antoninus himself who had granted the honor.

"Has Antoninus fared well?" I asked conversationally as we dined on salted sardines, olives, and bread. Primus ate with gusto. He was exactly the same, save for a few gray hairs sprouting above his ears. He sucked the salty oil off his fingers as he spoke.

"Antoninus is an impressive leader," he said. "Calm in battle. The men look up to him." The implication, unsaid, was that Geta was none of these things.

"How is the emperor?" I asked, genuinely curious.

"Not long for this world," Primus said bluntly. "I would not be surprised if they announce Antoninus as imperator any day now."

"But what about—" I stopped myself before saying too much. How would I know that Geta had been granted the title of Augustus? I needed to tread carefully. "But what about the Senate?" I asked weakly.

"The Senate stands with Antoninus, despite what Geta's loyalists proclaim," snorted Primus. "We shall all be under Antoninus' rule before long, Plautilla." Primus raised a glass and drank to this, as my stomach twisted into a knot. That night, I made a silent offering to Venus to keep Geta safe and ensure his continued authority over Rome.

Despite Primus' assurances, it was many months later when the news spread throughout the empire: Severus was dead, and Antoninus and Geta were to rule together as co-emperors. The emperor had died in Eboracum, his sons by his side. His last words to them had been to be harmonious with one another, enrich the legions, and scorn all the rest. So had passed Lucius Septimius Severus Pius Pertinax Augustus, who had risen to the highest position of power in the empire, only to provide the cudgel for his two sons to destroy each other in his shadow.

The knowledge that Geta was returning to Rome haunted my thoughts. The night I received the news, I spent the night in the temple. I stoked the fire as hot as it would allow and made an offering of a dove to Venus upon the altar. I prayed to Diana to provide me with strength, to Mercury to provide me with cunning, and to Venus to protect my heart. I recited the words of Geta's letter, which I had finally burned, lest Primus search my chambers and discover it. Cael flew erratically along the ceiling as the flames grew hotter. I shed my clothes and prostrated myself in front of the statue, sweating in the stifling heat. "Purify me," I chanted. "Make me worthy of my request."

Two weeks later, I was awoken before dawn by a sharp knock on my door. I sat up as Primus entered my chamber, holding a lamp. "Get dressed," he said, before exiting abruptly. I quickly pulled on my stola and shawl and followed him into the dim corridor. As we approached the front door, I saw two Praetorian guards waiting.

"Fulvia Plautilla Augusta," said one. "You are to accompany us to Messana, on orders from Augustus himself."

"I understand," I said. I dared not ask which Augustus it was. I looked at Primus, who watched with a quizzical look. "I will return soon," I said, almost believing it. Just then, a dark shape appeared in the corridor and flew through the doors. It was Cael, who landed upon my shoulder. I turned back to the guards. "My bird will accompany me," I said, with more bravado than I felt.

"Of course," said the other guard. "Quickly now." I knew then that these men were loyal to Geta. I followed them quickly to one of the smaller *liburna* ships, designed to ferry cargo and passengers quickly along the coast. As I turned to look back, Primus remained on the dock, watching us pull anchor with a shrewd look on his face. I felt uneasy, but there was little I could do except trust that Geta would protect me.

The wind felt cool against my face as we sailed into the sunrise. Cael rode the breeze above, swooping toward the deck of the ship before rising again. I clutched my shawl around my shoulders despite the heat, unsure of what to expect. I was too nervous to eat or drink. As we sailed, I thought of the ship that had brought Mother, Gaius, and I to Sicilia so long ago. Was it out there in the distance, ferrying more terrified exiles away from Rome's shores? Did Geta understand the risk of my undertaking this journey? Would Primus alert Antoninus?

I closed my eyes, trying to crowd out the jumble of unpleasant thoughts that swirled in my head. Instead, I called forth the memory of Geta's face, the way his cheeks dimpled when he smiled. My fingers longed to run through the curls of his hair. I would be seeing him soon, perhaps even before the day was done. Opening my eyes, I almost shouted in relief. Two swallows were flying near us, their wings flapping in synchrony with the rolling waves. It was as positive an auspice as any.

We arrived in Messana close to dusk and anchored the liburna in a small bay to the west of the harbor. My legs were unsteady beneath my feet as I was escorted to a lectica, the first I had ridden in since leaving the city years ago. I peeked out of the curtains as I was quickly carried toward a large villa located at the edge of the hills overlooking the bay. The road leading to the gates was guarded by dozens of soldiers holding torches as we approached. "Open up, in the name of Publius Septimius Geta Augustus!" one shouted, and then we were inside.

I was escorted from the lectica as Cael flew to my shoulder, and we were led upstairs, where several female slaves awaited.

"Domina Plautilla, we have arranged for you to bathe and refresh yourself while Augustus is occupied. This way."

It took a few moments for me to respond, as I was gaping at the ornate frescoes on the ceiling of the massive villa, like a peasant. It was overwhelming, being suddenly thrust back into the opulence of imperial life. "Thank you," I said, finally remembering my manners. "I am grateful for this courtesy." I donned the invisible mantle of Augusta once again and followed them to the baths.

After I enjoyed a light meal, I spent the next two hours luxuriating in fragrant water, allowing the slaves to scrape, clean, and anoint me properly. Cael splashed his wings in a bowl of cool water as I soaked. My hands were softened, and my nails were shaped. Sweet-smelling oil was rubbed onto my clean skin. The women trimmed, combed, and braided my hair, and a beautiful stola of deep green was provided for me to wear. Finally, the slaves presented me with a gold necklace that bore an emerald pendant. I gasped at the size of it. It felt heavy against my chest as it lay between the valley of my breasts. I viewed my reflection in the glass the slaves held up for me and did not recognize myself. Who was this creature staring back at me? Some days I still felt like a little girl, and on others I felt as exhausted as an ancient, but the glass revealed a beautiful woman. Were the gods playing tricks on me?

I was led to an enclosed garden, where torches illuminated a table placed next to a fountain. It was laden with fresh fruit and a pitcher of wine. Cael landed upon the table and snatched a strawberry before fluttering to a high alcove under the eaves to enjoy his prize. I sat down as a slave poured wine into my goblet before discreetly vanishing back to the kitchens. The garden was silent save for the sound of trickling water. I sipped my wine and closed my eyes in pleasure at the taste. I was momentarily in heaven, and I sighed deeply, letting my cares drift away for the moment.

"It's perfect, is it not?"

My eyes flew open. Geta was standing by the fountain, smiling down at me. He was dressed in a deep purple toga, the color of royalty. His curls bore gold laurels, and his wrists and hands were covered in gold cuffs. Each finger held a gold ring with a different gemstone. His face was covered in powder, making his skin appear almost alabaster in the torchlight. Beneath the finery, I observed how gaunt he was. His kohl-rimmed eyes looked haunted. I stood so quickly I nearly knocked over the wine. "It's really you," I gasped, and I threw my arms around him in an embrace. Geta's arms encircled my waist, and he squeezed me so tightly I could feel his heart beating against my chest.

Finally, we broke apart and took in each other's appearances. Geta reached forward, his long fingers lifting the emerald pendant nestled between my breasts before dropping it gently. "Emerald is Venus' gemstone," he murmured. "I had to honor my Augusta appropriately."

"It's beautiful, Geta. Thank you. But you didn't need to go to all this trouble."

Geta laughed, as his fingers moved to caress my cheek. "Of course I did. I have so much to make up for. Are you hungry?" He gestured to the table. "A feast has been prepared, if you want it. Any delicacy you could name, I will get it for you." He reached for his goblet and gulped the wine down in one swallow.

I placed my hand gently over his. "Let's talk, Geta. Tell me everything."

* * *

We talked deep into the night. Geta told me about Britannia

and the campaign, how Antoninus had slowly but surely assumed more power by securing the loyalty of the legions, and how he suspected that his brother had even tried to hasten Severus' death. Several advisors felt the same, hence the need to influence a feeble Severus to appoint Geta as co-Augustus. In the end, it was Julia Domna who had convinced the emperor, as she knew that it would be the only way to stop Antoninus from assassinating his father. "Antoninus and I do not speak anymore. We have taken up residence in separate areas of the palace. My brother has become obsessed with Alexander the Great. He thinks only of starting another war in the east, and conquering Parthia in some grotesque homage to Alexander's legacy." Geta grimaced, running his fingers along the edge of his wine goblet. "I have proposed a solution; that I rule the eastern portion of the empire and Caracalla rules the west. Mother opposes it." He signaled to the slaves to bring more wine.

"Caracalla?" I asked. I remembered Geta referring to Antoninus with this term when Father had died.

"It is the nickname he goes by now in the legions. It has to do with the long Gallic cloak he now wears." Geta waited until the slave replaced the wine jug with a fresh one and then dismissed him with a flick of his hand. "It suits him, for it's as base as he is." He poured more wine for us both.

"If Antoninus rules the west, does that include Sicilia?" I asked, fear rising in the back of my throat.

"Unfortunately, it does, my love. But it is the only way to prevent an expensive and unnecessary war with Parthia. But as I said, Mother opposes it. Therefore, it won't happen." Geta set the jug down with a thump, sloshing wine over its gilded edge.

I sipped from my refilled cup again, but I no longer found pleasure from the taste. I grew more terrified each with each revelation of Antoninus' behavior. I had always been somewhat fearful of my husband, but I had never imagined he would try to kill his father. My fingers gripped Geta's hand tightly. "Are you in danger, my love?" I asked softly.

Geta shook his head, but the tension visible in the muscles of his neck betrayed his words. "No. Mother would never allow it. I will not be cowed by Antoninus' madness. I am Augustus, and the rightful heir to the empire. The Senate is with me. I have worked long to establish alliances there. Antoninus is a tyrant, and he will drive Rome into the ground. I cannot let that happen."

"What do you mean?" I asked, alarmed. "Surely you cannot attempt to kill him yourself!" This was madness, and what I had always feared. "Geta, please, you cannot, for it is too dangerous."

"I have no choice, Plautilla, I must do what is right. It is the only way we can be truly free. Once Antoninus is dead, I will declare you as the rightful Augusta again. I will marry you at the Temple of Jupiter, in front of all of Rome. I will give you as many children as you want. I will give you everything." Geta slid from his chair to the ground and placed his head into my lap. "I will worship you," he whispered. "Please, let me worship you, my love."

My fingers wound into the curls of his hair, feeling the softness they had longed to touch for so long. Slowly, I lifted the laurels from his head and placed them on the table. "Come worship me then," I whispered. Geta nuzzled the valley between my thighs as I threw my head back and gazed up at the stars.

Geta's chamber was located just off the garden facing the back of the villa, away from prying eyes and ears. Once inside we undressed each other silently, drinking in the sight of shoulders, bellies, and finally sexes as they were revealed. The moonlight illuminated our bodies as we leisurely coupled, drawing out the act as much as we could. Geta's hands glided over my newly smooth skin as I kissed the powder from his face. The emerald bounced against my sternum in time with his deepening thrusts. Our foreheads touched as we moaned into each other's mouths. I was lost in exquisite bliss, yet my heart felt heavy, for it was bittersweet. The impish boy I had fallen in love with had transformed into something new, as if a wild eagle had been forced into a gilded cage and sprouted bejeweled wings that were too heavy to fly. "How I have missed this," Geta panted against my throat. "I have missed your sweetness, dear Plautilla." He began to lose control, moving faster as we clasped hands, until he cried out.

Afterward, we lay tangled together, our skin cooling in the soft air. The smell of night jasmine floated in from the hillside. I offered a silent prayer of thanks to Venus for granting us this moment in time. "When do you need to return?" I asked, my head pressed against his heart.

"Not yet," he said.

He played with my hair as I drifted off to sleep. I dreamt of Palatine Hill. In my dream, I was looking for someone. Was it Father? Cael? I entered my old cubicula and found Hortensia sleeping in my bed. I gathered her into my arms and ran frantically through the halls, seeking a way out of the palace. The hallways grew longer and dimmer as I desperately searched for the doorway to the outside. Just as I saw the glimmer of sunshine ahead, a wolf stepped into the doorway and bared its teeth.

I jerked myself awake, my skin chilly with sweat. Geta was asleep, snoring softly with his mouth open. I sat up and hugged my arms around myself. Despite Geta's assurances, I knew we were in danger. We had been too unguarded in front of others. Primus, Aurelia, the crew members of the ship, they all knew or suspected. If Geta did not kill Antoninus, we would never be safe. Yet I feared that the act of killing his brother would curse him and our love for each other. I shivered violently, waking Geta. He sat up and wrapped his arms around me. "What is it?" he asked gently.

"We should flee," I said. "Just the two of us. Let Antoninus have Rome."

"He would never stop looking for us," Geta said flatly, and my heart sank, for I knew this to be true. "Do you trust me?" he asked softly.

"Yes," I said. "But I do not trust your mother to protect you."

Geta laughed darkly then. "But our family is so loving." I wanted to cry at the ragged sound of pain in his voice. Instead, I burrowed into him once again.

* * *

We stayed in bed for the better part of the next day. The slaves placed food outside Geta's door, and we dined and bathed in privacy between bouts of coupling. Cael remained in the garden, stealing fruit from us. For a hazy day and night, we banished the rest of the world. Both of us were desperate to conceive, as if an unborn child in my belly would protect us instead of making us more vulnerable. In the end, our time together was too short. Geta was called back to Palatine Hill

236

on urgent business, and I needed to return to Drepanum and satisfy Primus' insatiable greed.

After a final bath together, I placed the heavy rings back on Geta's fingers, one by one. I then slowly removed the emerald from around my neck and placed it into his hand.

"Don't you want to keep it?" he asked.

"You know I cannot," I said softly, rising on my toes to kiss him between his eyelids. "Save it for me to wear when we see each other again, whenever that may be."

"I will try to send for you before the end of the year, my love. We will see each other again, I swear to it." Geta lifted my hands and kissed them gently. "Cast an auspice, you'll see."

"The gods will not let me see you," I whispered. "And I would not cast one even if they did." What I could not say was that I was afraid of what they would reveal. "I want you to know—" I began, but Geta silenced me with a finger pressed firmly against my lips.

"No last words, Plautilla. We shall see each other again."

I nodded, not wanting to upset him. Instead, I placed my hand over my heart, and Geta did the same, mirroring me. After a final moment, he called for the slaves to escort me to my lectica. As I began the bumpy journey to the bay, my last sight of Geta was of him standing at the window, stealing a glimpse of me from the shadows.

The liburna sailed back to Drepanum in a day. Traveling west was more difficult, as the ship battered against the current. This time, Cael remained close, his talons gripping the railing next to my fingers. "I'm sorry, little one," I said, though I did not know what I was sorry for. I licked my lips, salty from the sea spray. I missed the sweetness of Geta's tongue upon them. His absence was like a physical pain. *Soon,*

I thought. *He swore it would be soon.*

Could I truly be an Augusta again? Surely, Palatine Hill would be more pleasurable if I no longer needed to fear Antoninus or worry about my family. Yet a part of me knew it was folly. Julia Domna would never forgive me, and the half of Rome who followed Antoninus would seek revenge. The cycle of violence would continue, and Geta and I would most likely be poisoned or stabbed within a year. If we conceived, our child would not live to see adulthood. It saddened me to realize that Geta could not see this, and because of it, that we could never truly be together.

My wish was for Geta to forsake the laurels, but I knew he never would. He would never enjoy the simple pleasures of gathering fresh eggs, still warm from the nest, or walking barefoot in a shallow stream. He was too much a creature of comfort. We were fated to love in stolen moments, hiding our true selves from the rest of the world. This realization made me want to cast myself from the ship. Why couldn't I live the life I wanted with the man I wanted by my side? The gods were capricious indeed.

XVII.

It was raining in Drepanum when I finally stepped onto the dock after midnight. I followed Primus' guards back to the barracks and fell into a dreamless sleep. The rain continued for days, soaking the western slopes and causing mud and debris to tumble from the hills into the sea. I huddled under a blanket, listening to the pounding of the raindrops against the window. I felt drained and unwell after my journey. At least Primus couldn't demand auspices when it was impossible to see more than an arm's length in front of one's face. The birds had all taken shelter, like Cael and me. It felt as if the gods were lashing out at us. Sailors tried to prevent the ships from slamming into each other, and the roads filled with rushing water, sweeping away everything in its path.

Eventually, the sun returned, and Cael and I traveled back to the temple to cast my first auspice of the new month. I sought Primus out to see what query he had for that morning, but he had taken leave of the city for a few days. I rode with the guards to the top of the hill and entered the temple, setting some soldiers to work in sweeping out the water that had leaked onto the floor. Stepping out onto the portico, I gazed at the city and coastline below, dazzlingly bright in the late autumn sun. My mind was clear as I stepped to the ledge, feeling the sunshine upon my face. I closed my eyes, enjoying the sensation of the warmth on my cheeks.

Behind me, I heard a sound: *croak*. For a moment, I thought it was Cael. I heard the sound again, followed by *caw caw*. I opened my eyes to find Cael fluttering in front of the columns of the portico, appearing in distress. "What is it?" I asked, when a dark shaped streaked from behind and launched itself at Cael. It was an enormous raven, its wings battered and torn, slashing at Cael with its large beak. Screaming, I ran down the steps and tried to swat at it. The commotion drew the attention of two soldiers who hurriedly drew their swords. "No!" I shouted. "You'll hurt both!" Cael fought back, hopping away and swooping above, trying to get the advantage, but the larger bird was relentless. I tried to step in again, but Cael himself flapped his wings at me to stay back.

For some reason, the memory of the raven I had spoken to the morning I had observed the augurs at their auguraculum came to mind. I crossed my arms and stamped my foot. "That is enough!" I commanded. The raven paused its attack, swiveling to look at me. It emitted another bellicose *croak*. Of course, it was not the same raven as the one I had spoken to ten years earlier. And yet, it felt like the same bird. "Have you learned nothing?" I asked, holding out my hand. I held my breath as Cael escaped, flying in a raggedy line into the interior of the temple. The raven croaked again and then hopped toward me. Its coloring was dull, and its wings were missing several feathers. This bird was hungry and desperate. "Come," I said. "You can rest here. Come." I knelt, stretching my hand out even farther.

The raven took another step toward me, when the soldier's blade severed its head right at my feet. I fell backward; my hand pressed against my mouth. Blood pooled out of the carcass of the bird as the head gazed up with dead eyes at the sky. "What have you done?" I asked, but the soldier had already moved on. I suddenly felt a chill, despite the sun. I staggered to my feet and went inside to tend to Cael. I found him hiding behind the statue, agitated and hopping about. Mercifully, he did not appear to be gravely injured. Later, as we left to begin the journey back down to the shore, we passed the raven, still lying in the dirt. Its head was covered in flies.

That night, I dreamt of the villa above Panormus. As my family slept, hundreds of ravens landed on the roof, until it was a sea of black feathers. I was outside, trying to shoo them off with a broom. As I did so, I heard a wolf's howl in the distance. I startled awake and sat up in bed, gasping. Cael squawked softly, and I realized he was perched on my pillow. "Did you wake me?" I asked, my heart pounding. Danger was imminent; I felt it in every fiber of my being. Antoninus was coming. I did not care about my own life, but I could not bear to think of any harm coming to Gaius and his family. I needed to get to the villa as soon as I could. I quickly dressed and opened the door. The garrison was unusually silent. Where were the night guards? Why were no slaves in the kitchen? Something was very wrong.

I had earned a few coins from casting auspices for the local folk, and I hurriedly snatched my purse and exited the barracks. "Cael, come," I called as I ran to the docks. I approached several fishermen who were about to cast off for the day. "Please," I said. "I need to find someone to take me to Panormus. I have payment." I held up my small bag of sestertii.

A fisherman pointed to the far edge of the dock. "Good

morning, priestess. We cannot help you, but the shipmaster has horses." Thanking them, I set off and quickly arranged for a ride with the shipmaster's stable hand, using up all my coins. Soon we were galloping in the hills above Drepanum as the rising sun turned the sky orange ahead of us. *Hurry*, I thought, and I prayed to Venus that I was not too late. We reached the villa before midday, Cael leading the way. I thanked the man profusely and asked him to wait. Entering the doorway, I called out. "Gaius! Aurelia! Hortensia!" but no one responded. I rushed to the kitchen but saw no evidence of a struggle. The fire in the hearth was burning, and plates were on the table. Where had everyone gone?

I ran to the front of the villa and scanned the horizon above. Suddenly I spied several figures on the farthest hillside. They were working in the vineyard, as it was time to harvest the grapes. I turned to the horseman and pointed. "Take me there!" The sound of our hoofbeats drew the attention of Gaius, who raised his hand in greeting. His face registered surprise when he recognized me, and he handed a basket of grapes to a slave and hurried to greet us. "Plautilla? What brings you here?"

I dismounted the horse and ran to him, hugging him fiercely. "Are you all right? Is everyone all right?"

"Yes, what is it? What happened?" The others were hurrying to us. Aurelia was frowning, and I marked her growing belly. I was happy for her, but there was no time to congratulate them. I saw Hortensia scurry out from under a vine and run toward Cael, clapping her hands with delight. I grabbed Gaius so fiercely my nails left marks in his arm. "You need to flee," I said. "Now."

A short while later we huddled in the kitchen. It was just the three of us, as I had beseeched that we speak in private. Gaius ordered the slaves to tend to the horseman, and Aurelia asked Hortensia to collect eggs. "Don't go far," I begged, wringing my hands. Cael chirped and flew with her and I exhaled in relief. I quickly told them of the strange auspice with the raven and my corresponding dream. As I spoke, my heart sank, for it was clear that they thought I was mad.

Aurelia gave Gaius a look, and my brother took a deep breath, trying to placate me. "It was just a dream, Plautilla," he said reasonably. "We are not in danger. As you can see, we are fine. More than fine. We are expecting another child in the spring yet again. Hortensia cannot wait to play with it." He squeezed Aurelia's hand and she smiled weakly. I knew then what I had to say to convince them.

"Aurelia," I said. "This child is in danger. I have foreseen it."

"Stop it, Plautilla," she scolded, but her hand covered her belly reflexively.

"Please," I begged again. "You must listen. Antoninus is coming, and if he finds me here, he will burn this villa to the ground, and everyone in it. You must flee. Please. His anger knows no bounds."

Aurelia's face turned red. "If this is true, then why have you come? Why did you bring this evil to our door?" Gaius tried to place a calming hand on her shoulder, but she shrugged him off.

"Because he knows you are here," I said. "He will destroy everyone I love first, to punish me, before heading to Drepanum."

Gaius frowned. "Why do you think this, Plautilla?" he asked.

"You know why," Aurelia hissed. "She has cuckolded him with his own brother. Everyone knows this."

I almost vomited at her words. I turned on Aurelia, my fear morphing into anger. "Everyone knows? Who is everyone?"

"She doesn't deny it," snapped Aurelia. Behind her, Hortensia stumbled into the kitchen, her smile quickly vanishing at the tone of her mother's harsh words.

"Please—" attempted Gaius.

"I read his letter!" shouted Aurelia, triumphant. "I read the filth he wrote to you. I wrote to Father, to let him know—" Her words were cut off as I slapped her hard across the face. Aurelia lifted her hand up to her cheek as Gaius stared at me in shock. I was so angry I could barely speak. At least I saw that Gaius finally understood the grave danger they were in. My cheeks burned hot, but there was no time to feel ashamed.

"It's true," I said. "Geta wrote of his love to me. I traveled to meet him in Messana. Antoninus must have received word of it. I swear to you brother, I never intended for you to be in any danger—"

"Because you only think of yourself!" screamed Aurelia. "You have destroyed our life! You have destroyed our home!"

"A home I worked to build!" I shouted back; my hands balled into fists. Gaius tried to pull Aurelia back, in vain.

"A home tainted by your lies! By your behavior! Witch! Whore!" Aurelia was seething now, both hands clasping her belly. Her words cut me to the bone, but I had no time to grieve. I heard a sniffle and saw Hortensia was crying. I forced myself to remain calm.

"Gaius," I said, ignoring Aurelia, "You must send Aurelia to Panormus. Cornelius will find someone to ferry her to Leptis Magna. Send Hortensia with her. Use every coin you have. Free the slaves, or they will be killed. Do this at once. I will stay behind. I am not afraid." Suddenly, I felt the force of Hortensia nearly knocking me over. She hugged my legs with all her might. "Please don't go," she cried. "Please, Plautilla, please."

Fighting back tears, I knelt and cupped her sweet face with my hands. "I'm not going," I whispered. "You are. On a grand adventure."

* * *

Gaius was angry, but he did as I asked. We paid the horseman with nearly 100 sestertii, and he rode down the mountain with Aurelia. Hortensia accompanied them on the donkey, which also bore a bundle of possessions. The slaves scurried about, grabbing whatever they could before fleeing. Gaius retrieved the few gold coins he had hidden and sewed them into the inside pocket of his tunic. My heart was heavy, recalling our family's journey from Rome to Sicilia. I prayed that Cornelius could help us. The plan was for him to arrange passage for Aurelia and Hortensia first, and then Gaius separately, so that they would not be marked as a family.

"Cornelius will find a way," I said. "Our family has been very good to him."

"We'll see," said Gaius. Without another word, he stalked off to the vineyard and sat for a short while, marking the setting sun. I stood in front of the villa, anxiously watching the sky turn from pink, to purple, to blue. Once the sun finally dipped below the horizon, Gaius stood and took one last look around before descending the hill back to me.

"I was never a good winemaker, but I came to truly love this place," he said sadly. I felt a stab of shame for causing my brother so much pain.

"Will you be all right?" I asked.

"Yes," he said. "I will be there by morning. I know how

to hide if I encounter any riders. We will write to Lucius once it is safe. I hope you are right, Plautilla, for what has happened cannot be undone. But with all my heart, I hope you are wrong." My younger brother looked down at me, and for a moment, I saw Mother in him.

I took his hand. "I am not wrong," I said. "I'm so sorry, Gaius."

Gaius sighed. "Why, Plautilla?" He said no more, but I knew what he meant.

"For love," I said.

Gaius shook his head, then squeezed my hand and set off down the hill. I stood and watched him retreat back for as long as I could.

By nightfall, the air grew chilly. I stoked the fire and waited with Cael in the kitchen. A strange calm overtook me. I must have dozed off, for I woke to the dying fire and moonlight filling the room. Gathering my shawl, I stepped outside and observed the giant full moon, illuminating the hillside above. It was almost as bright as day, and the grass turned silvery in the light. Despite everything, I gasped at the beauty. It was a small gift from the gods.

My steps carried me eventually toward Mother's grave, and I knelt and cleaned some fallen detritus from her stone marker. "Do you understand why?" I whispered. The breeze was my only response.

A short while later I felt the vibration on the ground, and I knew they were coming. "Come," I said to Cael. I walked to the front of the villa and waited. Soon they appeared, a good forty Praetorians, holding torches. I was not surprised to find Primus leading them. He rode up to me and dismounted. We regarded each other suspiciously. "So that is where you went,"

I remarked as calmly as I could.

Primus bowed his head mockingly. "My apologies for my absence, *Augusta*. I went to inform Antoninus that his brother sought your company," he sneered. "He found it most interesting." Behind him, soldiers dismounted and began holding their torches to the eaves of the barn. Several ran inside, and I heard the cacophony of crashing plates and furniture. Flames were soon visible through the door. I held myself still, though I was terrified. I feared they would burn me alive in the villa, but they ignored me as they proceeded to destroy the vineyard. Eventually, a captain marched up to Primus. "Admiral, there is no one here," he reported.

Primus turned to me. "Where are they?" he snarled.

I shrugged my shoulders. "They left days ago. They turned away from me. I was no longer suitable enough to live with them, according to their morals." It was close enough to the truth that I hoped it would fool them.

Primus gestured to the captain nodded. "Ride to Panormus. Find them. A man, woman, and a girl." The captain nodded and whistled, and half the Praetorians quickly took to their horses and thundered down the mountain. The walls of the villa began to collapse. Out of the corner of my eye, I spied Cael, hiding high above on a branch nearby. The soldiers had attempted to light the tree on fire, but the wood was green, smoking instead of catching into flames. Primus marched over to me and gripped my arm, dragging me to his horse. I winced from the pain.

"Where are you taking me?" I gasped.

"You'll see," Primus jeered. "A place where you can talk to all the birds you'll ever want."

* * *

We rode hard through the night, reaching Drepanum at sunrise. I did not see Cael, but I clung to the hope that he was following us. Primus rode straight to the docks and dismounted, pulling me off the horse and dragging me behind him. Several of the fisherman watched as I was roughly shoved onto a liburna. My hands were bound, and I stumbled and fell, hitting my knee on the deck. I bit my lip to keep from crying out. One of the sailors tied my hands to the railing. As the ship pulled anchor, I watched the dock recede as Primus stepped to the edge. "All hail, Imperator Caesar Marcus Aurelius Severus Antoninus Pius Augustus!" he called out. The Praetorians shouted and raised their swords. If the situation were not so grave, I might have laughed at the sight of this small man basking in glory that was not his. I glanced over at the knot of fishermen, who said nothing.

The harbor was soon behind us, and we set sail for the open sea. At first, I thought we were heading to the islands that lay to the west, but we sailed past them, tacking north and then east. I tried not to struggle, but the constant rolling of the waves chafed the ropes around my wrists. Eventually, a chain of islands appeared in the distance. These were much smaller, and I saw that one bore the smoke of a volcano at its peak, rising to meet the clouds. The liburna tacked left, and soon we approached the middle island. It also featured steep mountains and a narrow, rocky shoreline. Unlike Sicilia, I could see no evidence of civilization. Before I knew what was happening, the rope holding my hands was cut, and a sailor hoisted me up onto the railing. "Welcome to Lipara," he said, before casting me into the water.

XVIII.

I reached the shoreline, gagging and spitting out seawater. Wringing out my stola, I sat on the jagged stones to rest. The sun blazed overhead as I tried to take in my surroundings. My mouth was parched, and thirst was nearly driving me mad. I looked around for a cave, or any source of fresh water, but saw none. I knew I had to find water quickly, or I would die.

I forced myself to climb, knowing that I needed to be farther from the sea. The endless expanse of water tortured me, so I didn't look at it, only looking a few paces ahead as I scratched my way upward through the scrub. I don't know why I didn't just lie down and surrender myself to the gods. Clearly, I would never see Geta again. Yet something stubborn in me refused to give up. Perhaps it was spite. I refused to surrender to Antoninus and Primus, who thought my life was theirs to control. As I climbed, the terrain grew steeper and cactuses appeared. I was practically crawling by then, whispering to myself to keep going.

After what felt like hours, I collapsed near a large stone and dozed off in the heat. I woke up to a strange sound. Unable to place it, I succumbed to torpor again. The sound returned; sharp and buzzing. For a moment, I thought it was the sound of bees, but then I realized it was the chattering of birds. I sat up and listened. There seemingly was a flock of birds nearby, chittering to each other. Perhaps they were near water. Slowly, I began to crawl again and saw a slight dip ahead and what looked like bushes. The land leveled off, and I stood to see a tree with large yellow fruit. I staggered forward and grabbed one off the branch, tearing it open and sucking it desperately. To my surprise, it was a lemon, though it was larger than my hand. I devoured several of them, until my thirst was quenched and my stomach roiled with acid.

I sat down underneath the tree and took stock of my surroundings. The sun was beginning to set, turning the sky a deep fiery red. I noted several trees in the grove that continued along the slope of the hillside. My thirst had been abated for now. But I would soon need food, and shelter. The chittering returned, and I looked up to see a flock of tiny birds landing in the tree, calling to each other. "Thank you," I said them. I then lumbered to standing and tried to figure out where I was.

The peak of the mountain rose above, but the grove spread out along a narrow gully that led somewhat to the northeast. I decided to follow this route in hopes that I could glimpse a view of the other side of the island. I took a lemon in each hand and set off, walking as quickly as I could in my still-damp shoes. I did not want to be exposed after nightfall, for I did not know what sort of creatures roamed these wild hills. The thought of creatures made me realize Cael's absence for the first time since I had left Drepanum. I nearly sank to my knees, worried that the connection between us had been severed. The little bird had been my constant companion for nearly a decade. Not having him near me was like losing a part of myself. I prayed to Diana to guide him to me.

The sun dipped below the horizon, and it grew eerily quiet,

save for the sound of the wind. I slowed my pace, afraid I would stumble off the mountainside. My head was faint with hunger, and I was thirsty again. I looked at the lemons but couldn't bring myself to eat any more. I was going to need to find a place to rest when it got too dark. The gully began to rise, and I turned the bend to see what appeared to be the wall of a villa. It was hard to tell in the dim light. I crept forward, unsure if there were people about. As I approached the structure, I heard music. Stopping short, I strained my ears. Was someone playing the lyre? It was now almost completely dark. "Hello?" I called out. No one answered.

I felt my way along the wall and found a round doorway with no door. Carefully, I stepped inside. The musical sound grew louder. I took a tentative step forward and almost fell straight into a hot plunge bath. Staggering backward, I crouched down and carefully felt the warm water with my fingers. Wind whistled along the windows of what I determined to be a *caldarium*, a hot water bathing chamber. There weren't any adjoining rooms, so this hot water must have been from a natural spring. It seemed to have been abandoned long ago.

The breeze blew again, and the musical sound returned, an echo from the wind blowing through the chamber. This was a sacred place. I placed the lemons along the edge of the pool as an offering before reciting a prayer of thanks to the gods for this gift of shelter. I then cupped handfuls of water from the pool to drink. I curled up next to the wall, feeling the mountain's thermal heat rise from the stone. I fell almost immediately into a deep sleep.

* * *

Hunger woke me. I was curled into a ball, clutching my belly. I couldn't remember the last time I had eaten. One of the lemons was floating in the water, and I lifted it out with shaking hands. I closed my eyes and prayed to Diana for guidance. Perhaps I could snare a rabbit or catch a fish. The thought of walking down to the beach almost overcame me, and I started to cry. Sorrow bubbled up from deep within my soul. I did not fear death, but loneliness I could not bear. Even when I had been trapped in Drepanum, I'd had Cael for companionship and had been able to cling to the hope of seeing Geta again. Now I had no one, and the feeling of loss was overwhelming.

Eventually, I wiped the tears from my face. If anyone was going to help me, it would have to be myself. I may die of hunger or thirst, but I would die fighting to survive. I came up with a plan: I would continue to walk farther, listening for birds. Hopefully they would guide me to more fruit trees. After that, I would look for rabbit holes. I tried to remember how Gaius had built the snares. I would need to find a plant stalk to create one.

I set off, and the gods blessed me almost immediately. Ahead, I could see several trees bearing red fruit. Stumbling closer, I plucked one off a branch with my fingers and shoved it into my mouth. It was a strawberry. I almost gasped in surprise. I proceeded to eat my fill, until my fingers were stained red with their juice. Glancing up at the mountainside, I saw several strawberry trees. I knew their fruit would bring animals, so I found a vantage point nearby to observe what creatures visited.

Over the next hour, I saw jays, sparrows, hummingbirds, doves, and a few brown mice that scurried up tree trunks before darting back into the earth. There weren't any mammals worth catching, so I decided to continue toward the far side of the island to see if there were any people. Someone had built that caldarium, long ago. Perhaps some of their descendants remained. As I continued along the path, the eastern side of Lipara fully came into view. Between my vantage point and the northernmost mountain range lay a series of structures situated on the hills overlooking a narrow bay. The structures converged into a town at the base of the hill, hemmed in by a massive fortress at the edge of the water. I almost shouted for joy. Surely, someone would help me. I set off, eager to reach the settlement as soon as possible.

I looked back to mark the path from which I had traveled, as I wanted to ensure that I could find the caldarium and trees again. As I did so, what appeared to be a dark wave rose from behind the hillside. It was as if the mouth of the mountain opened and a black cloud poured out, but it was not smoke. Suddenly, I realized it was a massive flock of crows, the most I had ever seen. I stood awestruck as they circled and flew in a gyre high above, cawing at each other. I raised my arms and called out to them. "Cael!" I shouted, daring to hope. "Cael! I am here!" The crows shrilled in response, but Cael did not appear. I watched as they migrated toward the sea before turning back to the village.

As I trudged on, the path began to descend. The first domus I came upon was empty. One of its walls was cracked, and the fireplace had collapsed into rubble. The next domus was still intact but also devoid of people. It was barely more than a hovel, with a firepit in the center and some odd chairs placed in various corners. Deciding that this one might be hospitable, I made a small mark with a stone against the front wall and continued on.

I had almost reached the village when I came across two children chasing each other. They looked a bit older than Hortensia. The boy stopped and stared at me with wide eyes, and the girl hid behind him. I smiled and knelt, realizing I must look like a *manes*, or dead spirit, to them. "Good morning," I said softly. "I am lost. Is your mother or father home?"

At first, I wondered if they did not understand me, but the boy shook his head. "No," he whispered. The little girl ducked behind him, shading her eyes from me.

"Oh," I said, trying to be as non-threatening as I could. I smoothed my hair away from my face. "I am very hungry, do you think I could have some bread?"

The boy shook his head and took a step back. "We don't have any," he said. I noticed they were both thin for their age. This was not an island of plenty. I closed my eyes, fighting dizziness. Behind my eyelids the image came of a hen. I opened them and smiled again.

"Do you have hens?" The boy nodded, and the girl smiled shyly. I direct my next question at her. "Do you have a favorite?"

After some coaxing, they led me to a makeshift pen behind a small barn where a few raggedy hens were pecking at the dirt. I held out my hand as the birds came to investigate. The children watched carefully as I smoothed their feathers and talked soothingly to them. "They are good birds," I said. "Do they lay eggs often?" I reached down and picked up the lightest-colored one. "Something tells me this one lays blue eggs." The children looked at each other in surprise, and the boy nodded. "What is her name?"

"Iubar," the girl answered softly.

"That's a beautiful name," I said. I stroked the hen's neck feathers, and the bird trilled contentedly. After a few minutes, I placed her back down, and she clucked before settling at my feet. The children looked at each other again, sharing a silent signal. The girl then slipped into the barn and returned with a blue egg in each hand, which she handed to me carefully. They were still warm. "Sometimes she lays more than one," she said.

I held them in my palms as if they were the most precious gold. "Thank you," I said solemnly. The children watched as I cracked the tip of each shell and drank the contents, trying not to gag. My stomach roiled once again but I felt my strength returning. I looked at the blue shells in my hands as the children watched warily. "My name is Plautilla," I said. "I will bless these birds, so that they lay more eggs for you and your family. I will ask Vesta to bless your home with abundance." I placed the shells upon a stone near the edge of the pen and plucked a few nearby flowers to present as an offering. Closing my eyes, I prayed: *Vesta, bless this home. Diana, reward this generosity threefold.*

I plucked another flower and gave it to the girl, bowing my head in gratitude. "This white flower is called Myrtus. It is sacred. If you burn it to create smoke, the gods will be pleased. I will be in the house at the very top of the hill. Perhaps you will visit me if the gods provide for you." I pointed toward the direction from which I had come. "Thank you again." The children nodded before scurrying off.

Walking farther, I passed through the remains of the village. There was very little to see, save a few sheep on the hillside and a stray goat braying in the distance. Most of the houses were abandoned. I approached the fortress warily, unwilling to encounter any legions or navy boats, but it seemed deserted as well. I carefully picked my way onto the beach, where I saw a few women repairing fishing nets and some boats in the distance. As I stepped closer, I realized they were cutting oysters from thick ropes. The women looked up at me but did not stop working. The brackish smell was overpowering.

"Who are you?" asked one.

"My name is Plautilla. I was brought here as punishment," I said, unsure of what else to say. It was the truth at least.

The woman grunted as if she were unsurprised. "Everyone has to work here. Take a knife." She indicated a low bench near the edge of their circle. I sat down, and before I knew it, a sharp knife and bowl of oysters were handed to me. The women showed me how to slice them from the thick rope and pack them tightly together in jugs of cool water. It was dirty and difficult work, but I slowly improved, shucking dozens before the boats returned and brought more. We worked in silence until one of the younger ones sat up and drank deeply from a jug, then handed it to me. I drank the watered-down wine gratefully, wiping my mouth with the back of my hand.

"Tell us why you are here," the young woman said. All eyes turned to me before moving back to their tasks. I thought about what to say—how could I make them understand what I was but not who I was?

Finally, I said, "I angered a powerful man, and he decided to banish me for it."

"Who was he?" asked the young woman.

"My husband," I said.

A silent ripple went through them, though of recognition or judgment I could not tell. I shucked with them until the sun was low on the horizon before departing back up the path, carrying a bucket of a few oysters and a small jug of water as my payment. I entered the marked domus on the top of the hill and set about trying to find something to sleep on.

A week passed. I journeyed to the beach every day to help the women prepare oysters and mussels for transport. Every morning, a boat traveled at sunrise from Lipara to the small port of Tyndaris to sell them at market. The women told me about the people who came to Lipara before the Punic Wars. Most bore Greek ancestry, though some were of African blood. The clusters of fishermen that dotted the northern and western coast of Sicilia and its islands to the north were all interrelated in some fashion. The Romans had defeated the Carthaginians and expanded the fortress that guarded the village from the sea, but the legions had departed long ago. All that remained were a handful of families who scratched a living from the land and the sea.

I was given a small knife of my own and a threadbare wool shawl to keep me warm. The next day, I returned to the grove and cut down dozens of lemons, bringing them to the village for all to share. That evening, the two children I had met, Tycho and Assia, arrived to gather strawberries. Assia left me three eggs upon the doorstep of my new domus, and I took it as a sign that my prayer on behalf of their hens had been fruitful. Another week passed, and then two. I was no longer starving, but I felt trapped. I had no money to travel to Leptis Magna or even Sicilia. I could not even imagine seeking passage to Ostia or Rome. Even if I could see Geta, he would barely recognize me, thin with matted hair and wearing clothes that were quickly turning into rags.

Worst of all, the calls of the birds were distant on Lipara. My domus was near a ledge that allowed me to view nearly the entire eastern coastline of the island, but the birds did not show themselves. I sat there with my feet dangling over the slope in the mornings and evenings, scanning the skies for Cael, but I began to lose hope that I would see him again. At night, stoking the branches of a small fire, I huddled under my shawl and wondered where Geta was and if he knew of what Antoninus had done to me. Were the brothers quarreling? Were they plotting each other's deaths? I was desperate to know if Geta was safe. I wished I could write to him again, though I knew it was dangerous. But I longed to tell him I loved him one last time.

The next morning, I woke and ate the last of Assia's eggs that I had roasted in the fire. I gathered my shawl and stepped outside to relieve myself and watch the sun rise. As I approached the ledge, I noticed a small pile of red fruit. I knelt to inspect it. Someone or something had left a small mound of strawberries there for me. I stood up quickly and scanned the skies. "Cael?" I called, hopeful. "Cael!" I raised my arms, feeling the bracing sting of the wind against my cheeks.

Out of the corner of my eye, I saw two dark shapes swoop toward me from the roof of the caldarium. I stretched out my hands and Cael landed in my right palm, followed by another crow in my left. The little bird squawked and flapped his wings, fluttering up to my shoulder to nuzzle my neck. I was both laughing and crying as he did so. By some miracle of the gods, Cael had returned to me. After a few moments of joyous reunion, I turned to take in the second crow, which seemed to be waiting patiently. She was slightly larger than Cael, her feathers so shiny they appeared almost blue in the morning light. "Who is this?" I asked, utterly astonished. "Did you find a soulmate, little one?"

As if in answer, Cael launched skyward, and the second crow followed. I clapped in delight as they circled, floating on the breeze and calling to each other until they swooped onto the ledge and proceeded to devour the pile of berries at my feet. I sat down next to them and hugged my knees, crying again. I bowed my head and said a prayer of thanks to Diana for reuniting us. Once Cael and his mate had finished eating, they spent several minutes preening each other. I reached out and stroked Cael's sleek head, feeling the softness of his feathers. Cael tilted his head, then hopped backward and let out a soft *caw*. Suddenly, I understood. Cael was no longer mine. He had found a new life, one with a mate. He was no longer confined to a cage, villa, or temple. He was free.

My heart filled with sadness but also joy for this creature who had comforted me through so much of my life. "Very well, lovebirds. Come visit from time to time," I jested, but there was a lump in my throat. Cael fluffed his feathers in response. He then flew off toward the hillside, his mate by his side. As they passed over the hill, dozens of other crows took flight and joined them. I gazed in wonder at the black cloud forming before my eyes as it wound itself higher and higher in the distance. My skin prickled for the first time in over a month, and I suddenly understood what this auspice was telling me. The course of my future was mine alone to determine.

XIX.

Time seemed to lose meaning. My days were filled with the same routine: wake, eat, walk, work, walk, eat, sleep. I even stopped visiting the ledge, though it was near. I was so focused on staying warm and ensuring that there was enough food in my belly that I did not have the desire to take any auspices. One morning, I walked into the village and smelled something I had not for a very long time—warm bread. A long table had been placed in the small plaza next to the fortress. The women were placing bowls of steaming soup upon them, and a few families were gathering, bringing jars of olives or smoked fish to add to the feast. My mouth watered at the tantalizing smell. "What festival is this?" I asked one of the women. I felt guilty for being empty-handed, though I would not have been able to contribute much.

"We honor the *Lares* today, for it is the start of winter," she said. "We make offerings in our homes but come the sea to make an offering to the *Lares Permarini*."

My mind raced as I tried to determine what time of year the Lares festival fell. It was after Saturnalia, near the end of Decembris. No wonder I had been so melancholy; it was close to the darkest time of the year. I sat at the table and feasted on the rich, salty fish broth, mopping my bowl with coarse bread. I had a sudden memory of Mother baking sourdough with Aurelia in the kitchen of our villa and smiled. Later, the children led a small procession to the shore, and we tossed small clay figurines of the ancestral spirits into the sea so they would continue to guide our ships safely.

As we stood at the edge of the waves, dozens of seagulls landed on the water, diving and splashing loudly. A few landed on the tables, lifting bowls and plates to see if any food remained. "They think we throw our scraps away," said a fisherman. "We have eaten them all, you scavengers." The villagers laughed, but there was an undercurrent of desperation. These people had endured hard times near to the point of breaking. Something stirred within me, and I stepped forward until I was knee-deep in the waves. The others began to murmur behind me. "Plautilla, what are you doing?" asked a woman, but I did not heed her, as I stood in the water and lifted my arms. Closing my eyes, I asked the Lares to convey my message to the gulls: *lead these islanders to the fish, and you will feast as you never have.* The gulls began to screech, flapping their wings and taking to the skies.

The sound of their cries was deafening as they flew in circles barely above our heads, screeching and buzzing past us. Some of the children ran back to their cottages. As soon as it started, it was gone. I remained in the waves, wet to my waist now, and called after them. "Remember your promise!" I returned to the shore, ignoring the stares of the others as I walked directly up to the captain of the boat that traveled to Tyndaris. He regarded me suspiciously as my thin stola dripped water at his feet. "The birds will show you where to fish," I said. "Follow the birds, and you will receive the sea's bounty." With that, I walked all the way back up the hill to the caldarium to soak away the chill from my legs.

The next day, when the boats came in, the men were shouting at us. "Neptune himself has blessed us! Bring pails!" We gathered around and helped them unload dozens of fish. There were so many that we sent the children for more bowls to gather them all. A second boat returned with so many oysters that we worked until late in the afternoon. The mood was celebratory, as this bounty would ensure full bellies that evening. I reminded the villagers to keep their promise to the gulls. Each family laid out fish and mussels for the birds upon the beach, and hundreds of gulls, pelicans, and other fowl gathered for a raucous feast.

Over the next week, the catches continued to grow larger. The fisherman regarded me differently now, bowing their heads in respect as I received my portion of the catch from the boat captains. The women provided me with an extra blanket and even some small loaves of bread. The catches had sold well in Tyndaris, allowing some families to trade for olive oil and flour, luxuries they had not enjoyed for a long time. More eggs were left on my doorstep. On the seventh day, they were laid upon a small cluster of dried myrtus flowers.

That night, I roasted the fish and eggs in the fire and ate them with the rolls, sucking my fingers like Primus. I gazed at the bundle of myrtus, and on a whim, tossed it into the flames. Soon, the room filled with the pungent fragrance, and I breathed in deeply, closing my eyes. The scent brought me back to the Temple of Venus, and memories of Geta. Now that the gnaw of hunger was no longer occupying my thoughts, my mind filled with images of him: laughing on the portico of the palace, dancing with me in the firelight of the Faunus festival, furrowing his eyes shut in pleasure during coupling.

Suddenly, my skin prickled, and a chill rippled down my spine, as if a blast of cold air had entered the room. I realized with a shock that an auspice was imminent, even though it was night.

With no shoes or shawl to protect me, I exited the villa and walked to the ledge. There was a mist in the air, dampening my hair and face. The grass of the path gave way to stone, and I stood inches away from the precipice, breathing heavily. I had not taken an auspice at night since losing my child, and the same fear and anger gripped me again. I waited in terrible anticipation for the bird to appear, for I already knew what it would tell me.

A large object appeared in the sky to my left, moving to the right. It was a lone white swan, flying eastward in the direction of Rome. The majestic bird moved at great speed, vanishing from sight almost instantly. It was gone before I could even cry out in anguish. Geta was dead.

I sank to my knees and screamed into the dark, pummeling my fists against the rock. Antoninus had won. He had taken everything from me: my name, my title, my family, my home, and now the love of my life. It was only rage that prevented me from casting myself off the ledge and joining Geta in death. At that moment, I only wanted to live long enough to see Antoninus killed in some terrible way. My heart was broken. What was the point of living without love? I would never look into Geta's tiger eyes again, seeing my soul reflected in them. My only reason to live had been stolen from me. I curled forward and lay my forehead against the cold stone, weeping. Eventually, the chill forced me to return to the villa and stoke the dying fire. I wanted to streak ashes across my face and tear out my hair. I was no longer a woman. I was only a vessel of revenge, seeking death.

I did not travel down to the shore the next day but rather lay on the floor, shivering under my thin blanket. I let the fire die out. My anger from the night before had been extinguished with the flames, only to be replaced by a heavy sadness. Perhaps I would die after all. If I crossed over, I would be with Mother and Father and Geta once again. I fell into a restless sleep, dreaming of a frenzy of birds feasting on human flesh. I was awoken by small hands shaking me. I blinked my eyes open to find Assia crouched next to the straw pallet, a concerned look on her face. "Domina Plautilla? Are you sick?" she asked. Behind her, Tycho was rekindling the fire.

"Leave me be," I said, but I did not protest as the children presented another egg. Assia cracked it into a bowl and placed it over the heat of the flames, enough to turn it white enough to eat. I forced myself to eat it and drink a little water.

"Our Mother asks for you," said Tycho. "There is more fish, and much work to do."

"I cannot help today," I said, but I felt a pang of guilt. These people did not care for my heartbreak. They needed to eat. I looked at these two skinny children, already more self-sufficient than I ever had been, and knew I could not forsake them. "Give me a few moments," I said. The children waited outside as I put on my shoes and tried to pin my hair as best as I could. Finally, I joined them and we walked slowly down to the shore, where the circle of women sat in their usual spot. Dispirited, I picked up a knife and bowl and worked in silence alongside them.

* * *

For the next few days, I said little as I continued the grinding routine. My heart lay as heavy as a stone in my chest. As my fingers worked, I ruminated on a plan. I would ask the villagers to transport me to Tyndaris, where I would cast enough auspices to purchase transport to Rome. Once there, I would find my way into the palace through a secret entrance I knew from my time living on Palatine Hill and hide until there was an opportunity to strike at Antoninus. Perhaps I would find him in the baths, or drunk late in the evening. I would slip my knife between his ribs, striking the death blow before his Praetorians cut me down. I would die with his blood on my hands and a smile on my face. My last words would be a declaration of love for Geta, so that Antoninus would know that he had never fully defeated me.

This was madness, but the idea of it kept me alive. I refused to give in to sorrow, pushing it deep within myself. I would weep for Geta once Antoninus was dead. If this fantasy fueled me during the day, sorrow took over at night. Unable to sleep, I clutched my knees by the fire, worrying I was missing Geta's funeral procession of mourners bearing *imagines*, the wax masks of his ancestors, as they paraded toward the imperial tombs. Or worse, worrying that there would be no procession at all, and Geta had been condemned to die in obscurity as Antoninus had damned Father. Geta's soul needed to be guided toward the underworld, but what could I do to ensure it did so? I hadn't been able to help Father, and Gaius had been there when we'd aided Mother.

I ruminated all night, wishing I had kept the emerald necklace as a token to sacrifice to the gods in his name. At dawn, I rose and bathed myself in the caldarium before gathering as much myrtus as I could from the hill and hanging it on the outside wall to dry. After the day's work was done, I returned and created a small altar with stones and a few shells on a small ridge across from the structure. I built a fire and cast the myrtus upon it, causing smoke to billow into the sky as the sun set. I knelt in front of the flames and bowed my head. "Jupiter, Apollo, Diana, hear my plea. Guide Geta to the underworld and reunite him with his ancestors. Accept my offering: I will use my gift to bless others. I will serve the gods with my heart and soul. Please, accept this offering on his behalf, and bring Geta peace."

I repeated the ritual for seven days, bringing what small offerings to the altar that I could: flowers, fruit, stones, eggs, and gifts from the sea. Eventually, my grief subsided a little, but I knew I would carry Geta's imprint on my heart for the rest of my life. At least with the continuing bounty of seafood, there was much work to be done, and the constant toil helped to further dull my feelings.

As word spread about the catches, other fishing boats from Tyndaris, Panormus, and even Drepanum began to arrive, seeking the same catches as the boats from Lipara. Soon the harbor was filled with the chatter of crewmen calling to each other and the musical squawking of seabirds. The town returned to life, and I noticed a few legions coming and going from the fortress for the first time. They paid no attention to me, as I appeared to be simply another fishwife, shucking oysters on the beach. I shook my head at the sight of them. "As soon as the people grow wealthy enough to thrive, the imperial soldiers arrive to tax them back into indentured servitude," I said darkly. None of the women commented, but another ripple seemed to pass through them in response to my bitter words.

On the Kalends of Ianaurius, the dawn was bright and cold. As I approached the beach, the bright rays of sun created a harsh glare on the surface of the waves. I shaded my eyes as I observed even more boats entering the mouth of the bay. Perhaps I would be able to find transport to Messana or even Ostia if this continued. I marked no seagulls but did not think anything of it, as the boat traffic had probably forced them to move farther out to sea.

I sat down and began to cut oysters, not looking up. The group was quiet, focused on the tremendous number of shellfish that were waiting for us. As my hands worked, my mind wandered. I wondered how Gaius and Aurelia were, and if the baby had been born yet. I felt a pang of yearning as I thought of Hortensia. She would be a young woman soon, and I would not be there to help her on the journey to womanhood. This thought filled me with almost as much sorrow as mourning Geta.

I was so absorbed in my own thoughts I didn't notice when one of the women pointed. "What ship is that?" she asked. The tone of her voice made me look up, and fear laced through me. An imperial warship was plowing through the water toward us. Nearly a hundred oars stuck out from either side, and its sail was larger than most of the villas on Lipara. A century of Praetorians stood upon the deck in full uniform. As the ship drew closer, I recognized the standard of the *Frumentarii*, the guards that served as the emperor's secret police. I hastily stood, dropping my bowl into the sand, the oysters forgotten. I couldn't believe what I was seeing. The women's mouths were also agape. Shouts could be heard from the various fishing boats in the bay, and the crewmen rushed to avoid being battered by the enormous vessel as it headed straight for the shore.

"Why have they come?" asked one of the women. I felt a fresh fear, not for myself but for these steadfast people, who would suffer misfortune due to Antoninus' need to destroy me.

"They have come for me," I said. "Do not interfere with them. Go, take shelter in your homes." The women stared at me. "Go now!" I shouted, and they scattered, leaving their bowls behind. I placed my knife on the bench and walked down to the edge of the water to wait. The enormous ship slowed as its oars pulled out of the water. It almost ran aground before it dropped anchor and a small tender boat consisting of a few Praetorians disembarked, rowing toward the shore. The other fishing vessels had moved out of the bay, and the harbor was deserted. I faced them alone. I was not afraid to die, but I was afraid of pain, and of what the legions often did to women. But I would not give them the satisfaction of knowing so.

The small boat reached the shore, and the soldiers jumped out into the shallow water. The centurion turned his head, surveying the empty beach. He held up his hand for the others to halt, as if he sensed a trap. He then turned his attention to me. "Who are you?" he asked warily.

"I am who you seek," I said defiantly. "Fulvia Plautilla." The men looked at each other, unsure of how to proceed. The centurion laughed, revealing rotting teeth.

"Fulvia Plautilla. Your execution has been ordered by Imperator Marcus Aurelius Antoninus Augustus, the one true emperor of Rome. Come with us."

Something snapped in me. "No! I will not." I was tired of taking orders from Antoninus and his minions. I was tired of being told what to do, what to think, and what to be. It was folly to resist, but I couldn't help myself.

The centurion shrugged. "Suit yourself." He raised a hand to signal the others.

My body reacted before I had time to think. I ran, racing straight for the path leading up to my villa. The men cursed and gave chase, but I was ten paces ahead and not standing knee-deep in water. I raced behind the first villas and ducked around a barn, using a shortcut that cut straight to the ledge. I had no plan; I was running on pure survival instinct. Behind me, I heard the shouts of the soldiers as they split up, trying to force me out into the open. I ran as fast as my legs would take me, my lungs burning. After a few minutes I heard shouts; they had spotted me. I kept running as hard as I could, refusing to look back. I passed by my domus, then the caldarium, then Geta's altar. I was soon cresting the hill that led to the western part of the island. Suddenly, my foot caught on a branch and I stumbled, tumbling down a gully.

Scrabbling with my fingers, I managed to stop my fall under a strawberry tree. I tried to quiet my breathing as the soldiers gathered at the spot where I had fallen from the path. The centurion knelt, inspecting the markings in the dirt. "She can't be far. Find her and get it done quickly." The men turned in my direction, peering down into the ravine. I remained as still as a stone, praying they would not see me. A strange part of my mind noticed that there was no birdsong. The birds must have gone silent, sensing the threat. Then one of the Praetorians shouted. "There she is!" My heart sank as he pointed at the tree I was crouching under. The men began to race down the gully.

I sprang up and ran in the other direction, screaming now as I scratched my way through the brush. Cactus tore at my clothes and grit entered my eyes, but I didn't stop. *Just get to the cliffs, and you can jump*, I thought. *End it yourself.* The crest of the hill that led to the rocky backside of the mountain was only a few hundred paces ahead. But I was exhausted, and my pace slowed as the terrain grew steeper. I knew they were almost upon me, for I could hear the panting of their breath.

Suddenly, the earth moved, and the sky turned black. Instinctively, I fell flat, covering my head with my hands as hundreds of crows lifted from the hillside as one. The air was shrill with their cries as they bore down upon the soldiers. I heard the men screaming as the birds attacked, pecking at their eyes and ears with their beaks, their sharp talons slashing flesh. Opening my eyes, I saw a path through the maelstrom and began to crawl forward on my belly. After a few minutes, I turned back to see that the soldiers had retreated to the bottom of the gully as the multitude of crows descended through the strawberry trees above their heads.

The centurion looked up at me, and I marked that he was bleeding from a slash above his eye. The rest of the men were tending to cuts of their own, spitting out feathers and wiping the blood away. I saw one look up and draw his sword, only to have the birds begin their screeching again. He sheathed his weapon, and the birds were silenced. The gooseflesh returned to my skin, and I slowly rose to my feet and gazed down at them from above. "This is not your place," I said, my words echoing down the mountainside. "Go, before they slash you to ribbons."

The centurion spat and kicked a stone in anger, but he knew he would not get twenty paces before the birds attacked again. There were now thousands of them, perched from pinnacle of the mountain down to the bottom of the gully. As far as the eye could see, the earth was covered in blue-black feathers. He looked back up at me. "You won't escape us, witch."

"Tell Antoninus you strangled me and tossed me into the sea," I said. "Tell him I begged for my life. Tell him what he needs to hear." The men glanced at each other, but they were silent.

A bird swooped down from peak of the mountain, and somehow, I knew it was Cael. He soared above the path that led toward the western beach, intending for me to follow. I looked back one last time, no longer afraid. "For the glory of Rome," I said, and then I flew after him.

XX.

Cael led me to the very same beach I had swum to months before. This time, there was a tiny boat moored beside it, its ropes caught in the jagged stones. I splashed into the water and pulled the rope behind me, pushing the boat farther out to sea. When the water reached my chest, I used the last of my strength to climb inside. The waves were relatively calm, but the current was strong, carrying me swiftly out into the open water. Cael flew above me until I passed the tip of the island. Then he was gone.

For most of the day, I watched the other islands in the archipelago drift past the tiny craft. I tried to cover my head with my stola as the sun beat down upon me, warming the boat but adding to my thirst. Eventually I fell asleep, praying to Neptune to guide me. When I woke, the sea was calm, and I sat up wearily, marking the sun as it hovered close to the horizon. I was now many leagues from Lipara. I worried for a few moments whether I would encounter the warship, but somehow, I knew I wouldn't. The soldiers would lie to save face and avoid Antoninus' wrath. I would not need to fear them again.

I did not see any seabirds, and this amplified my fear as dusk approached and the light grew dimmer. I decided that I

272

would mark the stars to try and determine where I was. As the sun dipped below the horizon, the breeze strengthened, and the waves began to grow bigger. I clutched the side of the small boat in terror as walls of water roared over me. As I rose and fell, another vessel caught my eye in the distance. I waved my arms frantically as it drew closer. Eventually, I could see that it was a fishing boat. I screamed as loud as I could and pounded the boat with my fists to draw their attention. Finally, I thought I heard faint shouting in the distance over the crashing of the waves, and the ship sailed closer. I fell back, exhausted, as the sailors gestured and pointed, throwing ropes overboard until I finally caught one. I clutched the damp rope with the last of my strength as the crewmen drew me alongside the ship. At the last moment, hands pulled me up into the vessel as the small boat smashed to pieces against the hull.

I sank to my knees, disoriented, as the men shouted to each other in a language that seemed familiar. A jug was handed to me along with a dry blanket. I gulped water gratefully as I huddled against the deck and issued a prayer of thanks to the gods. After much commotion, a man I assumed to be the captain approached and knelt before me. He had dark skin and the weathered face of one who had spent a lifetime on the sea. "I am Lebbaeus. You are on my fishing vessel. From where did you travel?"

"Lipara," I mumbled. My tongue felt thick in my mouth. I swallowed more water as Lebbaeus frowned.

"Lipara? That is many leagues. It is a mercy of the gods that you survived." He observed the scratches on my arms, and my torn clothes before murmuring something to himself in his own language. I recognized it as Punic. "Are you hurt? It will be another day before we reach land."

"No," I said. "Where are we headed?"

"Our home," Lebbaeus replied. "We sail for Leptis Magna. We do not usually travel in these waters, but word traveled that a powerful priestess has asked the sea to release her bounty to all fisherman who asked. So we traveled to the island, only to see Roman warships in the harbor."

If my hands shook, I hoped Lebbaeus would not notice. I kept my voice calm as I replied: "I have not heard of any such powerful priestess." Lebbaeus gave me a shrewd look after I spoke, but his face was not unkind.

"It is just a superstitious tale then," he said. "Have you traveled to Africa?"

"No," I whispered. "But my family is there."

* * *

I spent the night gazing at the stars, marveling at their icy beauty. As I grew sleepy, I thought I saw Mother and Father smiling down upon me from Cassiopea, and Geta playfully winking from Orion's belt. Below Orion was Caelum, where a tiny star watched over me. My eyes filled with tears as I felt their love, present even from so far away. The gods had spared me, so they must have believed I still held a purpose. Perhaps it was only to love deeply, and care for others when they could not care for themselves. I vowed to them that I would keep my oath. When I finally drifted off to sleep, I dreamt of Cael and his mate, forging a nest at the peak of the mountain, sentinels against threats to their home.

Early the next morning, the ship approached the rocky shoreline of Tripolitania. I leaned against the railing, gazing at the sprawling city of Leptis Magna stretching out along the horizon. Father had come of age not far from here. I hoped that Gaius, Aurelia, and Hortensia were somewhere within its borders. Even though Tripolitania was an important Roman province, no one expected me to be here. Antoninus would focus his attention elsewhere. For the first time in ten years, I was finally free of the Severan dynasty.

The sailors shouted, and I watched as the ship entered the harbor before anchoring along the jetty. Deckhands extended a wooden plank onto the deck for us to disembark. Lebbaeus joined me as I peered over the railing. "I trust your family is expecting you?" he asked. I shook my head.

"Ah," he said. "If not, you are welcome in my home. My wife and children will find a place for you, until you are reunited with them."

I was caught off guard, unused to such kindness. I gazed at his weathered face. "Why do you offer this?" I asked.

Lebbaeus did not respond at first but rather gazed out over the city. Finally, he answered. "Perhaps I feel that you are favored by the gods," he said. "And if they favor you, they will favor me in return."

"The gods are capricious," I said. "I cannot promise to bring good fortune to any who seek it from me."

Lebbaeus nodded solemnly before slowly breaking into a smile. "I will take my chances." He chuckled, then extended his hand. "Come, priestess. We are home."

I had inhabited so many homes, both grand and small, and lived so many lives. This was the first time I had ever been given a choice. I could refuse this invitation, disappear into the maze of the city, and try to find Gaius on my own. Or I could dare to trust this stranger, who had offered me comfort, but more importantly, respect. This was true power—the power to choose my own fate. It was both exhilarating and terrifying. Taking a deep breath, I placed my hand cautiously into Lebbaeus' large one. He then guided me carefully down the wooden plank.

As I took my first steps upon this ancient shore, I heard the songs of unfamiliar birds calling me. Their music pulled me forward, both into a homecoming and the unknown.

THE END

Afterword

While the characters and incidents portrayed in this book are based on historical facts, some creative liberties were taken in order to strengthen the story. Any errors, omissions or mischaracterizations of historical figures or events are my own.

Writing a book may be a solitary activity, but getting a manuscript published is a team sport. Once again, I am indebted to the professionals who helped me along the way: Luca Mercogliano, for creating another astounding cover, Greg Fisher, for his thoughtful historical analysis and story suggestions, and Flannery Wise, for copy editing that helped that final polish shine. In addition, I'm grateful to my beta readers Jody, Chandi and Ivan for their encouragement of my early drafts. As always, thank you to my family for supporting my efforts.

I would also like to acknowledge the female historians who provided much of the inspiration behind this book: Mary Beard (particularly her book *Emperor of Rome*), and Ashleigh Green, author of *Birds in Roman Life and Myth*.

When I began this story, I set out to center a woman who had been merely a footnote in the history of the Severan Dynasty. What little is written about Fulvia Plautilla is only that she was profligate and hated by her husband. Her life was too short, and she controlled very little of it. In some ways, I wanted to give her the ending she deserved. I hope by reimagining her story, we can more fully appreciate the lives of women who may not have been featured in history but certainly played their part in it.

#justiceforplautilla, now and always.

About the Author

Paloma Blue is the author of *The Saturnalia Queen*, the first novel in her duology exploring the Severan emperors, Caracalla and Geta. She lives in Los Angeles.

You can connect with me on:

🌐 https://www.palomablue.net

Also by Paloma Blue

The Saturnalia Queen

The Emperor Caracalla is feared throughout the Roman Empire as a cold and cruel tyrant. Yet when he travels with his Legions to conquer the Barbarian tribes in Germania, Caracalla encounters a young healer who refuses to be subjugated to his will. For Gelvira, who has spent her life dedicated in service to the goddess who guides and nurtures her people, this Roman Emperor fills her with both fear and desire as she feels a connection to him that cannot be explained.

As her feelings deepen, Gelvira must walk between two worlds: one of sacrifice to the goddess and one of decadence that beckons her in hypnotizing ways. But can she trust a man who has committed unspeakable acts against his own family?

As desire leads to passion and then love, Gelvira must risk everything to save not only her people but also Caracalla from those who would stop at nothing to claim Rome's power for their own.